WIFE
MOTHER
LIAR

BOOKS BY SUE WATSON

WIFE
MOTHER
LIAR

SUE WATSON

bookouture

Published by Bookouture in 2025

An imprint of Storyfire Ltd.
Carmelite House
50 Victoria Embankment
London EC4Y 0DZ

www.bookouture.com

The authorised representative in the EEA is Hachette Ireland
8 Castlecourt Centre
Dublin 15 D15 XTP3
Ireland
(email: info@hbgi.ie)

ISBN: 978-1-83525-703-6
eBook ISBN: 978-1-83525-702-9

PROLOGUE

She was always there for me, my best friend next door. Two new brides, moving into our two new homes in the spring of our lives, the future laid before us like a picnic rug on a bright-green lawn. We were so young and invincible back then; nothing could hurt us, or so we thought.

Over the years, we danced barefoot in the garden, drank too much wine, shared good times and bad, laughed, cried and argued, and made up. And that summer when we were both joyfully pregnant, we'd sit on our doorsteps chatting, drinking herbal tea, rubbing our bellies and dreaming of our babies, and dreading sleepless nights. And when later those two babies lay on the carpet in their nappies, we marvelled at just how much love we had for them both.

And their first day at school, we walked behind them as they held hands, with brushed hair and shiny shoes; excited and nervous, we gently let them go, with both hearts breaking.

Years later, when our children left together for the prom, we walked behind them as they held hands, with brushed hair and shiny shoes; excited and nervous, we waved them off in a big fancy car, our hearts breaking all over again. Young and invincible as we'd once been, me and my friend next door.

How could I ever have imagined that one day, I would want to kill her?

ONE

JILL

Friday

I'm currently waiting for my friend Wendy at the cottage in Wales that I've rented for our 'girls' trip, though we're hardly 'girls' anymore. When I suggested a January weekend away she didn't seem so sure, but then I promised her 'posh food, Prosecco, and starry skies', and she was sold.

My phone just pinged. That's her now.

Sorry, almost there, just delivered twins!

I smile to myself. Wendy's a midwife and whether she's late, tired, in a bad mood, or a good mood – she blames the births. Tim, my husband, used to joke whenever she was late joining us for the cinema or theatre. 'It'll be a breech birth, or quadruplets – and she isn't even working!'

The cottage I booked is lovely, so quiet and apart from the farmhouse opposite, no neighbours for miles. There's been a lot of noise in my life recently and I've been longing for this quiet isolation. I'm already loving the silence. And running my fingers along the mantlepiece and the TV for dust, I approve of the cleanliness. I'm a stickler for it. My husband Tim used to say, 'It isn't cleanliness with you, Jill, it's mental illness.'

He was exaggerating, of course. I'm not obsessed; I just like everything to be clean and tidy; nothing wrong with that. I've checked the bedrooms; one's a little bigger with a nice pale-blue colour scheme. I'll let Wendy have that one. I'm okay with the smaller, beige room, but I had to move the old teddy bear off the bed. Things like that can hold dust mites and bacteria; makes me shudder just thinking about it.

I sit on the sofa to check it out, stroking the soft fabric of the throw. I'm rather fidgety today so I go into the kitchen where there's a lovely Welsh dresser adorned in big bright pieces of pottery. I love it, but not sure it'll be to Wendy's taste; she likes contemporary minimalist interiors, which is hilarious for someone so untidy.

I gaze through the window. It's late afternoon, but the night's coming in fast like a huge dark blanket. There's no sign of Wendy.

'The stars in Wales were just magic, Mum,' Leo had said when he told me about this place. 'There's no light pollution and I saw *my* constellation clearer than ever!'

I smile, remembering his excitement. From being a little boy, my son loved to point out the Leo star constellation and claim the lion's head in the sky as his. After returning from a school trip here two years ago, he urged us to visit: 'I've never seen so many stars. There's no space between them. You *have* to go there.'

So I booked this trip for his dad and me, imagining us wrapping up warm and heading out into the darkness to watch *Leo's* stars. But that all went up in a puff of smoke last week when I saw the text on my husband's phone that changed everything. He was in the shower after work when his phone lit up. I wouldn't usually bother to read his texts, I was scared of what I might see. But that night something compelled me, and I moved quickly across to his side of the bed and picked up the phone. I could only see the beginning of the message, and I skim-read what I saw. The text, from someone called 'Pete at work', was congratulatory, commending Tim on something he'd done with his tongue the previous evening. I gasped and put the phone face down. Casting my mind back to the previous evening, I realised this 'performance' he was being complimented on had apparently taken place while I'd been waiting at home with a slow-cooked lamb casserole for dinner.

'According to "Pete from Work", you're amazing in bed,' I said casually as he staggered into the bedroom drying his hair with a towel.

He looked up and I threw the phone at him.

'Do I know her?' I asked calmly as he wrapped his towel around himself, obviously feeling vulnerable now. 'Is this just another fling?'

He shook his head. 'I'm sorry, Jill.'

I focused on the trickles of water making their way in rivulets through the hairs on his chest.

'You *love* her?'

He nodded.

This shook me. Tim never talked about love; it wasn't a word he used much, even with me. His indiscretions had always been about sex, or so I'd thought, but seemingly this was different. I knew something was creeping up on us, that this one wasn't the same, she pulled at the fragile threads barely holding us together.

There have been others, but as we were now in our late forties, married almost twenty-five years, I thought he'd finally settled down. But he'd been too careless, coming home late, going in other rooms to make phone calls, texting red heart emojis I could see from across the room. And now he'd gone in the bathroom and left his phone lying around in an attempt to end this marriage, now in its terminal stages. Me finding the phone made it so much easier than him having to tell me. How very Tim to choose the lazy way to let me know.

'Why this? Why now? What's special about *her*?'

He shrugged. 'She appreciates me; she *sees* me.'

I rolled my eyes. 'She *sees* you, what the hell does that mean? Have you been watching *Couples Therapy* on TV again, Tim?'

Wordlessly, he left the room, leaving a trail of water on the polished wood floor. As he slammed the bathroom door, I waited for the hurt to come; that familiar wave of pain was like a muscle memory. But this time, nothing; over the years he'd slowly turned my feelings off. I went downstairs, and later he appeared in the kitchen, fully dressed, sheepish.

'I'm sorry, Jill, I didn't want to hurt you.'

That was a joke coming from him. I'd spent most of our marriage in agony over his constant affairs. In some ways it was a relief that he was finally going; I couldn't have taken any more of his lies. I'd lived in a lonely marriage, my youth spent waiting for him to come home, never knowing whose bed he'd just left, or whose perfume I could smell. It was tortuous.

'*Almost* twenty-five years – we aren't going to make that silver wedding anniversary, after all are we?'

'Sorry!' He plonked himself at the kitchen table.

'So, you're actually leaving this time?'

'Yes. I think it's for the best.'

'I was never enough, was I?'

'You were always too busy with work, and especially after Leo was born, I felt like he always came first,' he replied.

This made me angry; he was trying to blame me caring for our child as a justification for his infidelity. How dare he? Anger plumed in my chest. I had to stop myself from slapping him hard across the face. I wanted to scream at him, tell him he wasn't a man, he wasn't a husband or father, he was just a womanising waster who'd ruined my and my son's life. But what was the point? I didn't have the energy, and it was all too late.

'Shall I leave tonight?' he said into the silence.

'Up to you.'

'I could stay tonight if you like?'

'No, go now, it's for the best.'

He looked a little surprised, awkward even.

'Did you think I'd beg you to stay?'

'No... it's not that, it's just that Angela's with her mother tonight; she's not well. And I don't have keys for her place.'

'Really? So, *Angela* hasn't given you keys but you're giving up your marriage for her? If I were you, I'd have made sure I could get into the next house before I left this one.' Sarcasm oozed from me, but it was lost on him.

'Look, I tell you what, why don't you stay for tonight?' I offered. 'I'll cook us a nice dinner, we'll drink our favourite wine. One more night together, and then we say goodbye?'

He didn't need time to consider this. 'That sounds perfect,' he said, willing to be unfaithful to the woman waiting somewhere else. I almost felt sorry for *Angela.*

'Okay, I'll get cooking then.' I stood up from the table and he reached out for me, his arms around my waist as I stood close to him.

'Thanks, Jill, you're so good to me. I don't deserve you.'

'No, you don't,' I said. 'But tonight is on one condition: no texting her, no secret calls or sending heart emojis. If you want dinner and a final night together, I want all your attention for the last time.'

'Of course.' He began kissing me on my neck, running his hands up and down my body.

'Let's have dinner first,' I said, gently pushing him away.

He chuckled. 'Okay, can I help?'

'No, I'm fine, you go and relax. After all, it's your last night here. She may not have all the sports channels; go and knock yourself out.'

He kissed me again, only this time it was the way a kid would kiss his mum for buying him a new computer game.

I smiled. 'Hey, and your phone?'

'I won't text Angela.'

'Mmm, just indulge me and throw it in that drawer.'

He was on too much of a promise to argue, and he immediately surrendered his phone to the drawer while I began melting butter in the pan. Then I started to cook the chicken for homemade pies, Tim's favourite. He could have a nice dinner with the outgoing queen while looking forward to the next day when he'd be with the new one.

As soon as he'd gone to sprawl over the sofa in front of a screen of balls and stupid men in fancy dress, I quietly opened the drawer.

'Jill.' He suddenly appeared in the doorway. I quickly shoved the drawer closed and looked up.

'Yes?'

'Thanks for being so understanding about all this.'

'I just think after all these years we need to end this properly.' I smiled. 'No hard feelings,' I added, going back to the chicken. After a few seconds, I turned around and he'd gone, so I quickly moved back to the drawer, and keeping an eye on the door, carefully took out the phone. I punched in his passcode. He was so stupid; he used his own birth date, and never changed it. I checked his messages, scrolling back for a while; so many nights he'd told her he would leave me, and the following day made excuses as to why he hadn't: 'Jill was drunk'; 'Jill was crying'; 'Jill begged me to stay'. I particularly liked 'Jill's mum's died; I need another week.' My mother's been dead over thirty years. Nothing was sacred for Tim; he was ruthless in the pursuit of his own happiness.

So I let my fingers do the talking, and using some of the phrasing he had in previous texts, I started one to Angela.

Hey Angie, I'm sorry. I was going to tell Jill about us tonight and ask her for a divorce, but I realise I still love her. We've had a long talk, and we're going to take a second honeymoon. We're going to have a few weeks just to be together and find what we lost. I know you'll understand I'll always love her, and nothing will ever change that. Good luck, babe.

I turned the phone off and left it in the drawer; it wasn't the first time I'd ended one of his affairs, but this would be the last.

So we had our final night together, a lovely meal, a bottle of wine, and we said goodbye on my terms. And then I packed my little suitcase and headed here, to the cottage in Wales.

I take out some of the groceries I've brought with me and make a cup of rose bush tea. I look at the chicken thighs in the fridge and wonder if I should have gone for something a little more fancy. Wendy's all about glitz and glamour, and though I've brought a couple of bottles of Prosecco and some posh chocolates left over from Christmas, I'm not sure it'll be enough for Wendy.

Slipping off my woolly jumper, I put on some lipstick. I want my old friend to see how being single suits me, and so I treated myself to some trendy new jeans and sneakers for this weekend. Wendy's always dressed young. She's got a good shapely figure, a fresh complexion and she's always been fashionable, though it can be a little *Love Island* sometimes. I haven't seen her for months, but when I last bumped into her at the supermarket, there was something different about her. I noticed it as soon as she waltzed towards me with a basket full of wine. Her forehead was so smooth and tight she couldn't frown. I'm sure she'd had lip fillers too; she could barely close her mouth.

'I may be in my forties, just, but I'm not done yet,' she'd announced in the baked bean aisle. I think she's reinvented herself; I'd heard that Robert had left her to go and live in Spain. Presumably Wendy and I are both now single.

I've only been alone for a few days, but I don't feel sad or defeated. I'm empowered, finally working out who I am and what I want for the first time in my life. Each to his own but, unlike Wendy, my salvation won't be in lip filler or Botox. I've decided to save myself in a different way, by finding some answers and taking my revenge.

So, gone is the mousy Jill with short greying hair, comfy shoes and neat little cardis. I've had my hair bleached, swapped my navy and black clothes for a splash of colour, and bought some amazing £90 sneakers online. I just knew I had to have them; they looked so 'cool', as Leo would say. Okay, the model was a long-legged twenty-something and I'm a short-legged almost fifty-year-old. Tim had always been the one who ordered stuff online. There were deliveries for him most days: new clothes, expensive aftershave, all sorts of stuff; I didn't even ask. But now it's my turn, so I put in my credit card details, and through half-closed eyes, clicked the *buy now* box.

I almost cancelled straight after I'd bought them, but convinced myself it was the right thing to do – even if it was mad and decadent.

* * *

It only took a couple of days for them to arrive. I was like a kid at Christmas, and when I saw them I fell in love all over again. Bright, neon orange; who'd have ever thought I'd wear footwear in neon? I read in a magazine at the dentist's that neon is in. I haven't paid much attention to the world recently, so I wouldn't know. The world kind of stopped the night my son and

Wendy's daughter went to the prom, and only one of them came home.

TWO

WENDY

I pulled up outside the cottage, and it looked nice enough if a bit twee. Within seconds Jill was in the driveway gesticulating, attempting to guide me in like some crazed air traffic controller. It was distracting rather than helpful, but it made me laugh. I wound the window down. 'What the bloody hell were you doing, the Argentine tango? That was like an audition for *Strictly Come Dancing!*' We both laughed at this. And once I'd parked the car, she picked her way through the icy ground, arms wide open in welcome. 'And now she's doing *Dancing on Ice!*' I called out in mock horror, which tickled her.

'I'd like to see *you* get across this icy path without sliding,' she called back.

'Stop skating, get over here and give me a hug!' I yelled, throwing open the car door.

'I've missed you,' she muttered into my neck while holding on to me, and in that moment I felt the years of our friendship; the days of joy and love and horror rewound in my head like clips from an old movie. It was the glue that bound us, always had, and in a weird way, always will.

'Come on, the cottage is gorgeous,' she said, taking a couple of my bags and going inside as I gathered the rest of my luggage from the car boot.

'Cup of tea first, or do you want to unpack?' she was saying as I entered the hallway and followed her through to the kitchen.

That's when I noticed her hair. 'Jill, you've gone blonde?'

Her hand flew up to the nape of her neck and she stroked it, 'yes, I wanted a change.' 'Suits you,' I said, but it didn't, bleach is too harsh at our age. I'm blonde, always have been but as I've got older I've taken my hairdresser's advice, and gone for a softer, more flattering tone.

I decided to unpack first; I was tired from the drive and needed a few moments to gather my thoughts. I headed upstairs to a blue bedroom, not to my taste, but that didn't matter; it was nice enough, and very Jill. I'd spotted a huge pine Welsh dresser in the kitchen that Jill had raved about; she was orgasmic over the monstrosity. Jill has always loved old stuff; most of her house is filled with furniture inherited from dead relatives. It's like she's never really discovered what *she* likes, never settled into her *own* life, just borrowed from others. I've always had definite tastes. I know what I like and I don't care what anyone else thinks. We're so different I often wonder how we came to be such good friends.

Jill and I are so chalk and cheese, other people never quite get our friendship; I'm not sure we did either, really. It's like those married couples who seem so happy but you wonder what they see in each other, what invisible thread binds them. Jill and I are like that. 'What on earth do you two *talk* about? Don't you find her a bit... *bland*? She's very uptight, isn't she? How do you stand it?' my other friends would say. Some even implied that she was boring, but I never thought that about Jill. I never analysed our friendship that much; it just happened, in the way a tree grows, or a sponge cake rises. We just happened.

I'll never forget the first time I saw Jill. It was almost

twenty-five years ago, but seems like yesterday. She and her husband Tim were moving in next door, and she'd pulled up outside in a big van, and when she climbed out, I was surprised to see how young and slight she was. I was in awe. I wouldn't have been able to drive a great big removal van with all our worldly goods inside, but this tiny slip of a girl had manoeuvred this heavy vehicle in traffic and was now parking it neatly outside her new home. Looking back, that was classic Jill – throughout our friendship, she was the coper, the DIYer, the gardener. She could move boulders around the garden, and once dug out a big old rhododendron bush in our garden that my husband Robert hadn't been able to budge. Jill plucked cats from trees, kids from ponds, changed tyres, fixed plugs and painted window frames swinging from a stepladder; nothing fazed her.

On that first day, I watched from our bedroom window while she attempted to lift huge, heavy boxes and bin bags into the house. I'd heard it was a couple who were moving in but with no sign of her other half I sent Robert out to help her. He grumbled a bit, but grudgingly went down our driveway and was soon helping her to unload the van.

I can still see her now in her tracksuit bottoms and loose T-shirt, which hid her slim, athletic build, as she carried a chest of drawers unaided. Later, we met Tim, who wasn't at all what I'd expected after meeting Jill; he was *look-twice handsome*, well groomed, worked out, with a permanent tan. Robert described him as flashy, whereas I thought he was cute. But Jill was the opposite; fresh faced, sensible clothes; the only hint at glamour was her hair, which looked like she'd been to a really good colourist. But when I asked her which hairdresser she used, she laughed and said the 'colourist' was just highlights from honeymoon sunshine.

Back then, I envied them; they were so in love. They'd walk down Lavender Close holding hands. The way he looked at her made me melt, and she only had eyes for him. They just sparkled.

One evening, I invited them over for drinks. We were similar ages, newly married, and we had some laughs, shared similar goals regarding kids and careers, and after that night, the four of us became friends. We were often at each other's homes for dinner and drinks, and barbecues; we even went on holiday together. At weekends Jill and I would go for lunch and shopping while the boys went to football, or the pub. In the beginning it was an effortless friendship; they felt like family and we had some really good times together.

We enjoyed years of long hot summers, sparkly Christmases, babies being born, and birthdays celebrated as four of us became five and six, then seven and eight. We couldn't believe our luck that the people who happened to move next door had become our best friends and enhanced our lives. I felt so lucky, I thought it would go on forever. If you told me there would come a time when I couldn't even bear to look at them, I wouldn't have believed you.

'Do you remember when we used to say we'd all live in the same care home when we got old?' I said. I'd unpacked and was sitting at the kitchen table drinking tea while Jill buttered some toasted teacakes. She had her back to me, but for a moment, she stopped and turned around.

'I wish we could turn back the clock.' She sighed, and the sadness on her face made me want to hug her.

'Yeah, me too. Some people never have friends like we all were. I'll always be grateful for that time.'

She didn't respond, just went back to the buttering.

'We were happy then and we can be happy again, Jill,' I offered.

'You're right.' She moved across the kitchen and, putting a

plate of teacakes down, brushed my shoulder with her hand. 'Thanks for coming, love... This weekend. I really appreciate it. I know being here in the middle of winter isn't the glamorous kind of weekend you're used to but—'

'Hey, I wouldn't have missed it for the world, I've been looking forward to seeing you,' I lied, picking up a teacake and biting into warm, buttery bread.

'It's a lovely place, isn't it, very clean, decorated nicely too,' she said brightly. But as she joined me at the table, I could see she was as lifeless as the watercolours on the wall. That bleach job had drained what little colour she had in her face. No honeymoon hair, no sparkly eyes.

We ate our teacakes in uncomfortable silence, something we never had before. I've come to hate silence; it reminds me of loss.

'Are those new?' I asked, pointing at the orange trainers she was wearing. They were very neon, and not very Jill.

She smiled, lifting her foot up for me to admire.

'You've always been a Sporty Spice; you suit that kind of gear,' I said, trying to be kind, but they were far too young for her.

'I wasn't sure about them. Do you think they're okay, not too young for me?' She beamed at my apparent approval, and my heart broke a little for her.

'No, don't be silly, they aren't too young for you,' I lied.

'They're great – really cool,' I added, assuming she must have got them cheap from one of the charity shops on the high street. Money was going to be tight now Tim had walked out; he earned a good salary as a fireman. Always looked good in that uniform too. If I'm being brutally honest, he was wasted on Jill.

I continued to eat my teacake as silence landed again. In recent times I think we'd both felt the weight of what we had to say and skirted around so many triggering subjects that we just did small talk now. We'd tried to have *that* conversation many times, but it had always ended in tears; now we couldn't even go there.

'Gosh, it's such a long time since you and I came away together...' I said blandly, to fill the aching quiet.

She smiled at the memory. 'Yes, I think it must have been that weekend in London – the last time you and I went away.'

'That was fun. It was always good to get out of the house and away from screaming kids and annoying husbands.'

She giggled at what she perceived as my irreverence around Robert. 'Remember that time we rented a cottage in Devon?'

I rolled my eyes. 'Yeah, the heating didn't work and the beds were rock hard.'

'The heating was so temperamental.' She hesitated, then said, 'Oh God! I just remembered, that was the time Robert thought you were having an affair!' She chuckled and raised her hand to her mouth in mock horror. 'He kept calling, and when you wouldn't answer, he started asking if I knew anything. "I know she's seeing someone," he kept saying; it was awful.'

'I *wasn't*.' I could feel my face flushing scarlet. 'I *wasn't* seeing someone.'

'You *were*.'

I looked at her. 'Why would you say that, Jill?'

'Because you *told* me you were.' She chuckled. 'You were seeing someone from work. I think his name was Dan?'

'I don't remember.'

'Yes, he worked in radiography, I think you said.'

I shook my head, pretending I didn't remember and feeling very uncomfortable. Meeting up with old friends who you aren't so close to any more is like seeing old lovers; the intimacy leaves its imprint, and be it sex or secrets, you can't go back. They *know*, and so do you – the curtain was lifted a long time ago.

'You don't *remember* someone you *slept* with?' she was now saying, without taking her eyes from mine.

'I remember *Dan*, but I don't remember having an *affair* with him. Robert blew it out of proportion,' I said, then quickly added, 'Hey, is it too early to open the Prosecco?'

She laughed. 'On a girls' weekend it's *never* too early to open the Prosecco.'

'I was going to take a shower, but first can I do anything to help?' I offered a little half-heartedly after I'd poured us both a flute of cold fizz.

'No, it's fine, you get off,' she said kindly.

The shower was as refreshing as the Prosecco, and padding back into the bedroom, wrapped in a towel, I looked up at the window, stunned to see so many stars. I'd never been anywhere so remote: no cars, no people, just darkness for miles, like living on the edge of civilisation.

I moved closer to the window, bringing my towel around me, and stared into the night sky. It was only when I moved to walk away and get dressed that I saw the outline of the house. It was hard to make out in the pitch black, but it was definitely a house, because I could see a light on in the downstairs window. I screwed up my eyes trying to see more, and as I raised my eyes up towards the roof, I could see the upper window was lit too. And though it was almost impossible to see, I could make out shapes in that window. Someone was sitting there; they were looking through a telescope. And it was pointing directly at my window.

THREE

JILL

Saturday

I couldn't get to sleep last night, but Leo's voicemail cheered me up. 'Mum, I just did my English exam. That question came up on *To Kill a Mockingbird* and I smashed it!' His sheer enthusiasm and optimism always make me feel better and eventually I drifted off, dreaming of a sky full of stars.

I woke this morning feeling more positive, like I can handle the situation I've found myself in, but first I need a cup of tea.

'Hey, Jill.' Wendy's standing in the kitchen doorway, all big hair and lipstick. Round her neck is a huge fluffy scarf with glittery thread.

'You look lovely,' I say, wistfully. I could never carry off a scarf with metallic thread. 'Do you fancy a walk this morning?'

'Thanks. Yeah, well, a bit of a wander around would be nice, nothing too strenuous. I'm not into hiking like you are.'

I laugh at this. 'If you call ten thousand steps a day "hiking" then yes, I'm a hiker. Tea?'

She shakes her head vigorously. 'Coffee, strong, please.'

'Hey, you know there's a big old house across the road, set back a bit?' She glances through the window.

'Yes, it's a farmhouse, it belongs to the Venables. They live there and they own this cottage too.'

'The owners? Bloody hell – well, last night they had this huge telescope at the window.'

'Yes, they're stargazers.'

'Well, the telescope wasn't pointing at the sky, it was pointing right in my window.'

I shrugged; Wendy can exaggerate sometimes, and as attractive as she is, I'm sure she doesn't get the attention she says she does.

'Perhaps they heard you were staying here and they wanted a paparazzi shot?' I joke.

'Can you blame them? I was in a white towel, totally naked underneath. A picture like that would make thousands.'

We both chuckle at this. So there's still a bit of the old banter left; I haven't seen that side of her for a very long time. I'm glad the old Wendy's still in there somewhere, under all that Botox. I might be able to reach her and actually talk to the old Wendy before we say goodbye this weekend.

We sit with our drinks, and as the steam rises from the mugs, I feel the small talk slowly drying up again, and replacing it is a tight rod of tension between us. It was there last night too, neither of us quite knowing what to say. It makes me sad and anxious. When did that happen? As if I don't know?

'We haven't spoken for a while. Your invite surprised me,' she says, without meeting my eyes.

'I know, we haven't kept in touch for over a year, have we? Not since...'

'No, it's been hard.'

'Yes, it has. I kept meaning to pick up the phone, but I didn't know what to say.'

'I felt the same.'

'I'm glad you came, though. I just think it would be good if you and I could try and get back to where we were. If you want to, that is?'

'Yeah, sure.' She doesn't; I can tell it's the last thing she wants.

'There are some things I'd like to ask, some things I'd like to explain... and I wanted to do that this weekend without any distractions.'

It's going to be hard, but we only have to get through the next couple of days, then we can say goodbye.

'Of course, I'm sure there are things we *both* want to talk about. Perhaps we should just settle in and... and go for a walk, take it from there?'

Wendy's never been good at difficult conversations; she makes light of them, or even ignores them, hoping they'll go away.

Two days after I miscarried my first baby, she knocked on the door and when I opened it, she was standing there, her hair blonde and shiny, in a crisp white shirt and faded jeans. She had a beautifully wrapped gift, which she held in both hands.

I couldn't think straight. The loss had hit me so hard, and that morning my milk had come, like some sick, cosmic joke that I couldn't process.

'My milk came,' I said.

In my distress, I guess I hoped my friend, who was a midwife, might comfort me, might know what to say.

'Oh. That happens with late term loss. I have some pads I can give you,' she replied, before thrusting the gift at me. 'It's a Jo Malone candle,' she said, like that would compensate for losing my baby.

'Thanks.'

'You said you'd always wanted a Jo Malone candle.'

I'd always wanted a baby too, and longed to talk about that – but she couldn't; it was too uncomfortable for her.

I remember closing the door and walking back inside. I was numb. I didn't open the gift, just sat alone and cried. Later that day, a pack of breast pads was pushed through the letterbox. I didn't see her again for several days, then she called me to say she was having a dinner party and Tim and I were invited. 'I thought I'd make my pavlova,' she said, but never mentioned my loss.

'It's like nothing happened,' I said to Tim at the time. 'She's a midwife, she deals with stuff like this every day, so why can't she at least address it, talk to me about it?'

He just shrugged; he wasn't much good engaging with real life either unless, I realised later, it was a woman he could sleep with.

At the time I didn't get it; I'd been too wounded by her apparent lack of concern. But now I understand that Wendy is a brilliant nurse *because* she can stay detached; she has to or she wouldn't be able to do her job. In the same way, she had to stay emotionally detached from what I was going through, but Wendy 'the nurse' offered practical help – a beautiful gift and breast pads. In her career she's seen some terrible things, suffered awful losses, and as she always says, 'It's harder being a midwife than any other nurse, because a midwife always has two patients.'

And now, many years later, she still seems to have difficulties with the awkward intimacy of friendships and talking about the painful stuff. So, I decide to give her the space she needs, hoping she'll eventually come around and we *can* talk. I know what happened is as raw for her as it is for me, but like the miscarriage, I *need* to talk about it. Besides, I can't go on not *knowing*, because there are things about that night we both need to explore, and I hope talking will make me feel better, exorcise some demons. But more importantly, between us, we might uncover something the police missed.

'So, how are you and Robert?' I ask.

She shrugs, and her newly fleshed-out lips clench slightly, an indication of her discomfort. 'I don't see much of him.'

'I heard he'd gone to Spain?'

'Yes, he's over there now. Ahh... these mugs are cute, aren't they?' She's pretending to like the floral mug she's drinking her tea from.

I smile. 'Wendy, I *know* what you're doing; your avoidance technique has always been clumsy.'

She rolls her eyes. 'I just *like* the mugs...' She's about to say something, then hesitates and, taking herself away from the conversation, pushes some bread into the toaster. There's something she isn't telling me about the kids, or is it something about Robert perhaps? I'm intrigued, but again I leave it or she'll totally clam up. If I make her too uncomfortable, she might invent an emergency and leave. She's clearly not happy talking about their break-up. I can read her like a book.

I remember the first time they invited us over. Wendy seemed delighted to see us. 'So glad you two came, everyone else is so bloody boring,' she'd whispered in my ear. I'd followed her into the kitchen, and once inside she'd poured us drinks and Robert had appeared, beaming. I'd immediately liked Robert. He was always smiling, and I liked that he was fair and kind; he didn't judge people. When Wendy and I had gossiped about the other neighbours, he'd jokingly reprimand us, but I could see he'd found it uncomfortable.

'He's too good for me,' Wendy would say, and I agreed with her; he was.

'I sometimes think about the people we were, those two couples living next door to each other, all the hopes and dreams we had,' I say, wanting to get her back on track. I need her to remember our friendship, how close we were in the hope she'll open up and *talk* to me.

Her hard expression softens. 'Good times,' she murmurs, and I know she means it. I glimpse the pretty young woman in pale lemon who came over with apple pie the day after we moved in. All these years later, and she hasn't changed much. Her hair is still blonde, her complexion fresh, though that might be the Botox? But essentially she's still the same woman who welcomed us with that pie. I just hope I can reach her before it's too late. Back then, as an insecure new wife with a handsome husband, I was slightly threatened by the pretty girl standing on the doorstep with a gift of food. But once I knew her, I soon got to like her and our husbands became great friends too. Wendy's husband Robert was a doctor, for Médecins Sans Frontières, providing medical care for people in crises throughout the world. He saved people's lives in war zones and areas of conflict and all Wendy could do was complain because he couldn't be around to take her to a party.

So if there was a party amongst our friends, we'd take her with us, and Tim would have one of us on each arm. I remember going to the house of one of Tim's work colleagues; it was around Christmas and we'd been invited for drinks. 'Let's take Wendy?' he suggested, and when we arrived, she soon found someone to chat to. I was stood near Tim and a friend of his came over congratulating him on his 'gorgeous' wife. He was referring to Wendy, and Tim had to explain that I was his wife. I was mortified. I'm sure if I hadn't been there he would have let his friend think he was married to Wendy, and the dismay on his friend's face made me want to cry. He looked from her to me without hiding his horror at how someone as handsome as Tim had ended up with me. Tim loved having her around; apart from being good looking, she was fun. 'Let's invite the Joneses,' Tim would say whenever we talked about doing something sociable.

'Do you fancy Wendy?' I sometimes asked, but he always denied it, said she was 'just a good laugh'. I assumed Tim found every woman attractive except me, and Wendy was a looker, with her curvy shape and flirty way of talking to men. She knew it too; I remember one of the neighbours referring to her as 'a maneater', which I felt was a little harsh.

I drag myself from the past and sip my tea. I'm doing that a lot these days, thinking about the past and getting lost. I have too much time on my hands, especially since Tim went.

'When I found out I was pregnant you were the first person I told,' I say to Wendy. 'Even before I told Tim.'

'Oh God, yes! I remember that day so clearly. I'd found out the week before that I was having Olivia, but just couldn't bring myself to tell you. I knew you'd be pleased for me, of course – but I also knew it might break your heart because you'd struggled so much.'

'Ahh, it would have been difficult, but Tim and I had always said that if we didn't have our own kids, we'd just borrow yours.'

'Yes, we were always glad of the babysitting you guys did... Well, perhaps not Tim so much, but you were so good.'

'I loved your kids, still do,' I say, and it sits between us, the thing neither of us are prepared to acknowledge.

'Our babies being born just days apart was like a dream come true.' I keep talking through it so we can come out at the other end. 'I remember thinking, "It doesn't get better than this." And it didn't!' I say, with a long sigh.

'I know, it's been a bumpy road, hasn't it, love?' she concedes.

'But watching our babies grow up was such a lovely time.' I put on my rose-tinted glasses, thinking about those exhausting, hellish, beautiful, horrible, heady days of early motherhood.

Olivia was born a couple of weeks before Leo, and from the moment she arrived, it was as if Wendy had no other children. She already had Josh and Freddie, but they seemed to fade into the distance as far as their mother was concerned. For Wendy there was only Olivia, and now the boys had to fend for themselves to some degree, while Olivia was treated like a princess.

'I wanted Olivia to have everything I never had. My parents

had nothing, so I had nothing, but I always said she'd have everything.' She looks close to tears.

'You were obsessed with that girl from the minute she was born,' I say. I always thought she saw Olivia as her chance for redemption; she would do well at school, have the great career, marry the right man, all the things Wendy privately felt she'd failed at.

'I was obsessed, you're right; after two boys I finally got my girl. But weirdly Olivia was also the watershed in our marriage.'

'In what way?'

'After she was born, Robert started to work away more. I realise that as a doctor working for the Médecins Sans Frontières there was always plenty of work to do. But he was offered postings here in the UK and he volunteered to go away; he actually chose a war zone over his family, Jill.'

'I know that used to get to you, but Robert's a good man; he just wanted to make the world a better place.'

'But he'd spend months on end away and we had three beautiful children at home who missed their daddy.'

'I know, but they had you, and you're a great mum. I loved hearing his stories about operating in a muddy field, delivering a woman's baby in a tent with bombs dropping outside.'

'Your husband saved people from fires, but he came home to you at night.'

'Sometimes he did,' I murmur.

'I just feel like once Olivia was born he abandoned us; our marriage was never the same.'

'I never realised you felt like that. Did you talk to him?'

'I tried to but he was never home. I sometimes wonder if that's why Olivia became a bit feisty as a teenager; there was no father figure.'

Olivia was a lovely child growing up, but when she hit her teens all Wendy's spoiling turned her into a little beast, always arguing with her mum when she didn't get what she wanted.

She would lose it at the drop of a hat, always getting herself caught up in trouble with other girls, until she got a little older and boys came along. That kind of trouble was quite different though.

'She seemed to become quite angry as a teen,' I offer, which is an understatement.

'She got her temper from her father. I tried to calm her down, but that seemed to make her worse. When she got close to Leo, that all changed. She became so much nicer.' I choose to ignore this. I don't believe Leo changed Olivia, and I don't think she became nicer; she was still entitled and stroppy the last time I saw her, which was the night our kids went to the prom.

My stomach drops just thinking about that night. I had such a feeling of foreboding I begged Leo not to go. I knew something would happen, but never in my worst fears did I think anyone was going to die.

FOUR

WENDY

After breakfast, Jill and I ventured out into the freezing Welsh morning. The cold blasted my head, and the air was so icy just breathing it in tightened my chest. 'Do you miss Robert?' Jill suddenly asked, out of the blue.

'Er... I miss the kids, miss living on Lavender Close – I miss our life,' I replied, deliberately ignoring her question. 'It's sad that everything changed. I thought we'd live there for ever.'

'Me too.'

'Has he met someone else?' she asked as we walked along the country road, sharp glints of frost twinkling in the tarmac, the air cold and crisp.

'No... we're just having a break.'

'Have *you* met someone else?' She turned to look at me, searching my face for clues.

I shook my head. I really wasn't prepared for one of Jill's interrogations. It was none of her business, and Robert and I had agreed not to talk to anyone about the current situation. After what happened, we were just trying to heal.

'Do you miss Tim?' I asked, keen to move the focus off me.

'He hasn't been gone long,' she replied after a few seconds

considering this. 'I'm sad because after years of wondering where he was and who he was with, I had this naïve and rather foolish idea that he might come back to me,' she admitted. 'I hoped age might wither his roving eye and we'd finally have the marriage I'd always dreamed of, but there was one problem with that – Tim. He loved falling in love, and after a little while, he got bored. It was the same with me, he is addicted to the falling in love bit of a relationship.'

'That explains a lot,' I said.

'I was stupid, I know. People don't change.'

'I think some couples just aren't meant to be together, and as sad as it is the only answer is to split, because the alternative is mutual sadness and regret.'

'Do you really think that the only answer is to split?' she asked, turning her head quickly to look into my face.

'Yes. At first you guys seemed so much in love, but then there was the stress over conceiving, and when you had Leo... things seemed to change.'

'Yes, well, everything changes when you have a baby.' She sighed.

'I mean *you* changed, and I know Tim felt that too.'

'Oh really? So Tim discussed our marriage with you, did he?' She smiles, pretending it's a joke, but I can tell from the tautness in her face this genuinely made her angry.

'He didn't *talk* about you, we just... we were all friends,' I said brightly, pretending to be unaware of the subtext here.

'My husband always had a soft spot for you.' And there it was, the subtext.

'Tim and I got along, he was always easy to talk to...'

We continued to walk, and I pointed at a bird in a tree bare of branches hoping to distract her, but I should have known. A nuclear bomb wouldn't distract Jill when she was focused on something. She never dropped a subject even when it became difficult; she was relentless.

'You and Tim would go off into the garden for a smoke and you'd be gone ages,' she started, going over her fears like it was yesterday.

'You and Robert would talk for hours; more than once Tim and I went off to our respective beds leaving you downstairs chatting.'

'Robert's polite, he just humoured me. I know he found me boring. Not like you and Tim giggling together, lots of in-jokes; I could hear you behind the garage when you went off to have your "cigarette break".' She had held on to so much over the years it was destroying her, but she wouldn't let go.

'It was *just* a smoke,' I murmured, like a resentful teen. Jill hated that Tim and I enjoyed each other's company, but he was irreverent, fun, and he made me laugh. He never took Jill too seriously; they were total opposites, and it was funny to watch them spar, which he did for sport, but Jill took it to heart.

Unfortunately Jill and Robert never had the same chemistry as Tim and me. Robert said her anxiety was infectious; she made him feel uneasy. Jill had always been slightly on edge but it had become much worse after Leo was born.

'Don't leave me alone with her,' Robert would say, but they objected to our smoking, so we had to do it outside near our garages like two naughty school kids. I liked a cigarette and enjoyed Tim's company. I wasn't going to stop doing that; it wasn't my problem that Jill made Robert nervous.

'I used to envy you,' she said. 'All the men wanted you, and all the women wanted to be you.'

'Oh, that's not true.' I kept my head down, continued to walk. It was flattering, but embarrassing.

'I thought if I looked like you, Tim might love me again,' she suddenly said. Then stopped walking to give more emphasis to this uncomfortable conversation.

'You were funny and bright and pretty. You know, I even tried to copy your hair, but mine was too fine. And your figure-hugging dresses... they looked ridiculous on my thin flat-chested body, though.'

I smiled, aware that a few months into our friendship Jill began to copy the way I dressed, the way I did my hair and even the shade of lipstick I wore. Even Robert would remark on it. 'I see she liked the dress you had on last time we met,' he'd say when she turned up in something similar.

I was thinking about the time she dyed her hair the exact colour as mine when I was suddenly startled by a man's voice behind. 'Hello there!'

Jill and I both turned around.

'Mrs Wilson?' A tall old man was holding out a hand awkwardly to shake Jill's hand. He smiled, revealing uneven, yellow teeth.

At first, she seemed confused, then must have realised he was the owner of the cottage we were staying in. 'Oh, hello, Mr Venables. The cottage is lovely, thank you for having us. Oh, and this is my oldest and dearest friend, Wendy Jones.'

'Oh, so it's you with the telescope trained on the cottage?' I said, unsmiling.

Something like anger flashed across his face, and his bushy eyebrows lowered as he turned to look at me. 'It isn't on the cottage, it's on the *stars*.'

I didn't want to embarrass Jill; she'd booked the cottage with them and obviously had email exchanges. But I was glad I'd let him know I'd seen him. Hopefully he'd keep his telescope on the bloody stars next time.

'I told Wendy that. I said you'd be looking at the stars, not us.' Jill smiled.

'I look at the stars most of the time, but it's handy to keep an eye on our tenants,' he joked. I didn't laugh.

'Oh no, we won't allow naughty girls in our property,' he continued, waving a long finger at us both. He must have been close to eighty; it felt inappropriate for him to be talking to us in this way.

Jill and I both glanced at each other; she looked as uncomfortable as I felt.

This was the guy who'd had a bloody telescope trained on my bathroom window the previous night. He was really creepy.

But Jill being Jill, she was on a mission and obviously keen to interrogate him.

'So, Mr Venables, have you lived here all your life?'

He looked from her to me and back again, clearly enjoying the attention. 'No, my wife has… I think she was born around here.'

I found this odd, why did he only *think* she'd been born there, why didn't he *know*?

'You don't sound Welsh. How long have you been here, Mr Venables?' Jill was definitely giving him the full shakedown. I didn't care about his heritage, I just wanted to go.

'No, I'm not Welsh.'

'Oh… so where are you from?'

'I'm from Worcester.' He looked at me, then back at Jill; his eyes were so bloody shifty.

'What a coincidence. That's where we're from, aren't we, Wendy?'

I nodded uncertainly, unwilling to give this old pervert any personal information.

'I used to live just down the road from you,' he said.

'Me… you lived near me? But how do you know where I live Mr Venables?' Jill asked.

He looked a little confused. 'You live on Lavender Close.'

'Yes, but how do you *know* that?' I had to butt in.

'I… I don't know,' he said, at which point Jill must have realised how he knew. 'Sorry, you've seen my address on the booking form, haven't you?'

'I was born near there; my dad used to work at the race-course.' He smiled, looking her up and down a bit too much.

Jill pulled her scarf around herself unconsciously, covering herself. 'Oh... when did you move here then?'

'Must be thirty or forty years ago.'

'I imagine it's all changed since you were there, you wouldn't know it.'

'No, I go back there a lot, I was there just a couple of weeks ago.'

'Really?' Jill stopped smiling. 'Why?'

'I have a cousin who lives in Worcester.' He was addressing Jill, but his eyes kept sliding over to me.

'Oh... you just see your cousin when you go back then?'

He was nodding and smiling, still looking from her to me and back again. I felt uncomfortable, and quite vulnerable standing on an empty road in the middle of nowhere with this stranger.

'Well, we should get on with our walk,' I said to Jill, fully expecting her to fall in with what I was saying. She must have noticed his lingering eyes and strange demeanour too. But it was as if she hadn't heard me and was concentrating solely on this rather odd man.

'Our children came here, on a school trip,' she started. 'They came to stargaze and camped somewhere nearby.'

My heart sank. So this wasn't a stargazing trip to remember her son and bond with her old friend as she'd told me. Jill was still looking for clues. After a year and a half, she was still asking questions, ferreting away trying to find someone to blame for Leo's death.

'Yes, we get lots of schools coming here. Perfect conditions for the stars. It gets very dark,' he added, glancing at me.

'It was this time two years ago, my son and Wendy's daughter were here with a school group. There must have been about thirty of them altogether. Do you remember a school group from Worcester? My son's name was Leo, his friend was called Olivia?' she added, looking into his face, desperately hoping he could give her something.

He looked at her blankly.

'Oh, I just wondered if you remembered any of them. They must have wandered around here?'

He shook his head.

'It's getting cold, perhaps we should go back now?' I said anxiously, reluctant to continue this exchange down the lonely, isolated lane. She'd already caused trouble and lost friends by accusing people of 'hiding something', in her constant need to dig up fresh evidence. Only this time, she'd dragged me along.

'Come on, Jill,' I urged.

'The last people who stayed said they were having problems with the boiler?' he suddenly asked, quite randomly. 'I tell you what I'll do, I'll pop over later with my toolbox.'

'I'm cold, do you mind if we get walking?' I asked Jill pointedly, and finally she seemed to get it and we set off.

'What was that about?' I hissed as we walked away.

'Something happened here, I know it did. Leo was never the same after that trip. The school won't talk to me, they say there were no problems on the trip and Leo was fine, but he wasn't.' She turned to me. 'I can't explain it, but when he came home, it was as if a light had gone out.'

'I had *nothing* to do with those kids.' The voice behind us startled me. He was still hanging around and had heard us talking.

'Shit, he's following us,' I cried, and my finger ends were tingling with fear. 'Come on,' I said, and we started to pick up our pace, and didn't stop until we'd reached the end of the lane. Only then did I turn around. He was standing in the near distance, staring after us, just like the night before as he'd looked through his telescope, aimed right at the cottage.

'Well, I don't trust him, especially the way he was so defensive about not having anything to do with the kids.'

'I don't know. To be honest, Wendy, I don't trust anyone after everything. But I'm convinced that someone, somewhere, knows exactly what happened that night,' she says pointedly. I feel my face flush.

'I understand,' I say.

'I don't mean to be rude,' she replies, 'but you can't possibly understand, because your child came home that night; mine didn't.'

FIVE

JILL

'You should have just ignored him, Jill; he is so weird, and if that telescope is out tonight I'm calling the police.'

'Oh no, we don't want any police hanging around,' I say as we go back into the cottage and I lock the door. 'I've had enough of police to last a lifetime.'

'But he's spying on us.'

'Mr Venables is weird, but I think he's harmless,' I say with little conviction. I don't want her too scared; she might decide to leave, and I need her to stay all weekend. 'I wanted to talk to him because he might *know* something.'

'I doubt he knows anything, seemed a bit gaga to me. I'm scared to go to bed tonight, Jill. He must have keys. We need to barricade the doors.'

'It was his wife who took my booking... I spoke to her on the phone, she manages the cottage, he won't have keys.'

'Did you have your suspicions when you booked the cottage? Is that why you booked it? I thought you genuinely wanted a weekend away.'

'No. Obviously I know this is the area where the kids came on the school trip, but I didn't suspect Mr Venables of anything.

It's just that when we saw him today it occurred to me he might have met Leo or Olivia. The youth hostel they stayed in wasn't far from here.'

'Oh, love, you're still going over and over it all, aren't you?'

'Yes, I am, as you would if it were your child who died that night,' I say before she can continue with what will no doubt be a buffet of platitudes and clichés about loss. How dare she tell me I'm 'going over and over it'? Of course I am. She sits there patronising me when she has three children living in the world, and my only child is dead.

'So please don't stop me from asking why my son was murdered and who did it.'

'I'm sorry, I didn't mean—'

'It's fine, I'm not playing the victim here. I *am* the victim. I'm not even a mother any more; all I'm left with are a few saved messages on my phone. I listen to them every night before I go to sleep – it's all I have.'

'I know, I know, Jill, and I'm so sorry. I think you misunderstood. I wasn't criticising or judging you for seeking answers, it's just – it can be self-destructive. When we've lost someone, it makes no sense, it's not rational, so our instinct is to seek a reason for that. I genuinely think that's what you're doing now.'

'I'm sorry, it's too convenient. The police *told* me that he had a head wound *before* he entered the river. Someone did that to him.'

'We've talked about this. That might be *why* he fell in the river; he'd had a drink at the prom, probably tripped and banged his head. Then he staggered in the wrong direction and fell in the water. I'll never understand why you're so convinced it was murder.'

'And I'll never understand why you're so convinced it *wasn't*! You can't categorically say it wasn't,' I add, 'unless you *know* something you haven't told me? Has Olivia said anything?' She shakes her head while registering surprise at my suggestion. My eyes are drawn to the paper handkerchief in her hand that she's tearing into tiny shreds as she starts to speak.

'The police.' She hesitates, clearly unsure of her footing here. 'The *police* have confirmed that Leo walked towards the river, Jill. His footprints were on the ground.'

'Olivia was the last person to see him alive, Wendy; she must know something.'

'She was with him when he ran out of the prom. Something or someone had upset him. He left her, but he could easily have met someone else before going to the woods and ending up in the river.'

'Olivia apparently told the police that she ran after him; she says she lost him. But did she?'

'Yes, she *did*! She lost him, never saw him again after he left her at the prom. Then she called me and... and I told her to call the police because she was worried about his mental state.'

She always tries to make Olivia seem innocent of everything; the implication here is that Olivia called the police and tried to save him, but I'm not buying it.

'Something happened that night to upset my son – and whoever upset him knows what happened,' I say. If Olivia is anything like her mother, cheating is in her DNA.

She takes a breath. 'This is hard, but have you considered that he might have... harmed himself?'

'Leo did *not* take his own life. He didn't fall in the river either.'

'But he sent a text saying he couldn't *take* any more,' she says gently, while pulling off her thick jacket and hanging it in the cloakroom.

'It's a turn of phrase. He was just using words he thought were grown up. He was *sixteen* years old. Wendy, he wasn't into drama; if he'd thought Olivia was planning to leave him for her ex he would have simply walked away. He was little more than a child. The complexities of relationships weren't paramount;

he was more concerned about how his football team would get on next season.'

She takes a deep breath, like she's tired of explaining life's basics to me. 'Don't you remember when *you* were sixteen?' she asks in a voice she probably stole from her therapist. 'Everything is intense. God, a broken nail would send me into an emotional frenzy.'

How can she use such a crass analogy when talking about my son's emotional state before death?

'I know there's a theory that he thought Olivia was seeing her ex – but that wouldn't have affected him. I knew my son, and I *knew* what hurt him,' I hear myself say, as guilt wafts through me like gossamer.

'We think we know our kids, love, but we don't,' she says, like she knew Leo better than me. 'It was probably just puppy love, but when you're in it, hormones raging, it can be the most intense thing you'll ever feel in your life. And if he saw Olivia talking to Rory at the prom, that was it – fireworks. If we could rewind and start again, we would. I feel guilty about it, and I know Olivia does.'

'If neither of you had anything to do with his actual death you mustn't feel guilty – there's no reason,' I add pointedly.

This seems to frustrate her, which convinces me her guilt is justified. 'I wish to *God* they'd never started going out together. It was a big mistake. You were against it and you were right to be – Leo was too soft, he couldn't cope with a girlfriend.'

'He wasn't *soft*.'

'He couldn't cope, and as soon as there was a problem, he freaked out. It wasn't Olivia's fault, but have you any idea of the shit that she's had to deal with? The whole school blamed her, Jill. I had to stop her going on social media – the trolls were so cruel, virtually accusing her of...'

I sigh, knowing in my heart that Wendy or Olivia hold the key to what happened. I can see it's going to be impossible to find out anything from Wendy, who's sticking rigidly to her script. And the more I probe, the more obstacles she throws into the mix and the more confusing it becomes.

'Look, you thought Olivia wasn't good enough for your son, and that's your opinion, but he may have had a different perspective. I'm telling you he was crazy about her, and that's why he killed himself.'

'Leo wasn't stupid. He had a huge crush on Olivia, but it wasn't debilitating love that he would die for; she wasn't the girl he dreamed of being with forever.'

'Stop, Jill, just stop!'

She doesn't speak for a while and we sit in silence, both convinced we know what happened, but in truth the only person who really knew was Leo and his killer.

I don't want us to fall out; we need to stay friends, for the weekend at least, so I return to our safe space, the early days.

'I often think back,' I say, 'to Olivia and Leo on a rug in the garden, little legs waving in the air, just starting to walk, and those baby giggles.'

'Yeah, while Robert and Tim hung out down the pub and the boys smashed their bloody football around the garden. I had to yell at them all the time, "Mind the babies," until I was hoarse.'

'And here we are now. The kids have gone, the husbands have gone, and we're in wet Wales.' She stops talking for a moment. 'Don't get me wrong, I appreciate why we're here. I just feel a bit... disappointed in life.'

She obviously doesn't have the same rose-tinted glasses as me. I always thought her life was perfect, and nothing really bothered her; she just laughed and danced through it all, and always came up smelling of roses. Perhaps it wasn't quite like that after all?

If I learned something from living on Lavender Close, it's

that you never know a person. Friends, neighbours, husbands, wives, and even our own kids – we were all strangers.

'I'll make some tea,' she mutters and walks through into the kitchen.

I watch her put the kettle on and rummage around the cupboard for tea bags. My only concern right now is her – because it's obvious she's keeping something from me. Is Wendy protecting her precious daughter. Or herself?

This weekend, I intend to find out.

SIX

WENDY

Saturday Evening

We were due to check out Monday morning, but I wanted to leave now. Mr Venables across the road had creeped me out, and Jill went from anxious and edgy to suddenly smiley and nostalgic for the past and the friendship we had. I was finding her hard to read, but she obviously needed some company, and as difficult as she could be, I felt for her. She'd lost everything and I felt guilty for abandoning her when Leo died, but I was concerned about Olivia. I had to help her.

I knew she felt I'd let her down, and I didn't blame her for that but, at the time, as a family, we had some issues of our own to deal with. I couldn't tell her about Olivia because she'd create a whole narrative around what happened to her and I knew she'd assume the worst. I couldn't risk that; she had already told the police that Olivia was cheating on Leo, which wasn't true. Olivia was devastated. 'I didn't cheat on him, Mum,' she said. 'I loved him!' And I believed her.

* * *

By early evening, we'd begun to slip back into our old selves. We had a pleasant afternoon talking about the past, mostly good times, remembering old friends and neighbours – we laughed a lot too. Jill seemed calmer as she sipped on her red bush tea, while outside it got darker and darker.

The smell of the tea reminded me of manure and I suddenly felt sick and wanted to leave the room. I couldn't be rude and tell her that her tea made me want to vomit, so I just sat there feeling trapped. I watched her scrolling on her phone, little animal movements, her neat nails, tidy V-neck jumper and tight smile. I had a rush of rising panic in my chest. Would I ever escape this place, this guilt, this old, anxious friendship that was no more?

I picked up my phone and mirrored Jill's scrolling, trying hard to hide the dread filling my mind. I kept my eyes on the newsfeed, headlines that made no sense because I couldn't focus. I was trying to avoid the shadows forming in neglected corners of the room. I saw Leo and was flooded with guilt and regret. Olivia's face hovered in my mind, her open mouth, her silent scream filling my head.

'How's Olivia? I haven't seen her for ages,' Jill suddenly asked, like she could read my mind.

'She's good.' I try to focus on my phone screen.

'Is she going to university in September?' I realise how poignant this is for Jill. Leo had been tipped for Oxbridge when he died.

'No, she doesn't feel ready.' I really don't want to get into a conversation about my daughter. Jill asks such searching questions. Tim always says, 'Jill's wasted in financial planning. She should have been a detective. She doesn't stop asking questions. In the end you just give in and agree to anything.'

'So she's not going, or is she just deferring?'

Christ. 'No, no, she isn't deferring. She may go later on.'

'I hope it doesn't have anything to do with—'

'No,' I say too loudly over her words, cutting her off. She raises her eyebrows and drinks some more of the vile tea.

'I saw her friend Sarah in Tesco; she said she's gone away, having a year out or something?'

If she knows, why did she ask?

'Yes, she's gone to stay with Robert for a while.'

'But I thought Robert lived in Spain now?'

I nodded. 'He does.'

'But why would she just go off like that? You and Olivia were so close.'

'We still are. She just wants to travel, starting in Spain. Can't say I blame her,' I offered flippantly.

'How do you feel about her doing that? I mean, you were both keen for her to go to uni.' Jill was never letting this go.

As my oldest friend, Jill knew me better than anyone, and my calm acceptance of the situation didn't make sense. I was the mother who constantly encouraged my daughter to dream big, work hard, finish her homework, revise for exams. 'Will she carry on doing media studies?' she continued, aware that a lot of money had been spent on private tutors with the goal of gaining a place at university.

'I don't know, she just needs some time to think about what she wants to do. She fancies art... some kind of art.' I was flailing around here. I longed for her to go to university, do something with her life. The idea of Olivia running away to Spain and bumming around just wasn't something I'd allow under normal circumstances. But things weren't normal for us any more, and Jill had guessed something was wrong.

'Art? That's a bit random... I thought she was set on university, then working in television?'

I was embarrassed; I knew exactly what she was referring to, and I heard the judgement in her voice. Mortifyingly, my only daughter's *only* ambition was to be on *Love Island*, and the only way we could get her to agree to university was if she could do media studies because it was the closest she could get to reality TV.

'Yeah, well, we can't choose our kids' lives for them,' I replied, trying to sound nonchalant, accepting, which I wasn't.

'I suppose she can learn Spanish while she's there. That would be useful?' she offered. I thought about Olivia, how she was – and it felt like a stinging slap.

'Yeah.' I went back to my phone, a sign to let her know the conversation was over.

'If you want to talk, Wendy, I'm here. We used to talk, didn't we? Couldn't stop us. Tim used to complain when I texted you. "Haven't you two spent most of today together? Haven't you said everything you need to for one day?" he'd say. But we always had more, didn't we?' She was now resting her chin on her hand and staring into my eyes. I knew she was searching for answers, which was why I couldn't look at her – because she might have seen.

After our encounter with Mr Venables, we decided to leave our stargazing walk for another evening. I was scared and Jill was tired. 'Tonight, let's just relax and chat over a glass or two,' Jill said. 'I'll make us some pasta. I found a lovely recipe.'

'Oh, Jill, you can't cook again. I'll cook for you,' I offered.

'Don't be daft, I love cooking. I don't get to do it any more. I miss that.'

'You know, all those years of cooking and cleaning, running around after Leo, dropping him off and picking him up, dashing home with armfuls of groceries. You can't wait for it all to slow down; you dream of picking up a book, watching a whole episode of your favourite soap, or taking a long bath. Then one day your kids grow up or leave and there's no rush any more; no one needs a lift and no one's waiting for dinner. Now you have all the time in the world, and you don't want it.'

I hear the emptiness in the silence.

'I know,' I said. 'I understand that feeling only too well – it's the loneliness that gets you.'

'I don't even have friends over now. You and Robert have split, the kids are gone and I don't get to do those big family suppers we used to love.' She sighed. 'Remember how we'd all sit down on a Saturday evening and watch *The X Factor*? You'd do one of your amazing French recipes one week, another I'd do a big pasta for eight people. Olivia used to call it "Jill's gigantic lasagne".'

'Oh, those Saturday nights were raucous and so much fun.'

'Yes, but when I think about it, we all drank in front of the kids.'

'Oh God, don't remind me,' I said, rolling my eyes and thinking about the way Josh had enjoyed beer too much for a sixteen-year-old. Now at twenty-two, his university life seemed to revolve around alcohol. Even Robert had remarked on it recently, asking me if I was worried about our eldest. 'No, I'm not,' I'd said, a little too defensively. 'It's what university is for, Robert!' But as a wife and mother whose husband had spent years working away, I hope my nightly glasses of wine haven't given the wrong message to my kids. Robert's work took him all over the world and away from his family for months on end. I needed wine, and friends... and lovers.

'Tim enjoyed my cooking,' Jill was saying as she added chopped peppers to the pot on the stove. She was smiling at the memory of him, like they'd had this wonderful life together; had she forgotten that I lived next door and heard the violent rows and screamed insults? More than once she arrived on my doorstep in tears after he'd stormed off over something nasty that had happened between them.

'God, he was a rubbish husband,' she said, like she knew what I was thinking. 'I don't know what I'd have done if you hadn't lived next door. You were my therapist.'

'I know, you needed one being married to Tim. You were always convinced he was having an affair, and I'd talk you down.'

'I remember, all the usual signs: "He's working late, smells of perfume, and he's bad tempered,"' she said, rolling her eyes.

'Sounds like every man I've ever loved,' I replied.

We both laughed. 'I think you said something similar then. You could always make me laugh, Wendy; you got me through some very difficult times.'

'Do you remember us sitting on our back doorsteps, sharing a bottle of wine?' I said, and her face lit up.

'Oh yes, or you'd bake a cake for the kids and by the time they were home from school, we'd eaten half of it. And Tim would say, "No wonder you're putting on weight, Miss Piggy."' She tried to smile at this, but the smile faded, and I saw the pain in her eyes.

'I probably shouldn't say this,' I started, 'but when I heard you'd kicked Tim out, I was proud of you.'

'I didn't kick him out, Wendy, he was planning to leave me,' she said in a really small voice. 'He's met someone else, someone he really loves who makes him feel seen.'

'Oh fuck. I'm sorry, I didn't realise.' I felt awkward, reaching instinctively for the bottle of red I'd placed on the kitchen counter earlier. 'Let's get that drink I promised you, Chef,' I joked, hoping to lighten the moment a little.

She emptied a can of tomatoes into the pot and began therapeutically stirring.

'But I heard you'd thrown all his stuff outside.'

She nodded and I saw a twinkle in her eye. 'I slashed a couple of his shirts too!'

This made me smile. 'Whoa, go Jill. All these years, I never knew you were a badass.'

'Oh, you'd be surprised,' she said, sipping her wine. 'No one gets the better of me.'

SEVEN

JILL

I thought Wendy was going to run off earlier; that would have ruined everything. I had to backpedal slightly and appear to be grateful for her 'support', and I think I've managed to convince her to stay now.

Spending time with her isn't unpleasant. She's a decent person; she just has her priorities skewed. Her values are different from mine. She'd rather buy her friend an extortion-ately priced, gift-wrapped candle than have a difficult or uncomfortable conversation.

Wendy has always valued *things*. Robert's family were wealthy, and they inherited a lot of money when his parents died. They used the money to buy flashy new cars and improve their home with architect-designed extensions, vaulted ceilings, and a staircase fit for film stars to glide down. If I'd had that kind of money, I'd have given up work and been home more for Leo, but that didn't interest Wendy. 'I need to be me, not Mum, or Doctor Robert's wife... for now. And one day I might just fall in love with one of the neighbours and run away.'

Wendy was being flippant, her default mode for most things – but I really believed she might.

I'm in the kitchen about to start dinner when she walks in. I'm reminded of how lovely she is, and why I was always so threatened by her friendship with my husband. Curvy, with a warm smile and shiny blonde hair that hasn't seen any grey yet, she's wearing a powder-blue jumper that brings out the blue in her eyes.

'That colour suits you,' I say.

'Thanks, my darling, you're always so kind,' she beams.

'You had a lovely dress that shade, must be ten or fifteen years ago. You wore it when we went to see *Les Mis* in London.'

'Oh yes, it was a wool dress, too fitted. I felt so fat in it.'

'Rubbish. I remember Tim remarking on how lovely you looked while I sat there in a brown wool dress looking like someone from the fifties – and not in a good way. I'd had my colours done and the woman said I was autumn.' I laugh. 'I really wasn't.'

'You look good in russets and browns.'

'Not as great as you do in blue, according to Tim. "You should ask Wendy where she got that dress from and buy yourself one," he said when we got home that night.'

She rolls her eyes. I'm embarrassing her; I don't mean to, it's just that I've buried these slights for so long, I feel like now he's gone they need airing. My problem was never with Wendy, it was with *him*. 'I sat there in my new brown dress and he never even noticed; he was too busy looking at you in blue.'

'I'm sure he didn't mean to hurt you.'

'No, I don't suppose he cared enough to hurt me. He was just tactless and stupid.'

'Of *course* he was, he's a man.'

I think about the night, just a few years ago. Wendy and Robert had been over at ours for the evening, and when they'd gone Tim found Wendy's glasses; she'd left them on the sofa.

I was waiting for him to say he'd take them there and then. They'd been giggling together all night and I thought he might use the glasses as an excuse to go round; Robert might be in bed. They may even have planned for her to leave them so they could see each other again. I had this vision of him wandering through the front garden, and her answering the door in her sexy nightie.

'I'll take them round tomorrow,' I offered, testing him. And to my surprise, he agreed, and when he came to bed later, he had them in his hand.

'Try them on?' he suggested, sitting on the bed.

'Why?'

'I want to see what you look like. It reminds me of a school teacher I used to fancy when I was sixteen,' he revealed.

I laughed at this, and enjoying his attention, which was rarely on me. I went along with it and put them on.

'I want to make love to you and pretend you're my old teacher.'

'Naughty boy,' I said, giggling and feeling slightly risqué as we kissed more passionately than we had in years. I wondered if this was the role play in the bedroom that I'd read about in magazines.

Later, as we lay next to each other in the dark, I said, 'Did you really fancy a teacher in school, or did you want to pretend you were sleeping with Wendy?'

He just patted my arm and went to sleep, while I lay there feeling uneasy, as I always had, knowing I was second best.

I'm thinking about this now, because like everything else in our lives since we moved next door to the Joneses, it shaped what we did and who we were. I have no proof that anything happened between them, but as a result of *his* behaviour, I've never been able to trust my friend.

It didn't help that Tim openly admired Wendy; he never hid his attraction for her, even to me. 'I really don't understand why Wendy is with Robert. He really is punching, isn't he?' Tim had said in the early days before we had the kids, when you looked at someone your own age and could still see the person, not the parent.

'You're just seeing the obvious,' I replied. 'Robert's attractive in a quieter way. He's kind and calm and he's a doctor; what's not to love?' I was openly trying to make Tim jealous, but he really didn't care.

I sometimes wonder if Wendy hadn't lived next door, maybe our marriage would have stood a chance. Perhaps I would have felt more secure, and he wouldn't have been constantly reminded of what he could have had every time he stepped out of the front door.

'Why would you want me when you can have her?' was my usual cry after I'd drunk too much at one of the neighbourhood parties and spent all evening watching him flirt with her.

'Not this again, Jill,' he used to say, and instead of reassuring me, he'd make some remark along the lines of, 'If you say it enough times it might just happen.' I thought it was his clumsy way of telling me to stop obsessing and stop blaming Wendy for our unhappy marriage. Now I think it was a warning.

After that I always held something back from her; I could never fully embrace our friendship because by then I didn't trust her. I hope I can make that up to her this weekend; I owe her that.

'Is dinner ready yet?' Wendy asks.

'God, I was miles away,' I chuckle.

'Just call me insignificant,' she jokes.

I check the oven; the pasta bake will take at least half an hour. 'Shouldn't be too long now.'

'Great, I'll get us another glass while it cooks. It's good to spend some time together, Jill.'

'Yes, seeing you again has brought the past rushing back,' I say, 'in a good way.'

'Yeah, it's been lovely to reconnect.' She's smiling and looking past me. Suddenly her expression changes. 'Shit.'

'What is it?' The fear on her face makes the hairs on the back of my neck rise, and I turn to look where she's looking. As it's now dark outside it's not easy to make out, but there's a shadowy figure at the window. Someone is looking in. All I can see are two eyes.

'Christ,' I murmur, picking up the just-boiled kettle and holding it high so whoever it is can see me and understand what I'm threatening.

'Get away! If you don't go *now*, I'm going to throw this boiling water right in your face!' With that, I march towards the door, and the figure seems to move away, so I open the door quickly. 'And don't come back!' I call loudly, walking out into the back garden, and from the light of the kitchen, I see what looks like Mr Venables scuttling off.

'That was *him*,' I say, marching back inside. 'Venables.'

Her mouth is open. 'Bloody peeping Tom. I *knew* he was a weirdo. I'm calling the police.'

I feel my whole body tingle as a slow fear runs through me; *not the police!*

'No, you don't need to do that. I'm sure he's harmless,' I add, concerned she'll freak out and leave. 'I mean, technically he's our landlord – he might have been checking up. I think we may have overreacted.'

'No, we didn't! What kind of landlord lurks around in the dark peering through a window?' She's right, and I'm as freaked out as she is, but I can't let her call the police.

'I spoke to his wife when I made the booking; she seemed really nice. Why don't I call their landline and tell her? I think it's probably better to do that in the first instance,' I say, picking up my phone.

'No, I can't sleep here tonight knowing he's wandering around,' she says, clearly terrified.

'Thing is, we didn't give him a chance to explain.'

'Explain what? He was *staring* at us, standing outside in the dark, just staring in!' she shrieks.

I desperately try to reassure her. 'It was my fault. I should have just asked him what he wanted. I thought it might be a burglar trying to break in and I started yelling and threatening him with the kettle.'

'I hope to God he was telling the truth when he said he didn't meet our kids,' she murmurs.

I also wondered if he'd lied about that, but I've buried it deep; I have enough on my plate this weekend. I feel like I might faint; *why did I come here?* But I know why I came here. I would investigate him afterwards.

Suddenly there's a loud banging on the front door, and we both let out a yelp.

'He's back,' she says, grabbing my arm, a whimper escaping under her breath. She's shaking. We both stare back at each other, and together move to the kitchen door that leads to the tiny hallway. And at the end of that little hallway, the tall, shadowy shape of our landlord stands waiting for us to open the door. Then there's a rustling, a movement, and we hold on to each other as the sound of a key going into a lock grates through the silence.

'He's got fucking *keys*,' Wendy's groaning quietly, her voice loaded with terror.

Now even *I'm* scared, because out here in this remote cottage, with no streetlights outside, and no one else for miles, no one will hear us scream.

EIGHT

WENDY

'I'm calling the police!' I hissed, almost crying as I started punching numbers into my phone. Something was now pressing, shuffling against the glass of the door. Then a hard rapping on the glass, which shook me so much I yelped. Jill and I stood close, both rooted to the ground as the front door slowly opened, and as my phone rang, I waited for the response in my ear.

'Hello, police?' I was shouting, but the signal must have gone because it went dead. I was about to start dialling again when someone emerged from the pitch black, into the dark hallway.

'Hello?' It was a woman's voice. 'I don't think there's anyone in, Derek.'

I was confused, but as Jill turned on the light, I saw the tall outline of Mr Venables, and behind him a small woman.

'Oh, you made me jump!' She clutched her chest like it was us who had intruded upon her.

'I'm sorry, who are you?' Jill asked, remaining calm and polite while still on edge, I was huffing and puffing.

'I'm so sorry, dear, I'm Margaret... Margaret Venables,' she said. 'I do apologise for just turning up like this with Derek. He came over a few minutes ago to fix your boiler but he said there was no one in. So I checked and saw both your cars here and was concerned you might have ventured out on foot.' She was looking from me to Jill, studying our faces. 'We decided to come and check on you, and when there was no answer we used our keys; we didn't mean to scare you.'

'Well, you did!' I replied angrily. 'We thought it was a burglar or worse. We were terrified. He was staring through the glass door at us.'

'So sorry, dear,' she murmured again. In complete contrast to him, she was stout with a smiley face *and* a full set of fairly white teeth, though I imagined they came out at night.

'I'll go and check the boiler,' he muttered, trudging up the stairs. I felt so uncomfortable, it was like an invasion. They'd let themselves in and he was now wandering up the stairs.

'We haven't had a problem with the boiler so far,' I called after him, but he carried on up the stairs. I wouldn't have been surprised if he took the opportunity to check out my lingerie drawer while he was up there. I stood at the bottom of the stairs watching him and shuddered as he disappeared from the landing; God knows what he was up to.

Jill was now fussing around Mrs V, making her a cup of tea while the two of them engaged in a fascinating conversation about the weather. I was one glass of pinot away from booking a flight to Spain and getting the hell out of there when Jill abruptly changed the conversation.

'Our children were here, about two years ago,' she said, and I braced myself as her interrogation began, *again*. 'They were on a stargazing holiday with the school, camping just down the road.'

'Oh, I think I remember them.'

'Really?' At this we both looked at each other in surprise. This *was* interesting considering her husband apparently *didn't* remember them.

'Yes, some of the kids turned up at our farmhouse. They'd been walking and got lost. I remember them because they came from Worcester, and Derek's family come from there.'

I turned around. 'But Mr V said he didn't recall—'

Jill shot me a warning look, jumping in. 'Do you remember a boy named Leo, and a girl called Olivia?' She was being very intense, right up in Margaret's grill as my kids would say. According to our old neighbours, Jill was constantly doing this, interrogating people, even sometimes accusing them of being involved in Leo's death. Seeing it for myself was quite disturbing, and Mrs V looked a bit taken aback.

'Yes, I remember them both,' she said. 'Nice children.'

Jill and I looked at each other. 'Olivia is Wendy's daughter, Leo my son,' she said, without using a tense to indicate he wasn't with us any more. That must be so cruel for a bereaved mother, that your child *was* instead of *is*.

I put my hand on Jill's arm in an attempt to show my sympathy, and comfort, and leaned forward to hear what Mrs V had to say. Jill was desperate to pin Leo's death on someone, and if the focus moved to these two weirdos who lived in the wilderness, Jill might stop trying to drag Olivia's name into it. There's a silver lining to everything if you look hard enough.

'Why would you remember *our* two children specifically?' I asked, abandoning the green peppers in the sink and walking over to the table where they were both nursing mugs of tea.

She turned to me and shrugged. 'Because they were nice kids and Leo talked about the Leo star constellation with Derek.' She stared at us both.

'So Derek *talked* to them?' I snapped. 'Because he told us he didn't, which seems very odd to me.' I tried not to sound anxious, but I couldn't help it. Jill said that Leo changed on that holiday, and I was concerned this might come back on Olivia.

'Yes, we both talked to all of them. Derek gave Leo a lift back after.'

'After *what*?' Jill asks as I brace myself for something, though I wasn't sure what.

'You're Leo's mum?' she asked, looking at Jill.

'Yes,' Jill replied eagerly. She was tapping her feet on the floor. Her fists were so tight I could see the whiteness of her knuckles. I could feel her desperate, visceral need for knowledge about her boy. In that moment my heart went out to her, and I had to move closer and put my arm around her skinny, now hunched shoulders.

'Leo was talking about the lion's head constellation?'

'Yes,' she said quickly to waste no time.

'Well, Derek took him to look through his telescope.'

Jill looked uneasy at this. 'The one you have at the upstairs window?'

'That's right, my Derek is fascinated by the night sky. Leo loved the telescope.'

'Did he?' Jill wanted more. I realised this need for evidence wasn't just about Leo's death but also his life – it was a primal need to know everything she could about her son. And to hold him to her one more time.

'Did all the kids go upstairs with him?' I asked, alarmed at this. 'Were there no teachers with them?'

'No, just Leo,' she replied. 'The others stayed downstairs with me. I gave them cake and mugs of hot chocolate. Lovely kids.'

Olivia had never mentioned this to me; she'd been fifteen then and had been in a stranger's house miles from home. Miles from anywhere! *What else had my daughter not told me?* But selfishly, I breathed a sigh of relief; at least my daughter had been safely downstairs with the wife eating cake with her friends. It also meant Jill couldn't implicate Olivia if whatever happened that 'changed' Leo took place alone upstairs with Mr Venables.

'Leo loved the telescope. The one their teacher hired for the trip wasn't half as powerful as Derek's.' She stopped talking and, looking at the doorway, said, 'Hello, love.'

Derek was standing there; he looked angry, and they stared at each other across the kitchen. I felt like I was watching two animals about to fight, and I wasn't sure why – or who would pounce first.

'You remember Leo, the boy from the school trip from Worcester? They were here last year. This is his mum.'

His face turned from anger to confusion.

'He was called Leo and you showed him the lion's head constellation, with your telescope?'

'Oh... yes, I remember now,' he said, which seemed rather odd. Jill clearly wasn't buying this and, keen to pin him down, she offered him a cup of tea.

'Was Leo... okay? Did he like using the telescope?' Jill asked, her eager face waiting for a crumb as he sat down at the table.

'Oh yes, the telescope.' He looked at her and we waited for him to elaborate, but he didn't offer any more. I got the feeling that he didn't remember Leo, that he was just saying he did to appease his wife. I couldn't work out the dynamic between them, but she seemed to be in charge.

'I think Leo felt a bit left out,' Mrs V suddenly announced.

Jill's head whizzed round to face her, and tilting it to one side, she asked, almost in a whisper, 'Why do you *say* that?'

She half-shrugged, seemingly put off by the penetrating stare her remark had triggered.

'What do you mean, left out?' Jill really was relentless.

'Some of Leo's friends wanted to go to the pub. They had fake ID, but we tried to stop them, and said if they got caught, they'd be in trouble. Leo didn't want to go to the pub, he was a good boy but the others were trying to persuade him.'

'Leo's always been a good son, never caused me a moment's trouble,' she said smugly. I knew this was aimed at me because Olivia was a bit of a tearaway, and Jill obviously thought my daughter was a bad influence on her son. But poor Leo had no choice but to be 'a good son', because Jill never gave him a chance to do anything; she mollycoddled him.

'So the others didn't manage to persuade him to go to the pub?' Jill asked hungrily.

'We didn't do anything with them,' Mr V piped up.

Mrs V immediately put her hand on his, squeezed it and continued. 'No, he stuck by his guns; you should be proud of him. The others all went to the pub, and he stayed behind and looked through the telescope. Derek wouldn't let Leo go back to the campsite alone, so he drove him, *didn't* you, love?'

She was looking into his face, staring intently until he said, 'Yeah,' while nodding uncertainly over his mug of tea.

'I took Leo home; I looked him up the next time I was in Worcester visiting my cousin.'

Before either of us could say anything, Mrs V swooped in.

'No, you didn't, love. You haven't been back there for years.' She rolled her eyes at us and stood up. 'I think we'd better go; it's getting late and these ladies want their dinner.'

Jill was clearly disturbed by this, as was I. 'Just you and Leo, none of the *other* children?' she asked Venables, a deep frown creasing her forehead.

He looked up at his wife, who was now standing over him. 'No, just Derek and Leo, chatting away about stars, they were. They got along so well, didn't you?'

'You told me off,' he said.

'I didn't, Derek...' Then she hesitated. 'I was a bit cross because I was worried. You were ages coming back, over an hour for a ten-minute drive. But you and Leo were chatting, weren't you? I nearly sent a search party for you, didn't I, love?' She bent down, smiled into his face, and the hairs stood up on the back of my neck. Was she trying to shut him up?

'Come on then,' she urged, helping him to stand up, keen to get him out of the cottage.

This didn't feel right to me. Leo was a schoolboy, and quite sheltered thanks to Jill's helicopter mothering. Did something happen on that lift back to the campsite that freaked him out, and caused the change Jill said she'd seen in her son?

I looked from the Venableses back to my friend, who looked shell-shocked. I didn't even want to formulate a guess as to what might have happened. Was *this* what Jill had been searching for?

I turned to Jill; her face was white. I thought I might be sick.

NINE

JILL

After meeting Mr and Mrs Venables, I'm having serious concerns about what happened here with my son. I feel so anxious, it's very confusing. Why didn't Leo mention this encounter, even if it was just to tell me about the telescope?

I thought all I had to do was get the truth out of Wendy this weekend, but now I'm worried about the Venableses too. There's something not right about him, and the way she seems to shut him down. What's she trying to hide?

'Why would a seventy-something man take such an interest in a fifteen-year-old boy? What did they talk about that they spent over an hour chatting, in his van?' I say to Wendy after they've gone.

She's shaking her head. 'I don't even want to think.'

'Me neither.' I feel nauseous. One half of my mind is saying Mr Venables did something inappropriate; the other is frantically searching for a more innocent answer.

'Is he just a nice old man who's kind to kids?' I ask.

'Teenage boys?' she replies, horror edging her words.

'Were they really talking for over an hour in a cold van in

January? And *did* he meet up with Leo in our hometown as he said? If so, why didn't Leo ever say anything to us?'

She shrugs, now opening a bottle of Prosecco.

'I mustn't get carried away. I do think Mr V seems confused.'

'Confused? *Lying* more like. He was definitely hiding something,' she says, struggling to get the cork out of the bottle.

'Yes, I felt the same; there was something shifty about him. He was determined to go upstairs and fix the boiler, but I don't think there's anything wrong with it.'

'Yeah, I only realised after they'd gone that the boiler's in the kitchen.' She raises her eyebrows.

'What was he doing upstairs then?'

'Again, I don't want to even think about it – but he's probably wearing one of my lacy thongs as we speak!'

In spite of everything, we both giggle at this, just as she finally pops the cork and spills fizzing Prosecco into two glasses.

'Cheers!' she says, and clinking her glass with mine, I'm suddenly transported back to the first summer we met. Another time, another place, another bottle of fizz, the same women. My pretty barefoot neighbour was wild and rebellious; she drank too much and flirted with everyone's husband, but I loved her. It was only later that changed. Should I forgive her, let her go? But how can I, after what she's done?

'Wendy,' I say once she's sitting with her drink, 'can I ask a favour?'

'Anything,' she replies, a big, beaming smile on her face, always happiest with a glass in her hand.

'Could you ask Olivia what she knows, and what she told the police? Ask her about the Venableses, about the night we lost Leo? I don't feel it would be appropriate for me to call her and ask, and besides – she's changed her number, hasn't she?' I say, locking eyes with my old friend.

The smile instantly disappears, and she puts down her

glass. 'Yes, she's changed her number. After Leo, she started receiving abusive messages and calls; she was terrified.'

I let this hang in the air. I know she blames me for that. I told people – including Wendy – that I thought Olivia was hiding something, and I believe that.

'We don't talk to Olivia about that night; it upsets her too much.'

'Oh, we can't have that...' I say sarcastically.

'Jill, I hate to keep saying this, but the police and the coroner are agreed... it was an accident. Either that or suicide.'

'No, it was an open verdict; no one in authority has mentioned anything else.'

'Jill...'

She's trying to spread lies to cover it up, but I won't let her.

'No one *knows* what happened. The head injury caused his death; he was gone by the time he went into the water. That doesn't suggest an accident or suicide to me.'

'It happens, Jill. You need to stop torturing yourself.'

'I'm not, you're torturing me. If you spoke to Olivia and asked her, she might be able to put my mind at rest. But you won't. Why, Wendy?'

Silence.

'Could you give me her new number so I could call her? Could I call her in Spain? Will Robert let me speak to her?'

'No, she's left Robert, she's gone *travelling*... to the mountains. There's no signal.'

'I thought you said she was *living* with Robert?'

I'm aware I'm being a bit pushy, but Wendy is actively trying to stop me from speaking to her daughter. She's done this since Leo died, and it's one of the reasons I know Wendy's hiding something. Why is she scared of me talking to Olivia, the last known person to see my son alive?

'She *was* with Robert, she was... She's gone travelling around with a friend. I've no idea where she is.'

How unlike Wendy to not know where her daughter is, and how convenient.

'Oh well, she wouldn't tell me anything anyway. Always a bit of a dark horse, that one.' I take a sip of Prosecco, while Wendy puffs her chest out, clearly offended by this.

'You were always complaining she never told you anything, Rory Thompson's arrest sheet, for one.' I chuckle to myself at this. 'And she hid her tattoo for ages. Even I knew about that before you,' I say defiantly.

'That's not true, we talked about it before.' Each word has a little spike on the end.

'You didn't know, you told me you were horrified when you saw it.'

I hate throwing back confidences made when we were friends, but my son is dead. There are no rules.

'I wasn't horrified, I just thought about how it would look when she gets married, in a white dress.'

'Yes, it didn't look great with her prom dress.'

'It's a lovely tattoo,' she says defensively. 'They're fashionable now, not like when we were younger, Jill,' she adds, talking down to me like I'm some old lady.

'She had "Rory Forever" tattooed over. It's now the Leo constellation... She had it done after...' Her voice drifts away.

'I might get one,' she says.

Now she's really pushing my buttons. 'A tattoo? For *Leo?*' The look of incredulity on my face must say it all because she positively shrinks.

'No, not for Leo – for *me.*'

I roll my eyes theatrically and go back to my phone. *Leo's constellation...* More like *Olivia's guilt.*

It had always been my worst fear that she'd lure him away with her skimpy skirts and too-tight tops. Wendy always dressed provocatively, and she'd allowed Olivia to do the same from a young age. I remember her coming over to Leo's thirteenth birthday party with a gift; she was wearing a very tiny skirt and her top was far too low for a young teen. I saw him noticing her though, and she seemed very much aware of him, causing my stomach to do a flip. The Joneses had caused enough problems in our lives without those two getting together.

'You have a great future, don't do anything stupid with some girl,' I used to say, meaning Olivia. I didn't want to be specific; no point making her forbidden fruit and even more tempting.

Wendy's put a glass of wine on the little side table for me, so I turn off my phone and take a sip.

'God, don't you sometimes wish you could turn the clock back to your twenties, just for a week, a day even?' she says, obviously wanting to change the subject, clear the air.

I'm still thinking about Venables and Leo. I can barely focus on anything else, but the wine is soothing. 'No, I'd hate to turn the clock back to my twenties, they were horrible,' I say. 'That age is almost as brutal as being a teenager. You're judged mostly on your looks and the clothes and make-up you own, and being plain and poor, I wasn't exactly popular. I just felt worthless, until I got into my thirties when I felt appreciated for other things, like my career, and being a mum.

'But your twenties were probably a joy. You've always been pretty and know how to wear clothes,' I add, trying to make up for my unkind remarks about Olivia's tattoo.

She smiles a little sheepishly; only women are embarrassed to admit they're attractive; a man would wear it with pride. 'I did okay. I had this one guy... The one that got away.'

'Oh, I think we all have one of those,' I say, thinking of mine as she pauses and drifts back into the past.

'I almost left Robert for him.'

'Oh, I had no idea.' I knew she had 'gentleman callers' when Robert was away, but she said it was just a drink or dinner. 'Male companionship', she called it.

I see her in my mind's eye with Tim, the two of them whispering, and my stomach churns. *Now our marriages are over, will she finally confess?*

But then frustratingly, she takes the conversation back to her Robert. 'He was a good husband and a great dad – when he was there – but as you know, his work took him away from us.'

'Yeah, he's a great dad, Robert,' I agree, remembering the way his kids used to run into his arms whenever he came home. 'But those early years were hard on you, being alone with the kids,' I offer, still trying to compensate for the mean comments I made about Olivia.

'Yeah, it was tough! I remember walking through the close with Josh in his pushchair and almost everyone I bumped into was expecting their next one. "Ooh, when are you having another?" they were asking as they waddled down the road. Jesus, he wasn't twelve months old, but there was real pressure and I got caught up in it all, like there was this race on to have the next one before our ovaries shrivelled or our husbands left. The close was like a bloody baby farm.'

'Tell me about it,' I sigh, remembering the grief and sadness, whingeing women complaining about their bulging bellies. I'd have given ten years of my life for what they had; I was suddenly excluded from the club. And I wanted to punch the well-meaning trolls with bumps telling me, 'You'll be next.'

'But you always seemed to take everything in your stride, had easy pregnancies and you just coped, where I failed.'

'Rubbish, you probably only saw the good bits. After Freddie was born I became a secret smoker. I used to sit having a fag on the back step while Freddie screamed inside in his cot and Josh ran around like a lunatic in the garden bumping into things. I just breathed in all that calming nicotine and let it wash over me.'

'You wouldn't have left Robert, though, would you?' I ask, eager to get back to her earlier comment.

'I might have, but the guy was married. I just wanted romance, passion, but I'd never really had that with Robert.'

'Anyone I know?' I ask, frustrated at her dismissal.

'No, just a guy I worked with. It was probably lust – Robert and I never quite gelled in the bedroom. I bet you and Tim did. I imagine he was a real romantic too?'

I shrug. I never saw my husband as romantic, but he was obviously different with Wendy. They were easy together, while Robert and I edged around each other cautiously. I always dreaded them going off for a smoke, leaving Robert and me alone in awkward silence avoiding each other's eyes. We'd be like that for what felt like an age until he'd make an excuse to leave. 'Just popping to the bathroom,' or if we were at ours I'd say, 'Let me fetch you another drink.' And hide in the kitchen until the others returned.

I feel uncomfortable even now just recalling those moments. And the relief when the other two returned soon changed when Tim's hand would creep onto Wendy's knee, or he'd rest his head against her neck with his eyes closed, like he was home. It was all so open, and jokey, the flirtatiousness, the teasing, the exclusive fun they always seemed to have, whoever else was there. And now, as we sip our wine in silence, my mind wanders through the years, and I wonder whether Wendy had once considered leaving her husband, for *mine*.

TEN

WENDY

After we'd had a glass of wine, Jill seemed out of sorts, but that was to be expected, I think the whole Venables thing had shaken her.

'We really are in the middle of nowhere,' I murmured, feeling a bit creeped out after our encounter with our strange landlords.

'I know, but that's the point. Tomorrow we're going stargazing like the kids did.'

'Jill, are you looking for something here?' I asked. 'I mean, apart from the Venableses, I can't help but feel you're still looking for answers that aren't really here.'

'Ooh, I need to check on dinner,' she said, standing up and going into the little kitchen. I followed her to try and convince her to let go. I genuinely wanted my friend to find peace. And yes, it was in my interests that she stopped her witch hunt, because she'd pointed the finger at Olivia, implied I knew something, and also blamed Tim for not turning up in time to collect the kids. But it wouldn't have made any difference because Leo left the prom early and according to Olivia he was in an emotional state. Jill didn't seem to be concerned about that, but kept calling Leo's friends and quizzing them at all times of the day and night; she wanted to know where they were, who they saw, what they knew. Early on in the investigation she even told the police that one of the teachers might be responsible. It was Mr Shelton, one of the nicest, kindest teachers who happened to have been on the trip to Wales. As it was early days and the police still believed her 'evidence' was legit, they had interviewed him, but dismissed him. But apparently, she continued to openly accuse him of knowing something about Leo's death.

'What more do you need, Jill?' I asked her now as we sat down to eat. 'You can't keep accusing innocent people, and harassing Leo's friends; it's damaging. You're upsetting others who loved him too, who want to let him go. Please, Jill, let him rest in peace,' I begged.

'I'm his mother, and I need to know the truth, that's all. Call it maternal instinct or just an educated guess. Every fibre of my being is telling me it wasn't an accident, and it certainly wasn't suicide. I'm sorry if it makes you uncomfortable, Wendy, but I'm not giving up.'

It was no use; she was like a dog with a bone. I knew Jill well enough to know she meant it: she wasn't going to give up. This filled me with dread, because I had a horrible feeling that Olivia was going to be right in her line of fire soon, if she wasn't already, and that was terrifying.

I'd been prepared to spend time with Jill that weekend, because I'd wanted to be there for her. I knew that this visit to Wales and the dark sky reserve that Leo seemed to love so much would be tough, and she'd need a friend. I'd looked forward to the walks, the chats, the shared memories, and for a little while be the friends we used to be.

Jill didn't want to see or speak to anyone in the days after Leo's death. We all sent flowers and cards, but no one ever opened the front door and they were left to rot on the doorstep. It was a warm July, and without water the flowers didn't last long. Each day I'd look out and watch them die before my eyes, until they turned brown and shrivelled.

The funeral was horrible. There were so many people, they filled the church and spilled out into the hot August day; no one could believe it and had to see for themselves the coffin of a sixteen-year-old boy. Robert and I went to the funeral together. I'd say the shock of Leo's death brought us closer. We both cried at the loss, but I'd never seen Robert cry like that. I guessed we were both thinking of our own boys, and remembering Leo the baby, the toddler, the little boy, the teenager. We'd been on his journey with him, and it was heartbreaking to see it end too soon.

It was those memories that bound us. Jill and I had a past, but we didn't have a future. I doubted I'd ever see her again after that weekend, but before I moved on with my new life I wanted to try and make sure she was doing the same. I'd really hoped that this short time together would be a watershed, and I might convince her to have a change of heart and stop looking for someone to blame. Only then would she be able to begin the agonisingly slow move forward into some kind of life. I'd heard she was having a hard time accepting this, but I didn't realise the whole point of this trip seemed to be about quizzing me, the Venableses and anyone else she might bump into.

'Jill, I know it's early days, it's only a year and a half since you lost Leo, and you will never truly move on; how could you? But I believe that accepting it was an accident will *help* you. We may never know exactly how he fell, or what happened, but what we *do* know is that no one else was there.'

'Do we?' she snapped belligerently.

'Well, unless you know something I don't, no one else was there,' I repeated, to test her.

'Someone *was* there, Wendy; I just need to find out who. When in those first few days he was missing, I asked the police to check all the cars in the school car park that night. They eventually told me the CCTV only covers half the parking area.'

I tried not to register a reaction to what she'd just said, but breathed a quiet sigh of relief.

'I mean, what kind of security is that? Only half the car park, so anyone could have turned up that night, in a car or on foot, and made their way to the woods behind the school.'

'That's bad,' I said, shaking my head.

'Those few days, before he was found, were hell on earth, but at least there was hope, a tiny chink of hope that he might just turn up, that whoever had taken him would drop him by the side of the road. But when the police came that morning and stood on the doorstep, I knew, I just knew!'

I remember hearing her blood-curdling scream from next door, and I also knew. The sound of another mother's scream is the worst sound in the world. It chilled me to the bone then, as it still does to this day.

'He ended up in that river, and if I can find out what happened that night to make him leave the prom in such apparent distress, then I might be able to find out who put him in that river. And whatever you, or anyone else, say – I will spend the rest of my life looking for that person.'

'I understand, Jill, as much as I can. I can't imagine how you must feel; how do you ever accept that your child died in some random accident? As human beings, we're always looking for reasons, for neat endings, but sometimes in life there are no neat endings, and not everything makes sense.'

'Please don't speak to me like I'm a child, Wendy; I'm well aware of what life is like! I'm also aware that it doesn't suit neighbours, teachers, pupils, or anyone else that might have a grudge against Leo.'

'Oh, Jill, it's not like that, he was just a kid; a popular kid too. No one had any reason to harm him; everyone *liked* him.'

She turned around and looked at me. 'What about Olivia?'

My blood ran cold. We only had Olivia's word that she and Leo didn't argue or fight; she insisted she wasn't present when he died. I couldn't prove to anyone that my daughter was innocent, and Jill knew this.

I picked up my glass of wine and took a long drink before responding. 'Olivia has nothing to do with Leo's accident,' I said firmly and with as much conviction as I could muster.

'What about Rory, her other boyfriend? She'd been playing one off against the other for weeks, and he'd been involved in a knife crime last year.'

'Olivia finished with Rory long before she started seeing Leo,' I replied, trying and failing to be drawn into this.

I had no idea when Olivia had finished seeing Rory, or if she even had. She knew I didn't like him; he was bad news and she may have kept it from me if she was cheating on Leo with him. Who really knows their kids?

I wasn't going to let Jill know that I had doubts about my own daughter that plagued me, kept me awake at night. I also wasn't going to let her know that I was aware that only half the school car park was covered by CCTV; that was why I parked my own car where I did that night, *after* Leo had left the prom.

But I wasn't the only mother waiting for her child outside the school that night. I can't ever ask her about it, because then she'd know that I was there too, but it was Jill. She was sitting in her car, parked behind a clump of trees out of sight of everyone, on her phone.

Why was she there, and why had she never told the police, or anyone else? Did Jill know more than she was letting on about Leo's death? And did that somehow explain her desperation to point the finger at someone, *anyone*, else?

ELEVEN

JILL

'Was Tim the love of your life?' Wendy asks out of the blue as I make coffee after dinner.

Pouring hot water into the cafetière of ground coffee, I breathe in the rich, nutty aroma and think for a moment. 'I suppose he was. As you know, I was an only child – my parents both died when I was young – and I'd always been on my own until I started seeing Tim. He had three sisters, all with families of their own by then, and I loved the idea of being part of that extended family. Being Tim, he lost touch with his sisters over the years, and when his parents died, I was back to being without a family.

'I certainly believed he was the love of my life early on, and as I never met anyone else, I supposed he's kept his crown,' I joke, pouring cream into a small jug and placing it on the table.

I put the lid on the cafetière, and resting my hand on the plunger, I try to remember what love was like. 'Tim was everything I wanted in a man; he was bright and funny and confident. Yeah, I *adored* him.'

'He was attractive too. Still is,' she reminds me as I put the cafetière and cups on the table.

'Yes, I often registered the surprise on other women's faces when they met him for the first time,' I say, joining her now at the table. 'They didn't expect mousy old Jill with her short hair and tracksuits to have someone like Tim, but I guess the clue is in the word "have" – because no one ever *had* Tim; he didn't belong to anyone.' I glance over at her to see if this landed, but she's looking down into her cup of coffee.

On our wedding day, it never occurred to me that my handsome, funny, charming husband would ever have eyes for anyone else. We were now married, and married people made vows to God promising all kinds of nonsense, which at the time I truly believed. I had what I thought was my perfect husband, and when we moved into Lavender Close, I finally got my white picket fence too. I remember one summer evening, we'd been married just weeks, and he was walking up the drive after a shift at work. It was that newly married stage when every time I saw him, the sun came out, and I couldn't believe he was mine. Then right on cue his face broke out into a smile and my tummy fizzed with love as I smiled back, until I realised his smile wasn't directed at me. My husband was looking over at the Joneses' house, and there she was, in the window, all pretty in pink. Wendy had been watching him come home too.

New people have moved in next door. It feels strange to me. They seem like pale imitations of Wendy and Robert, body snatchers who've taken over them and their home. It will always be Wendy and Robert's house, and when I glimpse the new people in their garden, I feel like I've been left behind in another life.

Everyone else has moved on. Tim has gone. Wendy's moved into a flat with Freddie, their middle child; it's temporary until he finishes his exams, but it looks like she and Robert have come to the end of their rainbow. Meanwhile, he's in Spain with Josh, their eldest, and Olivia. Whoever would have believed that we'd all move on, live separate lives.

It's as if a bomb had gone off and everyone scattered except me, and I'm the only one left now. The problem is, I can't leave number eleven Lavender Close because it's Leo's home, where we brought him just days after he'd been born. The vase he made for Mother's Day still stands in the kitchen, his drawings and photos adorn the wall, his magnets are all over the fridge, family photos, school photos, posters; that's his life, right there. I even hear his voice echo in the walls; his face reflects in the windows, and his bed is made and ready for him. If I moved, where would he exist?

I always had this fear of losing him. I imagine all parents are the same, but for me it became part of my anxiety. Tim tried to reassure me: 'Look at him; he's fit and healthy and we live in a nice neighbourhood. There are no gangs that teenage boys can get involved in around here. There's nothing to worry about. We're the lucky ones.'

But it turned out he was wrong – we weren't the lucky ones after all.

As much as I loved being a mum, my basic anxiety was exacerbated by post-natal depression. And having suffered previous losses with several miscarriages, I had to see a psychiatrist for a while, then have counselling. I sometimes felt like I had a death wish, but as the post-natal depression took hold, this became a lot darker, and more serious. This baby, this life, this marriage, felt so precious, yet so fragile, and the happier I was, the more I feared losing everything.

My feelings started to affect my ability to eat, sleep and look after Leo. I was scared of touching him, and terrified of being alone with him. Tim had to extend his paternity leave to stay home with me, but I didn't want anyone to know; I felt ashamed. I'd longed for this baby, jumped through hoops to have him, and now he was here, I couldn't even bathe him.

In truth, I was becoming more and more scared – of myself. I had terrifying, intrusive thoughts, imagining Leo drowning in the bath, suffocating in his cot. I was scared to take him out in his pushchair in case a car reared onto the pavement. Tim had to do pretty much everything for him while I looked on, safe in the knowledge that if I wasn't involved in his care, he'd survive.

I'd never imagined in my worst nightmares that this was what motherhood could be like. I'd gaze out of the window onto Lavender Close and see other young mums passing by, pushing their babies. One mum even cycled with her little one strapped in a seat behind her. I couldn't look; it made me feel dizzy just thinking about that tiny little one strapped into a bicycle that might encounter a lorry.

It was all so competitive too, and while the other mums planned parties, held playdates, went to Mummy and Me this and that, I just stayed at home to keep him safe. I felt like such a failure, which wasn't helped by the fact that my next-door neighbour sailed through pregnancy and childcare, or it seemed like that to me. Wendy's babies never seemed to scream through the night, and she breast fed like Mother Earth, while I cried and Leo completely refused to latch on. In the end I gave up and had to do the walk of shame through the aisles at Boots buying formula while other mothers looked on, pity in their eyes.

On the rare occasions that Leo slept, I'd sometimes watch Wendy in her garden from an upstairs window. She'd be running barefoot across the lawn holding newborn Olivia aloft, rubbing her face in hers, and singing to her. She'd often sleep on a sun lounger, leaving her daughter on a mat on the grass, in the dubious company of her wild and unpredictable brothers.

'How come she can do it and I can't?' I'd asked Tim, who'd struggled to answer me.

'I try so damned hard, I ate well during pregnancy, I looked after myself, and now he's here I keep everything spotless. I puree organic vegetables for him, wash his sheets most days, and his nappies because it's healthier and better for the environment than disposables. I'm washing, scrubbing, cleaning and pureeing until my hands bleed. While she' – I gestured angrily to the house next door – 'she dances round the fucking garden!'

He tried his best to comfort me but it was as insensitive and tactless as ever.

'You can use disposable nappies and dance in the garden too if you want to. Stop comparing yourself to Wendy; she's a different person to you. She doesn't overthink it; she's laid back and she's... spontaneous,' he added, in a voice that suggested he was listing what he was looking for in a woman.

During those first few months with Leo, I'd gone into a kind of hibernation. I couldn't bear to see anyone. I was too embarrassed at what I perceived to be my failure as a mother. I didn't want Wendy and the other mothers on the close advising, patronising or pitying me. Of course, it would have been so different if Mum had been alive, but both my parents died when I was so young. I so envied the others that parental support. Wendy's mum had helped her with the boys and now Olivia. 'The cavalry is coming,' Wendy would say, relief in her eyes and a bottle of white chilling in the fridge.

The only person I could talk to was my midwife, who tried to be reassuring when I told her I worried all the time about Leo dying.

'Lots of new mums have those thoughts,' she said in her lovely, lilting Welsh accent. 'It's perfectly natural for you to worry about your baby's safety. You think of the worst thing that could happen then dwell on it until you think it really will happen. Trust me, nothing bad will happen, it won't. It's just your hormones postpartum, but I think it would be helpful for you to talk to someone, so I'll put you in touch with a counsellor who specialises in post-natal issues.'

I didn't want to be patronised by some well-meaning therapist who'd expect me to talk to them. How could I? How could I tell someone that when my husband put our new baby in his cot and we left him to sleep, I went back and sat on the floor by his cot listening to his breathing and praying he wouldn't die in the night?

TWELVE

WENDY

'I don't think I can go on, Wendy.'

Jill was sitting in the easy chair opposite me. We'd eaten dinner and I thought we were having a pleasant time drinking coffee and talking about old neighbours when she suddenly blurted this.

'Now that's silly talk,' I said, trying to hide my alarm. Standing up from my chair, I walked over to her and knelt on the floor, resting my hand on her arm.

She stared ahead, in her own world, like I wasn't there. 'Now Tim's gone there's nothing. He thought he could end nearly twenty-five years just like that.' She clicked her fingers. 'All the betrayal, the money problems caused by his spending on other women and himself. He once spent over a hundred pounds on aftershave, and I was scratching around trying to pay the mortgage. But you know what's really stupid? I could put up with all that if he'd just loved me, shown me some affection.' She finally turned to me. 'He hadn't loved me for years. Sometimes I wonder if he ever did.'

'I'm sure he did, Jill—'

'You don't know anything about my marriage, Wendy. The damage was done early on.'

I didn't understand what she was saying, but she'd always seemed fixated on Tim and me, and I wasn't getting into that now.

'Look, I know he hurt you, so why don't you try to see this split as a positive? Being with him made you unhappy and anxious. You guys weren't good for each other, and in leaving he may have done you a favour. Now you can be happy. He's actually given you back your freedom.'

'I never *wanted* freedom,' she snapped. 'I was an only child of two only children who'd both died by the time I left university. To me, freedom means being alone, and I always wanted to *belong*, to *need* people and for them to *need* me, but they just go and leave me.'

'I'm so sorry, love, I know you're hurting. Perhaps it might help to talk to someone?'

'I am, I'm talking to *you*.' She was staring at me with such coldness it made me shiver inside.

'I mean someone *objective*, who isn't *involved*.'

'But *you're* involved.'

What was she saying? I hesitated, lost as to how to respond.

'I mean, you know me better than most,' she said, a slight warmth suddenly returning. 'You were a big part of my life, my marriage, my *past*.'

'I wasn't part of your *marriage*, Jill.' I smiled, showing my surprise at this. 'You and I were good friends, we shared a lot, but you had your marriage and I had mine.'

She was slowly shaking her head. 'Our marriages were entangled, but only I could see it.'

'I don't agree, we were all just friends,' I insisted, wanting to avoid this before she went off on one about Tim and me being 'too close'. 'After Leo was born, you and I were barely even friends, you just shut me out.'

She shifted uneasily at this. 'I'm sorry I made you feel like that. I didn't mean to.'

'You'd just had Leo, you were a new mum and you weren't well. Please don't apologise, I'm just pointing out that our friendship became distant, and our marriages *weren't* entangled.' Experience told me that it was sometimes necessary to be clear and firm with Jill or she'd hold on to ideas, create her own narratives and make them bigger.

I stood up, went back to my armchair and opened up my phone; she was now scrolling through hers. Our conversation was terminated, but it had triggered the memory of Leo's birth and how she'd pushed me away.

Olivia was two weeks old when we got the call to say they'd had a seven-pound baby boy and they'd be home soon. They'd been through so much: IVF, miscarriages, and if anyone deserved a perfect baby, they did. I was thrilled for them.

'I can be at the hospital in ten minutes?' I said to Tim.

There was a tangible silence. 'Well... she had a difficult time, and he's slightly jaundiced so the hospital said no visitors.'

'Oh, of course, we'll see them both when she's home then?' I said, knowing it was highly unusual for the hospital to ban visitors, but sent the biggest, most beautiful basket of fruit I could find. And to my absolute delight, just three days later, I saw their car pull up outside the house with Jill and the baby inside.

Holding Olivia in my arms, I watched through the window as Jill delicately climbed from the car. Tim opened the passenger door and took the baby carrier out so carefully it touched me to tears. My heart hurt for them. They both looked so tired and fragile and their little cargo was precious. I remembered what it was like with our first baby and wanted to just hug them and tell them it was all going to be fine. So, still carrying Olivia, I rushed out of the house and through the little front garden to greet them.

'Hey, how are you all? Can I see him?' I cried.

Jill was clinging to Tim, who lifted the carrier so I could have a peak, while I swooned at how beautiful he was. 'Oh, Jill, I'm so happy for you,' I said, clutching her arm. 'I can't wait for him to meet Olivia.'

She didn't respond, just stood on the pavement staring ahead. Her skin was grey and she looked so frail; I thought she might fall.

'I bet you're exhausted, but all worth it, eh?'

'She'll be fine, Wendy, just a bit tired,' Tim said, and he rolled his eyes as he guided her up their front path and through the door.

'See you soon,' he mouthed as he turned around and disappeared into the house. I called and turned up on her doorstep, invited her for lunch, coffee, anything I could think of. I even asked if Olivia and Leo could meet up, but she simply ignored my calls, never answered the door and didn't even acknowledge my invitations. When I heard she'd met up with some of the other neighbourhood mums, I was so hurt. Why would she do that? She was my best friend, and I didn't see her or her baby again until he was six months old.

And now, eighteen years later, we were sat drinking wine in a cottage in Wales and I still wondered what was going on with her back then. Yes, she was a new mum and she wasn't 100 per cent, but how could she see other friends, and not me? Perhaps she felt even more protective of her marriage now they had a baby? But why keep me at arm's length even when Tim wasn't around? We'd been so close, like family, and babies usually brought friends closer – but our friendship never really recovered after Leo was born. And she had always refused outright to discuss it, but I suddenly got this urge to talk to her about it.

'Jill, I know it's all in the past now, but you've never told me why you stopped seeing me when Leo was born... From the moment you found out you were pregnant, you just seemed to close down our friendship.'

'I guess it was my hormones. As you say, it's in the past; no point going over it, trying to understand it.'

'I just... it still hurts and I asked at the time if it was my fault, but you wouldn't talk to me. I just wonder if you can tell me now if it was something I did?'

'I was ill, Wendy.'

'I know, but I was your friend. I wanted to share your joy.'

'There was no joy! I was poorly and I didn't need you turning up looking like a commercial for the perfect mother and telling me to chill.'

'I'm sorry you felt that way,' I replied, knowing in my heart that it was more than this.

'At the time, there was a lot going on in my head, Wendy. Forgive me.'

'I forgave you back then. Like I say, we were best friends, that's why I threw you a surprise birthday party after Leo had been born.'

'Oh... that?'

'I hadn't seen you for six months. I thought it would be the perfect opportunity to bring you back into the fold. Olivia was only two weeks older than Leo, and having three kids by then, I understood what it was like to try and keep the wheels on. When I'd suggested the party to Tim, he was thrilled, said it would really help to lift your spirits.'

'*His* spirits more like; he was bored of staying in with me and Leo.'

'I also felt it was important after a baby to celebrate the mother,' I continued, rejecting her negative remark about Tim.

'I need to get to bed,' she suddenly announced, and stood up shakily from the chair. 'I think I've drunk too much. I blame you,' she joked, and staggered up to bed, leaving me with half a bottle of wine and memories.

* * *

The night of her surprise birthday party, Robert lit the barbecue, I put fairy lights around the garden, and we filled a table with booze. We'd invited all the neighbours, with instructions to come down the side of the house so she wouldn't see, and everyone arrived quietly with gifts and bottles and love. I really thought this was going to bring her out of herself.

But when she finally arrived, she was arguing with Tim and clutching the baby, and as she appeared in the garden, everyone screamed, 'Surprise!'

This shocked the baby, who started crying, and she just stood there, her mouth half open, unsmiling. The ensuing silence was deafening. It was as if time had stood still. The fairy lights swayed gently in the breeze, all other sound and movement frozen. I started panic-singing 'Happy Birthday' to cover the sticky silence and eventually everyone else joined in. It was messy and awkward and I knew I'd made a huge mistake.

Robert's mum had our children for the night, so we were ready for a party of loud music, dancing and lots of fun. I'd suggested to Tim that Jill might appreciate letting her hair down so Tim should get a babysitter organised. But he told me he'd mentioned it to Jill and she hit the roof, said she wasn't leaving Leo with a stranger. So I tried to make the best of a bad situation and found her a quiet spot to sit with the baby and went to get her a drink. On returning, she'd disappeared, and now I was worried, so I searched the house and was surprised to find her in our ensuite alone.

She gasped and turned around so fast she almost fell over when I appeared behind her in the mirror.

'Sorry I startled you,' I said, wondering why she hadn't used the family bathroom, or the one downstairs.

'Where's Leo?' I asked, and for a moment she hesitated.

'He's... I hope you don't mind, he's on your bed.'

'No, not at all,' I said, realising I must have missed him when I'd walked in. I peered into the room, and there he was wrapped in his blanket fast asleep, but was awoken by a sudden smashing sound in the ensuite. The baby started crying, and I ran back into the bathroom to find Jill picking up shards of glass off the floor. 'I'm sorry,' she was saying, 'I broke a glass, I broke one of your glasses... I'm so sorry, Wendy.'

'It's fine, only a glass. Come away. I'll sort it.' I guided her into our bedroom, sitting down next to her on the bed, putting my hand over hers.

'I'm fine, just a bit overwhelmed,' she replied, pulling her hand away on the pretext of checking Leo's forehead. 'Thanks for doing this party. I don't deserve you as a friend.'

'You know, you could always bring Leo round here one afternoon if you need a nap,' I offered gently. But at this, her arms instinctively tightened around him.

'It's okay.' I was smiling, speaking softly, aware of the sheer panic in her eyes.

'You're not having him, Wendy.' The panic was now real, eyes darting around the room like she was looking for an escape.

'Hey. No one's going to take Leo from you, darling,' I murmured in hushed tones. 'You don't have to cope alone. You have Tim, and you have us.'

'Tim?' She looked bemused at this.

'We're here, and we can help any time, so please ask,' I said, ignoring her dig at her husband. 'Your little one is relying on you, which is why you need to get some sleep and eat properly. Have you seen the doctor, Jill?'

'No, I haven't, because I'm fine,' she snapped, 'and don't try telling anyone I'm not.'

'I remember feeling like this about Josh,' I continued calmly. 'Right now, it feels like a mountain to climb, but trust me, by the time you've had baby number two it will all be quite different.'

She picked Leo up, holding him to her chest. 'There won't be any more babies, Wendy, I promise. I'm so sorry.'

'You don't have to apologise or promise me anything, love, just that you'll look after yourself.'

Jill took Leo and left her own party early that night. She never had any more babies, but doted on her precious only child, whose body was recovered from the river just four days after his first prom. He was just sixteen years old.

THIRTEEN

JILL

Sunday

I'm standing outside the Venableses' house. I woke early this morning, and while in the kitchen, I happened to glance across the road and saw the Venableses' old van pulling out through the gate. Mrs Venables was driving, and Mr Venables was in the passenger seat as they trundled off down the road. I sat in the deathly quiet of the cottage wondering if this was meant to be; should I go over there and have a look around while they were out? I just have a feeling about them, especially him, and if I can find out anything that might be connected to Leo, I'll go straight to the police.

So here I am, in the pitch dark in their back garden looking for a way in. It's crazy, and dangerous and stupid, but as I've said before, losing a child means nothing can ever scare you again.

Shining my phone torch at the windows, I can see they're all in a state of disrepair, and I choose the kitchen window. Levering it open with my keys causes the rotting wood of the frame to break, and soon the window opens enough so I can slide my hand in and lift the latch.

I feel weirdly elated at this small achievement and lift myself up onto the window ledge. On the first couple of tries I lose my grip, but eventually, with an almighty physical effort, I make it onto the ledge. I slip in through the window and slide over the sink, almost landing on my head.

The house hits me with the pungent aroma of porridge and urine. I feel like some ageing goldilocks in a horror version of the fairy tale as I make my way through the dark kitchen. I run one hand along the wall and by shining the torch from my phone, I eventually locate a light switch. With one click, a sickly yellow light floods the room.

I stand here in a stranger's kitchen questioning what the hell I'm doing here, but Leo's with me all the time and he's guiding me. He urges me on; I know he's as angry as I am that everyone thinks he fell in the river drunk. That's what they're all saying – but I know that isn't true, because Leo is telling me it isn't.

My eyes skim over the old Aga oven, and a *very* old fridge, then a pine Welsh dresser, old pots piled on shelves, all very dusty. I open drawers, look through bits of paper, run my hands under the sofa, on the top of cupboards without knowing *what* I'm looking for. I stop for a moment; I'm looking for secrets. And where do people hide their secrets? Their bedrooms?

Moving swiftly through the kitchen, I carefully mount the rickety staircase, each step creaking and complaining like old bones. I wander into the first two bedrooms and nothing draws me, but as I open the door to the next one, the telescope is standing by the window. It's still quite dark, and through the lens I look out onto the milky blue morning at the tiny leftover stars, like diamonds in pale velvet. I imagine Leo standing here, looking through this lens, and I hold it as he must have, feeling close to him again.

I look around the room and through the window onto the back yard. It's then that I notice the shed; perhaps the shed is a place for secrets?

I check my watch; they've been gone about half an hour and could be back in minutes or gone all day. I can't hang around, so I run downstairs, open the kitchen door and head for the shed. But when I get there, breathless from running, the bloody door is locked, and in my frustration I give it a sharp kick. Slowly, the door creaks open. This is starting to feel really creepy, like someone *wants* me to look inside. Are they watching me? I instinctively look behind me but don't see anyone. 'Shall I go in?' I murmur under my breath, and Leo says yes.

Inside, my torch alights on a small chair, some magazines and a small, single bed. What the hell is this, a homemade prison cell? I take a few steps closer. The bed's been made, but by torchlight the covers don't look too clean. I look up and the walls are lined with photos. I'm just about to take a closer look when something leaps out from under the bed. I squeal and almost fall as something furry whips past my legs, disappearing off into the morning. In the silent aftermath, I hope it was a small cat and not a giant rat.

I try to calm myself by breathing deeply, but the air is damp and acrid. What have I found here? There are piles of paper all neatly stacked, but I can't stay and look through them, so I just glance at the top ones. I see star names; the words are a stream of consciousness about God and the stars. 'He will come down from space and save us from man's evil and pull us into the fires of hell.' Along with the words are detailed drawings; they're so disturbing all I can think is, *Whoever wrote these needs help.*

What if Leo saw some of this? Was he disturbed? Is it some kind of cult and he came home a different boy? He could barely look at me when he returned from the stargazing trip, and I've never understood why. Perhaps this is the answer?

Suddenly, the door creaks and starts to open, a whiny

groaning sound. My heart feels like it's in my throat, thumping like a drum. Is it the wind, or something else?

I'm really uneasy, and I go to the door to leave, but something drags me back. *Is that you, Leo?*

I'm drawn to the photos, but before I can focus on them, I hear footsteps crunch on the gravel outside. I quickly turn off my torch and stand as still and as quiet as I can.

'What are *you* doing here?' a voice calls out. It's Mr Venables' voice, but I never heard the van.

'Hello?' he's saying gently from the other side of the door, like he's trying to entice me out. How does he know I'm in here? He must have seen the torch. What if I was mistaken and he *wasn't* in the van with his wife? Was he here watching me all the time?

My heart's beating so fast and loud I swear he can hear it. 'You are lovely, aren't you, girl?' The voice is deep and dark and spine-chilling. Then suddenly, he says in the same weird gentle voice, like he's talking to a little child, 'Let's close this door, shall we, so you don't get into any more trouble?' Then the wooden door creaks shut, and the bolt slams across with a heavy thud. I want to scream, but I know there's no one else around for miles.

Venables' boots continue to crunch on the gravel. He's pacing, round and round and muttering, but his words aren't audible; all I hear is a strange lightness, as if he's talking to a child.

While trying not to breathe in case he hears, I carefully take my phone from my pocket; there's one dot of signal. So I text Wendy.

HELP! Venables locked me in shed. Call police. Come asap.

I press send then panic. What if she comes running here from across the road and he's waiting for her? My blood runs cold at this. I look down at my phone; the message has delivered. It's too late, she'll be on her way, so I stand by the door waiting to hear her footsteps, then I'll call out to her. He's not a big man; Wendy might be able to fend him off. Where's Mrs Venables?

Then I start with the dark thoughts again. If Wendy is hiding something about Leo's death, it wouldn't be in her interests to rescue me. Self-preservation is a strong instinct, and she has it in spades.

Self-interest is high on her to do list too. Like when she insisted on hosting that horrible drinks thing on her lawn before the kids went to the prom. Both husbands were still at work, and I was glad not to have Tim there fawning all over Wendy, but I was uptight, and so unhappy. While Wendy and her daughter posed for the professional photographer she'd *commissioned*, I took Leo into the house.

'You don't have to go with Olivia tonight. Even if you go in the car with her, you can be with your friends when you get there. She doesn't have to be your date,' I said.

'Mum, I've told you I *want* to go with Olivia. I like her.'

'I... I told you, Leo, she's not for you. Please don't get caught up in things you don't understand...' But before I could finish, he'd pulled away from me to join her in the garden. Reluctantly, I followed him outside where Wendy was barefoot on the grass, laughing with them, sharing this special time. She was wearing a new dress; it was floaty and floral, and her hair shone in the evening sunshine as she sipped on fizz and threw her head back, laughing at something Olivia had said. How I envied her ease, her happiness, her innocence, and their innocence too. How I longed to grab a drink and join them, but I couldn't.

That was a year and a half ago; a lot has changed in that time. Leo's death impacted all of us in different ways. Local people were scared that a killer was on the loose and their children's lives were in danger, and in the four days it took to find

Leo, everyone was on red alert, picking their kids up outside school, making them stay home at night.

I know it wasn't completely his fault but I often think, what if Tim had been waiting outside the school as he was supposed to be on the night of the prom? He might have seen something. Leo might have simply got into his car instead of running away.

I can't forgive him for that, and I told him. Just a few nights before he left, I said that our son's death could have been avoided if he'd just done his job as a father. I'd always picked Leo up from school when he was younger, and I'd never let him stay out after 10 pm. And on one of the rare times *he* was supposed to collect him, he was late, he let him down.

I'll never forget his face, it was red with anger; 'Stop it, Jill, STOP IT!' he'd yelled and stormed off to the pub, or to meet his current other woman. It had always been like that; even before we lost Leo, he blamed me for his late nights in the pub, and for his infidelities. He never took responsibility for anything, even Leo; the one thing he had to do that night was collect his son from the prom, and he couldn't even do that.

When the police found Leo's body in the river, I told them my suspicions, gave them names, motives, tried to convince them it wasn't an accident. But they told me they couldn't arrest anyone just because I *thought* they might be guilty. Then people began to avoid me in the street; friends stopped calling and messaging, scared I might accuse them of murder. Tim told me I sounded unhinged. He was as caring and supportive as ever: 'You're nuts!' he yelled as he stormed from the house, leaving me alone, nursing my grief.

Several months after they discovered Leo's body in the River Severn in Worcester, the police made a statement to say as far as they could see it was 'a tragic accident, with no evidence of any third-party involvement in the incident'.

After learning that there was no serial killer on or near Lavender Close, parents were back to their old carefree ways within a couple of weeks. Their kids were back playing on the street again unsupervised, and teenagers made their own way home at night instead of being driven. Friends and neighbours carried on with their lives. But I couldn't. I'll never be able to carry on with *my* life. But I can fight for my son's; I can find out who took it and why. And as I stand in Mr Venables' shed with him prowling around outside, I wonder what I've got myself into.

It's half an hour since I texted her; it would take about two minutes to dash across the road from our cottage. So where is she? Where the fuck is Wendy?

I look again at my phone, and to my horror, I see the little red exclamation mark by the messages I sent to her. Not one of them have been delivered.

No one knows I'm here!

FOURTEEN
WENDY

Jill was missing! I hadn't seen or heard from her since the previous evening when she'd abandoned our difficult conversation saying she was tired and going to bed. This morning I'd woken up early for me, about 8 a.m., so I'd dressed and gone downstairs, hoping Jill had made porridge. But no warm porridge smells, no golden syrup melting in hot oats; the kitchen was deathly quiet. No one was around. I'd assumed she'd gone for one of the 'brisk morning walks' she loved so much so put the kettle on, bread in the toaster and waited. But after I'd eaten the toast, read some of my book and scrolled through my phone, I started to get this little sting of worry in my head. The night before she'd said she couldn't go on. Did she mean it literally? I knew she'd invited me here for a reason; was she planning to kill herself but wanted a medical professional in attendance? Fuck! I dropped my phone, jumped off the chair and ran two at a time up the stairs, calling her name, then bursting into her room. In that moment, I fully expected to find a body, either lying on the bed or hanging from the light fitting. God, I was so scared, I plonked down on the bed and had a little cry. It was relief mostly, but also guilt for what I'd put her through. How long could I continue with this charade, the lies, the pain and poor Jill's endless suffering? I hated myself, but what could I do?

The visit from the Venableses the previous evening had disturbed her, made her even more determined to find out what had happened to Leo leading up to the night he died. I didn't like the weird couple but was grateful for their presence because it took the spotlight off Olivia and me for a while. Jill had been constantly implying I knew something. But now Jill was concerned that her son had in some way been abused, something she hadn't even considered. Whether this was true or not or relevant to his death, she was now torturing herself with the idea of it.

When she wasn't around this morning, I assumed she was having a lie-in. That wasn't Jill's style; she was usually up around six, but we were away and I hoped she was perhaps chilling out. So I made coffee, hung around in the kitchen and sat with my thoughts, which at that time always seemed to find Leo's death.

In the aftermath Tim tried to hold Jill up, but he wasn't exactly a strong support, never had been; besides, he was also shrunken and lost and needed someone to hold him up. 'I never wanted it in the first place, your daughter and my son,' Jill said to me in the aftermath. 'Those two should never have been together. She was so controlling, and so much more worldly than Leo. She had him mesmerised, wrapped around her little finger; I just hope to God they didn't do anything illegal.'

She sounded like some 1950s evangelist, her accusations based around the evils of sex, and her thinly veiled rather misogynistic swipe at my daughter's sexuality was hurtful. It made me very angry, but I had to be gentle; she'd just lost her son. I also didn't want to escalate this because she'd already started pointing her finger in my daughter's direction.

I had no problem with our kids being together; in fact, I

embraced it. I'd been surprised and delighted when Olivia told me they were going to the prom together.

'As friends?' I asked.

She rolled her eyes and swept out of the room, which was her default move back then. I was elated; hopefully this would be the end of Rory Thompson, the boy she'd been hanging out with for a while. I was pleased to God that was over, because I'd heard rumours he was in trouble with the police. Consequently, the news that she was going to the prom with Leo was music to my ears.

'So what about our kids going to the prom?' I said to Jill next time I saw her. 'Shall we order the kids a limo from yours or ours?'

She looked confused.

'Olivia and Leo are going *together*... to the prom,' I added, suddenly realising she didn't know.

'Oh dear, we can't let this get out of hand,' she said, as if to herself.

'What do you mean?' This had immediately made my hackles rise. 'They're young, no harm in having fun, they're both good kids.'

She took a deep breath. 'Yes, but Olivia's idea of having *fun* is quite different to Leo's. Don't take this the wrong way, but Leo has a lot of work to do. I haven't said anything but he has an interview at Cambridge... for medicine,' she added. I saw the thrill in her usually sad eyes.

'Olivia's got work to do too; we're hoping she gets on a prestigious course for business studies,' I replied defensively. Since when was her son too good for my daughter?

She sighed, then smiled weakly, like she pitied me and wanted to be kind but I was trying her patience. I was furious, and I knew this was going to cause some trouble; it was simmering underneath every conversation we had that summer.

I pushed the past from my mind for a moment; these days if

I thought too much about Jill's behaviour it made me angry, and I didn't want to fall out with her that weekend. She was so preoccupied, and it wasn't just about Leo's death; the obsession had started with his birth. She had no time for anyone, not even herself. 'Kids need to know you're there, but you have to give them space, love,' I used to say. But she wouldn't listen.

Like now, she'd probably just gone for a walk, but why not wait and I would have gone with her? She'd told me specifically that she wanted to spend time with me this weekend, and I was annoyed she'd just gone without texting me or even leaving a note.

I went back upstairs to see if I'd missed something; had she packed and gone home? I hoped so; that meant I could go too. I was staying at that godforsaken place to be with her, support her, and how did she thank me? By disappearing. Now I had to twiddle my thumbs until she came back. I had other people in my life who needed me; it wasn't just about her. I felt wretched; what the hell was I doing here pretending to be this woman's friend to save my own skin?

Suddenly my phone started to ring, but it wasn't Jill. I picked up.

'Sorry, I had my phone off. I wanted a lie-in.'

'Good, you probably need it.'

It was so isolated, so far from home, I needed to hear a familiar voice, to talk to someone who *knew*. Someone I didn't have to hide the truth from.

'Hey,' I murmured. 'I miss you.'

'Me too.'

'You okay?' he asked, sounding on edge.

'Yes, are you?'

'I'm okay, I'll just be glad when you're finally here.'

'Yes, I know, I can't wait. How are things there?'

'Okay...'

'You don't sound sure?'

'We've been through a lot, it won't happen overnight.'

'No, of course not.'

'How are things there?'

'Awful. I hate the way Jill looks at me.' I brought the phone closer to my lips and whispered, 'I sometimes think she *knows*.'

'That's impossible.'

'Yeah, but she's making me *so* uncomfortable.'

'Just hold tight, don't say anything that she can reinterpret – or misinterpret.'

'No – I won't. I'd like to leave right now. She's not here. God knows where she is. I'd better go, she'll be back soon.'

I clicked off the phone. The room was extremely tidy, and all her stuff was put away except for a small photo in a frame by her bed.

I picked it up. It was Leo in his school uniform; he'd have been about twelve. It was the same school photo we all had in our homes, on dressing tables and mantlepieces. A bright young boy with an awkward smile in a shirt and tie that looked far too big, his hair combed across his forehead like you'd never see in real life. Except this photo was different, because he was dead. I tried to look away but was drawn to his eyes; they stared out from an unremarkable face just like his mother's. And, just like his mother's eyes, his looked right at me, staring, accusing.

I shuddered and placed it back on the bedside table. Just looking at the photo brought that evening back to me, the summer wind blowing the trees, the air of expectation. The tinkle of laughter. The clink of champagne glasses.

Then just a few hours later, Olivia screaming. Blood on her prom dress. That was just the beginning of my own personal horror story.

FIFTEEN
JILL

Until now, I've been waiting for someone to turn up, but as each minute passes, I'm starting to wonder if this is it. Will my days end here in a shed in Wales?

When I couldn't get through on the phone, and Wendy didn't respond to my text, I had panicked slightly. But I soothed myself with the thought that she might be sleeping late, or had even called the police and was waiting for them rather than turn up alone. But now I know my messages haven't reached her I'm seriously panicking and becoming quite frightened. I just can't see a way out of here, *ever*!

I move towards the door, pushing at it, then kick hard, again and again. I don't care if Venables hears me. If he comes in, I'll just dodge him, run past and get out of here; he's an old man, and I'm fitter than he is. But I'm crying now and scared, as for the first time I realise there's a chance I might never get out.

The door isn't budging, so I keep my phone torch on to see if there's anything in here I can use to smash the door. I can't see anything in this weird little room with its creepy single bed and piles of strange papers. I turn around and around on a few square feet, feeling like I'm going crazy. But then the light catches what look like photographs on the wall. For a moment I'm distracted from my plight as I lift my torch closer to see what the photographs are, if they can give me any clues. At first, I can't make them out, but slowly something starts to emerge and to my mounting horror I can see that every picture is of the same person, a young boy, about Leo's age. To my relief it isn't Leo; this boy has lighter hair, a slightly bigger build. Even in this light I can see it isn't him. Several of the photos are from the waist up, and the boy has no top on; his chest is completely bare. As I move the torch slightly to the left of the photo, I see Mr Venables standing with him, his arm around the boy's waist. The telescope in the background. My stomach turns upside down. They are upstairs in the Venableses' bedroom.

I gasp, still not sure what to make of this, but something stirs in the pit of my stomach. This man spent time with my son, who for some reason never told me about the encounter. I just keep thinking how Leo left that cold day in January, a happy, excited teenager. He couldn't wait to go on that trip and see the stars. But when he returned, he was quieter. He didn't want to engage with me or Tim; in fact, he avoided us.

I was obviously concerned that Venables may have had something to do with the change in Leo, but how could I find out what it was? I hate to think of Venables alone upstairs with Leo, then driving him back to camp in his van, which according to his wife had taken far longer than it should have. But before I go to the police, I need proper evidence, something tangible, not my wild theories based on conversations with the strange couple.

I learned my lesson after Leo died. The trauma of losing him had made me paranoid, and I believed that everyone and anyone had a motive, a reason to kill him. I'd been foolish, calling the police about every little thing, because now I had a reputation for being hysterical. But this shed is weird, the little bed, the strange words and drawings on the piles of paper, and now, on the wall all these photos of a young boy, half naked. Then there's the connection with our housing estate; Mr Venables has a cousin there. It could just be a coincidence, but what are the chances?

But even if Venables is weird, even if he scared Leo or was inappropriate with him, Leo was big enough to fight back. He was also old enough to take action, call us or tell a teacher. I just couldn't see Leo being Mr Venables' victim, whatever form that might take. And who's to say he had anything to do with my son's death?

Thing is, I still can't get Olivia out of my head. She chased after him that night when he ran from the prom upset, so surely she caught up with him? And why was he upset? Was it something she said or did? She isn't admitting anything, says she never caught up with him and has no idea why he left. And what makes me more suspicious is that after she was questioned, and released, she went away. She was his girlfriend, his prom date – but more than that, she'd known him all her life. She'd lived next door, and she was like a sister – but she didn't come to the funeral. I haven't seen her since the night of the prom, when they were excited and all dressed up and Wendy was fluttering around them like the cat that got the cream.

I'm confused; my world is blurred with grief. Am I just barking up the wrong tree again? I'm not the first mother unable to accept her child's death, and I understand why people think I'm going mad; that's because I am. But he was my everything, my reason to live. I adored him. And call it mother's instinct, but I know this wasn't an accident, or drug-related, or suicide, or anything else they want to throw at me. But to prove it, I have to find something to back up that gut feeling that someone knows something, someone did something. And one thing I'm sure of is that Wendy Jones knows who and why.

I check my phone. The battery is really low, and no messages. The signal is so weak. What if no one finds me?

Perhaps I should have shouted out to Derek Venables, told him I had called the police or something equally threatening? But I was scared, I *am* scared. What if he's alone and Mrs Venables is away for the day, or longer? What if he's just keeping me locked in here until he has the time, or appetite, to come back and do whatever he's planning to do with me? I'm pacing around the shed; it's no bigger than a small bathroom, so I'm just going round in circles.

According to my phone it's 10.30 a.m., and I've been here for more than three hours. I'm now on the edge of panic and my instinct is to scream for help, but I'm in a shed in the middle of nowhere and the only person who'd hear me is the man who locked me in here. And where the hell *is* his wife? Perhaps he dropped her off somewhere before coming back here? But I have no way of knowing *when*, or *if*, she'll return. Then it occurs to me that she could be here; what if she's his accomplice and as crazy as he is? She seemed to be covering for him a lot last night, answering questions when he stumbled, stepping in to stop him incriminating himself. The more I think about the dynamic between them, the more my chances of ever leaving here seem to diminish.

I'm standing in the pitch black, and I'm filled with a rising panic. A crescendo of fear and noise is thrumming through me, and I'm scared I might lose control. Despite my battery having only four per cent left, I *have* to turn on the phone torch just to stop me from losing it.

Now the torch is on, I have to do something in case I don't ever get out. I could write my name on the wall; I could take a photograph of myself in here. But what would that do? If Venables does intend to hurt me or worse, he'll just destroy my phone and cover up or erase anything I write.

With just minutes left of light, I go back to the wall where all the photos are and skim the torch across them, looking again to see if there are any clues. I hold my breath as the light hits each photo, my mouth dry with dread at what I might see now I'm taking the time and looking more closely. What I'm really afraid of is seeing a picture of my son, but as I move the light along the newspaper clippings of stars and shiny, ageing photos, I see something even more shocking. I have to step closer and shine the torch right into the picture to make sure what I'm seeing is correct and it's who I think it is. The photo is of a group at a family wedding, with kids and adults all dressed up, a bride and groom, some little bridesmaids, and I can see from the clothes it isn't a recent photo. But right in the bottom left-hand corner, I see him. He's much younger, but I'd know him anywhere.

'Tim?' I murmur as my teenage husband smiles back at me.

SIXTEEN

WENDY

By 11.30 a.m. I was beginning to wonder if Jill was playing a game with me; was she testing me? Where the hell *was* she? I checked my phone again: nothing. What if she'd gone for a walk and fallen, was injured and now couldn't get back? When do you report someone missing? All these thoughts were running through my head at such speed, I couldn't concentrate on my book. So I put on my jacket and wrapped my scarf around my neck and set off to find her, but as I opened the front door, the freezing cold air took my breath away, and it was starting to rain. She'd been gone now for at least three and a half hours; surely even she wouldn't want to stay out that long in weather like this?

I walked down the lane, wrapping the scarf round my face as stinging rain was now coming down fast. I walked quickly while keeping an eye out for any signs of her, a dropped glove or an umbrella, anything to show she was out there.

To my relief, my phone suddenly pinged, but when I checked, it was a text from Robert asking if I was okay and what time I'd be leaving Wales. He hadn't felt it was a good idea for me to go that weekend. 'I don't trust her; I think she might be up to something,' he'd said when she'd invited me on the weekend, but I could handle myself with Jill; I knew her well. I genuinely believed at the time that she was telling the truth, that she wanted to rekindle our friendship. How naïve I was.

Leo's death had changed us all. Robert had always been the one who trusted people, took everything in his stride, and here he was worrying about me spending a weekend with Jill. It had always been me who was suspicious, worrying about what might happen, especially regarding the kids. I remember being distraught over Olivia going out with Rory Thompson and Robert saying, 'Leave her to make her own mind up, and she will. If you ban the bad boys now, she'll always have a hankering.'

But I didn't agree, and my attempts to dissuade Olivia from seeing Rory had merely strengthened her feelings, as my husband had said they would. So when, after a few months, she turned her attention to Leo, the boy next door, I was relieved and delighted. I couldn't wait to tell Robert. But he wasn't so sure.

'I don't think it's a good idea for Olivia to go out with Leo,' he said.

I was shocked. 'Why, for heaven's sake? Leo's a damn sight better than bloody Rory Thompson, who'll be going to prison when his classmates go to university. And Leo's a nice boy, from a decent family. And he's going to be a doctor. What's not to love?'

'I just have a feeling about that boy, he's... Leo isn't what he seems.'

'Oh, he's fine, it's just a daddy-daughter thing; you don't want Olivia to have a boyfriend full stop.'

'No, actually, I *don't*, Wendy,' he said, getting all stroppy. 'And I definitely don't want that boyfriend to be Leo Wilson. If he's anything like his dad he will break her heart.'

'What are you *talking* about?' I asked, feeling a bit uncomfortable. 'Not like you to concern yourself with affairs of the heart, Robert,' I added, trying to keep this light and jokey.

'You know what he's like, has an eye for the women, and the fruit doesn't fall far from the tree.'

'Bloody hell, what's got into *you*?' I was almost smiling; it wasn't like my husband to be like this. He was always non-judgemental, fair. Robert took people how he found them, but he obviously knew something about Leo that I didn't. 'Why are you saying this? You've always said what a nice, polite boy he is; you even helped him with his university applications. I thought you liked Leo? I thought you'd be thrilled to see him with Olivia. He's taking her to the prom, it's like fate...'

'There's no such thing as fate, and I still like Leo, but... I wasn't going to say anything, but Marek told me that Leo's got in with a bad crowd. They're into drugs. I never said anything because I didn't want you to tell Jill.'

Marek and Lena were our neighbours. I was fond of them both, but they could be a bit gossipy, and I found this hard to believe.

'Drugs? No.' I was amazed. 'I don't believe that. Jill would hit the roof.'

'Exactly, it would upset her and cause problems for Leo, because – as you say – she'll just hit the roof. So please don't say anything to her.'

'But Robert, he might be in danger. Jill and Tim need to know.'

'No, they don't, Leo just needs to be able to make his own choices, the right choices.'

'That's rubbish—'

'No, I mean it, Wendy. I was sworn to secrecy; Marek just mentioned it in passing. He hasn't even told Lena because he can't trust her not to blab, and if it got back to Jill...'

'She'd be devastated, but she needs to know, Robert. She needs to help him.'

'Yes, but he needs to be squeaky clean for Cambridge – and if Jill finds out she'll be straight to the school blaming them, blaming the other kids. Then the school may be obligated to notify the university, and it could impact his application. We don't want to be the catalyst for anything like *that*.'

He had a point; it could have caused Leo more trouble, and ruin his future.

'I managed to catch up with Leo, and I've spoken to him about the consequences. I was very discreet. I don't want the kids hearing about this either, especially Olivia.'

Having two boys ourselves who were slightly older, Robert was used to a bit of teenage trouble, and I hoped he'd managed to nip it in the bud. But still... 'Anyway, how does Marek know about Leo and drugs?'

'He's a pharmacist.'

'I *know*, but Leo's hardly going to go to the bloody pharmacy for his drugs, is he?' I was laughing now. 'Honestly, Robert, leave the village gossip to me. I reckon you've got it all mixed up, love.'

'Do you ever take anything seriously? Do you think I'm a fool?'

'No, but I do think you're being dramatic, and you know what Marek and Lena are like.'

'I just don't think it's a good idea for Leo to be taking Olivia to the prom.'

'Well, I think you're being overprotective. Olivia can look after herself, and trust me, a Leo Wilson on drugs is preferable to a Rory Thompson threatening people with knives, which is the reason for his current school suspension.'

At this he shook his head and stormed out of the room.

'Anyway,' I called after him, 'it's not like they're getting married, they're only going to the prom together. They're only just sixteen!'

'Exactly, they're far too young,' he snapped back.

He could be a pompous ass sometimes, especially when it came to his precious daughter. I guessed it was the dad and daughter thing; no one would ever be good enough for his little girl, and he didn't want her exposed to anything potentially harmful, be it boys or drugs. As her mum, I was with him on that, but I had a more realistic take on our beautiful, burgeoning woman-child. I had a feeling that where boys and sex were concerned, that train had already gone – with the dreaded Rory Thompson.

Jill had an obsession with Rory from the get-go and came round to see us at the house a few weeks after Leo's death.

'I need to speak to Olivia,' she said, refusing to come in and just standing on the doorstep saying, 'I need to talk to Olivia.'

'I'm sorry, she's gone travelling.'

'What? Have the police allowed her to leave the country?'

'Of *course*, she isn't a suspect. She's free to go wherever she wants to. She needed to get away.'

'I can't believe they let her go. I know she knows something, Wendy, and I think it has something to do with Rory Thompson. I imagine he was very angry about Olivia going to the prom with Leo; was she playing one against the other?'

That was when I slammed the door in her face. I couldn't take any more. I burst into tears, and Robert came running into the hall asking me what was wrong.

'She's blaming Olivia, implied that she was making Rory Thompson jealous, that somehow he was angry and… Jill's determined, you know how she is. If she gets the chance, she will destroy Olivia. We *can't* let that happen.'

Suddenly there was a noise at the top of the stairs. We both looked up, and Olivia was standing there; she'd heard everything.

My instinct was to get Olivia safely away when we could and put the house up for sale; we couldn't live next door to them any more. But in the meantime I would speak to Jill. I couldn't allow her to say those things about Olivia. If I did, she would only add to it and I had to nip it in the bud before she caused more trouble.

So a few days later, when things had calmed down, I went round to their house and knocked on the door. I stood there for a long time, but eventually she answered, and I could see by her face it was going to be a tense conversation.

'I'm sorry I slammed the door the other day,' I started and handed her a bunch of flowers, hoping it would soften what I had to say. But as I offered the flowers and reached out to hug her, she recoiled and pushed them away like they were contaminated.

I felt tongue-tied and confused; the Jill I'd known would never have been so cruel. She'd have invited me in, made tea and been open to talking a problem through. But this Jill was impenetrable, and the disgust on her face when she looked at me made me feel unclean.

That was why I was amazed she'd invited me to spend the weekend with her in Wales just a few months later. It didn't make sense. Unless she wanted to get me on my own to try and wheedle information out of me, some kind of confession on Olivia's behalf? Jill was relentless. God knows what she was hoping to achieve by keeping me in that little cottage with her all weekend.

But standing on her doorstep that day, she'd made me feel like rubbish, and as I started to speak, she just turned and walked back inside, leaving the door half-open. I wasn't quite sure what to do, but I had no choice. I wanted to put a stop to this, so I had to follow her inside, still clutching the flowers.

Jill's house was always clean, but now it had a clinical cleanliness. The strong smell of bleach hit me, stinging my nose as I breathed in.

She walked into the sitting room. Leo's pictures were all over the walls and on the sideboard and mantlepiece. She'd always had one or two framed family photos around the place, but now there must have been dozens all over the room. It was as if she'd collected every photo they'd ever taken of him, framed them and filled the walls, the sideboard, the book shelves. I had this urge to run away. How could I face this pictorial montage of grief, knowing what I did? But as much as Jill was fighting for her son, I had to stay and fight for my daughter.

Everywhere I looked his eyes were watching me, even as I sat down on an armchair in the corner. Inside I was trying to get away, but Leo was everywhere, the same eyes that had looked at me the night he died now following me around the room.

'So what did you want to say?' she asked. Her eyes were cold, searching.

Silence. Just staring, waiting.

'Jill, I... I just wanted to ask you to stop this... this campaign against Olivia. It's hurtful and damaging to imply that she's somehow involved in what happened to Leo.'

She just sighed heavily. I knew she had her mind set and wasn't listening to me.

'We don't want it to get out of hand, because soon everyone's talking and a nasty rumour suddenly becomes fact,' I said, desperate to change her mind, which was never going to happen. 'We don't want our daughter's life ruined before it begins by people telling lies about her. She's just a child, it's cruel and unfair.'

At first, she didn't respond, then she slowly breathed in, gathered all her anger and hatred and calmly blew it out at me.

'Cruel and unfair, is it?'

'Yes, Olivia had nothing to do with what happened. Leo had had a drink; he'd fallen into the river. Olivia wasn't there, Jill – she wasn't *involved*!'

'Really?' she said calmly, still watching me with those cold eyes. Leo's eyes were on me too. I felt exposed, scared.

'When someone sends a text saying "I hate you, I wish you were dead!" and that person is then attacked, murdered,' she hissed, 'I think it's safe to say your daughter *is* involved. Up to her pretty little neck!'

SEVENTEEN

JILL

This feels like a fever dream. I'm in a stranger's shed in the middle of nowhere, staring at a photo of my husband as a teenager. Nothing is adding up, and however hard I try to find a connection, it seems impossible, because none of this makes sense.

Suddenly, I hear a car engine; someone's pulling up outside. My heart lifts a little; is it *Mrs Venables*?

I'm about to start screaming and shouting when I hear her voice; she's calling to her husband.

'Derek, DEREK! Have you found her, is she here?'

He doesn't answer. My heart is thumping, my mouth dry; is she talking about me?

'No... I can't see her anywhere, love,' he responds, his voice getting louder as he walks into the yard. Presumably he's been inside waiting for her.

'Have you checked everywhere?'

'I have, but no sign; she'll come back, she always does. But guess who I found in the shed?'

I swear my heart is pumping so loud they'll hear it.

'This little one,' he says, which doesn't make sense to me, until I hear Mrs Venables' reply.

'Oh, what a little sweetie. Where did you come from?' she asks in a baby voice. And I hear the tiniest sound. A cat meowing. In an instant, it all makes weird sense. Mr Venables doesn't *know* I'm here; he was talking to a bloody cat!

'The shed door was open, she must have crept in there,' he's saying. 'Can we keep her, Margaret... please?'

'Well, she's just a kitten; we can't leave her to fend for herself in this weather. I think we'll have to give her a home. Come on, let's take her in and get her warm.'

Despite my lingering fear and doubt, there's nothing else for it. I have to let them know I'm here. The alternative is even scarier.

'Hello! HELP!' I yelp. 'Please let me out, I'm locked in the shed.'

There's a moment of silence when I imagine them both looking at each other, surprised.

'You've locked someone in the shed again, Derek?'

'I don't remember doing that.'

'No – you never do. You locked the bloody postman in last week, he was only putting our parcels out of the rain. I bet this little kitty was your doing too,' she's saying, her voice close now.

'Hello, I'm so sorry,' she's calling.

'Get me OUT!' I yell.

'I am, hang on. I'm trying to undo this padlock. I'm afraid my husband's forgetful. Do you work for Royal Mail?'

'No, it's me, Jill Wilson. We're in your cottage across the road.'

'Oh dear, I'm so sorry, Mrs Wilson.' She's obviously struggling with the keys; I can hear them jangle as she curses under her breath. 'Nearly there... I think I've got it. Derek, please keep the torch still.'

'I need to find Kitty...'

'You took Kitty *inside*, Derek!' She sounds at the end of her tether. 'Bring the torch back now! The lady staying at the cottage is in here and I can't work out the padlock; have you put a code number on it again?'

'Yes, it needs to be securely locked.'

'No, it *doesn't*! Not always, Derek,' she adds. 'I keep taking the code off, and you keep putting it *on*, then you forget what the number is. Oh *Derek*.' She sounds as close to tears as I am. But hearing this conversation, I'm beginning to work out what's going on here, I think.

But it still doesn't explain why there's a photo of my husband on the wall.

I glance back, flashing the torch and photograph it, just before my phone dies.

After a lot more huffing and puffing and bickering, the door is pulled open. Daylight and relief floods in, making me tearful and shaky. The light's too strong after hours in darkness, and I want to hug her, but I resist. I'm not a hugger.

'I am so very sorry!' she says the minute she sees me. I must look terrified. I'm shaking with both fear and cold, tears of anxiety and relief running down my cheeks.

'Let's get you out of here and in the house,' she says kindly, stepping into the shed and taking hold of my arm.

'What happened?' she's asking me as we walk across the yard to the farmhouse, her husband following behind. 'Derek didn't force you inside the shed, did he?' She looks concerned.

'No... I don't think he realised there was anyone in the shed.' I turn to him for confirmation, but he isn't listening.

'What were you *doing* in the shed?' she asks, looking right into my face. I'm desperately scrabbling for a reason to be in someone's shed as she helps me up the step into their kitchen. I feel so guilty where I'd opened all the drawers and probed into their lives without their knowledge.

'I'm sorry, I was just coming over to say hello. I saw the shed and thought someone was in there and before I knew it the door had been closed. I suppose it serves me right,' I add, feeling guilty.

'Derek's always locking that shed door. I mean, as if some-one's going to take anything from his shed. There's nothing there, it's all his personal stuff... his man cave.'

I smile uncertainly, thinking of the photo of Tim and the half-naked boy.

'One or two?'

'I'm sorry?' I still feel like this isn't real.

'Sugars. I think you're in shock so I'm putting some in your tea.'

'Thank you, one is fine,' I say gratefully as she hands me a warm mug and sits down at the table with her own.

'Now, you sit by that fire and don't you dare move until you feel better. I think the cold got to you. How long had you been in there?'

'I... about four hours, I think.'

She nods. 'Just after Derek had dropped me off at my sister's. She's broken her hip and I go over there most days.' She smiles. 'Poor Martha.' Then she leans forward and says to me in a whispery voice, 'Take no notice of Derek.'

'Oh?' Is she covering for him again?

'He hasn't been himself for a while. He keeps forgetting things, losing things. And sometimes he seems... frightened. I was telling Martha; she thinks he might have that Alzheimer thing, you know?'

'It could be.'

She nods. 'It's not a problem. I worried at first, but now I just go along with him; he gets upset if I question him too much.'

'Do you think he should see a doctor?'

'Probably, but let's face it, I'd have more chance of getting an appointment with the king than a doctor these days.' She smiles defeatedly. 'No, Derek will be fine. He's looked after me for fifty years; it's my turn to look after him now.'

She says this with such commitment and love in her voice, I'm almost moved to tears. I watch her stoke the fire, and see the way her face lights up when Derek comes back into the kitchen. He's carrying the kitten that scared me to death in the shed, and she goes to him, stroking the cat and smiling up into his face.

'I just saw Sheba out on the field,' he says triumphantly. 'You hold Kitty and I'll go and get her.'

Mrs Venables turns to me. 'Sheba's our dog. We thought we'd lost her, didn't we, love?' she says, looking back at him as he goes out through the kitchen door.

Holding the cat in her arms, she moves to the window, watching him head off over the field. I can hear him calling the dog, and she turns to me. 'Sheba died ten years ago, but I can't keep telling him, because he forgets then cries all over again.'

To grieve is one thing, but when the mind forgets, it's fresh and constant grief. I feel for him.

My mind is drawn back to the photos; before Derek returns, I need to ask her about them.

'I couldn't help but notice the photos on the wall of Derek's shed,' I say.

She suddenly looks uncomfortable, and gently placing the kitten down on the sofa, she walks towards the window, obviously looking for him. 'I wonder where he's got to?'

'I just wondered who was in the photos... I know this sounds mad, but I think my husband is in one.'

She turns around, surprised. 'Really?'

'It's an old photo... I don't know anything about it, looks like a wedding, a family celebration?'

'I've no idea, you'd have to ask Derek.' She shrugs. 'He's like a mysterious magpie these days, always finding treasures and animals. He takes them to his shed and forgets about them, which is fine if it's a lost earring or glove, but when it's a kitten...'

She smiles and looks back at the window, clearly more concerned now about Derek's whereabouts than unexplained photographs on the shed wall.

'I saw pictures of a young boy too, quite a few of them. Does someone sleep in the shed, only there's a bed in there?'

She's now really on edge, her eyes darting everywhere, wringing her hands. 'Oh, thank goodness, he's here.' She marches to the door; I know she's trying to avoid my questions, so I ask her again.

'You must understand, I'm confused about my husband being in the photos... And the boy, who is he? And' – I push, aware I'm asking too many questions – 'and the bed... who sleeps in the bed?'

'I'm sorry, Mrs Wilson... please don't think I'm rude, but I'd really rather not talk about it.'

'But why? I'm confused. Why can't you answer my question?'

She stops at the door and turns around slowly. 'Because you might not like my answer.'

EIGHTEEN
WENDY

I walked for at least a mile that morning looking for Jill. I tried to call her, but there was no signal, and I'd sent texts, but they just kept bouncing back. By now I was seriously concerned about Jill's mental state, and as tempted as I was to call the police, I wanted to try and find her first. I was worried what contact with the police might do to Jill; she might have started ranting again about Leo's death and hurling accusations. As concerned as I was for Jill, I had to protect my daughter.

I realised that at some point I might be forced to call the police, but in the meantime, I would check out likely places. First I headed down to the river, to check if she'd gone for a walk and got into difficulties. Since Leo's body had been found in a river, I approached water with dread, reluctant to look too close, scared of what I might find. Once I'd reached the banks, I followed the river downstream, going over our conversation the night before. I'd so far failed to convince Jill that Leo's death was an accident, and it was exhausting. I'd forgotten just how determined Jill could be. That small wiry frame, that mousy hair, was just a front; she was the most single-minded ferocious woman I'd ever known.

I remember walking home from school with her one parents' evening after she'd publicly blamed the Head of Science for Leo's slightly low grades.

'Underneath the polite and quiet façade you're quite the fierce tiger mother, aren't you, Jill? Poor Mr Shelton, I felt quite sorry for him.'

'He's an *idiot!*' she'd snapped. 'He couldn't see potential if you kicked him in the face with it.'

'At one point I thought you might just do that, Jill.' I'd chuckled.

'That's where you and I are different Wendy. I will always fight for my child, even if it doesn't look pretty. He's my priority, and I don't care how that looks.'

'Hey, I'm as fierce as you, I just do it with tact and a smile. I find I get better results that way; you should try it some time.'

Jill thought I was a neglectful mother because I let my kids make their own choices. I wasn't constantly in their faces, always telling them the 'right' way, I was more lenient than she was. I never disapproved of her parenting, but she did mine.

I always thought our friendship benefitted from us being such different people, but in fact that's what created the tension, along with all the secrets we kept from each other.

Robert had told me not to go on Jill's weekend away, he said it would lead to trouble. But I wanted to go, I felt guilty about everything and in truth, thought I might be able to steer her in a different direction than the one she seemed to be going in.

If only I'd had some indication of the price I would pay for being in Wales with mousy Jill, tiger mother whose maternal inner rage and determination knew no bounds. It had driven her on to continue her campaign against my daughter. Only days before she invited me to Wales, I'd spoken to our old neighbours Lena and Marek, who still saw Jill from time to time.

We'd all been friends and neighbours, with children of

similar ages at the same school, and Robert and I were fond of the couple, sometimes having discreet dinners with them without Jill and Tim, who had no idea we did this. Sometimes Jill was just too much, especially the way she watched Tim and me like a hawk, and often made remarks about our closeness. It was uncomfortable.

'Jill's still hell-bent on finding someone to blame for what happened to Leo,' Lena told me. And it seemed that after a whirlwind of accusations, she'd settled on Olivia as the prime suspect.

'She's hurting and I think she blames you,' Marek warned.

'She thinks you're involved at some level too,' Lena added.

'She was my friend. I just don't understand why she'd turn on me like this.'

'Who knows?' Lena shrugged. 'It's probably just her grief; she's looking for someone to blame.'

'I don't understand why she's chosen Olivia... or me.'

That's when I saw a look pass between them, and I realised I may be on enemy territory. Had she convinced them of Olivia's guilt, and mine? Jill was a tragic figure; everyone felt her grief and wanted to be there for her, and if that meant taking sides against us, so be it. I decided after that not to trust any of my old neighbours.

The fact that Jill could turn good friends against me made me wonder what else she'd been up to behind the scenes. The fact she was still forcing her narrative about Olivia being responsible for what happened to Leo might explain the abuse Olivia had received online. I couldn't recover from the vile comments and accusations that Olivia was still receiving. We'd even bought her a new phone with a new number, but the trolls had found the new number and were continuing to hound her. Olivia was beyond hurt by then; she was beyond perception really, but Robert and I were distressed on her behalf. Then one night a woman actually called her, said she'd kill her and put her in the river, 'Just like Leo'. After that we took Olivia's phone from her and were shocked when she didn't object, didn't even flinch. For once I genuinely wished our daughter had kicked off about us taking her phone. I longed to see my feisty daughter again, but by then her spirit was crushed.

Before Leo died, Olivia was all about rainbows and sparkles and fun. She wasn't perfect; she had a stinging temper, but she could also make me laugh like no one else. That night when she dressed for the prom I couldn't have been more proud. She was standing in the garden, barefoot, her long pale gown wrapped around her, tall and slim, young and beautiful; she looked like a model.

'Mum, do you fancy a quick game of hoops?' she suddenly asked then, and within seconds we were both screaming and hurling the ball into the boys' basketball hoop. Both barefoot, both in our finery, just laughing and, though I didn't realise it then, happy, just bloody happy. I'd been taking that happiness for granted all my life.

'Let's have a quick Prosecco before Auntie Jill turns up,' I suggested. Jill never approved of anyone under eighteen having alcohol, and I knew it was going to be difficult for me to offer Leo a beer with her watching. But it was my daughter's prom night, she was going with a lovely boy, they were young and in love and I wanted to celebrate with them.

I continued to walk along the icy riverbank. No sign of Jill, no sign of anyone; I decided to head back towards the cottage, see if she'd arrived back.

As I walked, my mind returned again to that night, Olivia and me sitting on the grass in the sunshine drinking Prosecco in our best dresses.

'Thanks, Mum,' she said.

'What for?'

'For buying my dress and liking my friends and never objecting when I went out with Rory.'

'Nothing wrong with bad boys, as long as you don't marry them.' I chuckled, thinking of all the bad boys I'd known before Robert.

'Well, I'm with a good boy now.'

'Yes, and long may it last. You're happy, aren't you, love?'

'Yeah, I really like Leo. It's just...'

'What?'

'He can be a bit moody sometimes. Like when we went on the trip to Wales, someone said something to him and he just changed, like that.' She clicked her fingers.

'Who was it, and what did they say?'

'It was Kai. I don't know what he said, but it pissed Leo off.'

Kai was Marek and Lena's son. He was a nice boy and a friend of Leo's, so it was hard to imagine him saying something mean.

'Yeah. Kai and Rory were talking, and Kai whispered something in Leo's ear, I think he was repeating something Rory had said about Leo.'

'Oh... so Rory was involved?' My heart sank at this; I was hoping he was off the scene but obviously still hanging around Olivia.

'I thought Leo was going to punch Kai, but then he went for Rory. Some of the other lads stopped him. I didn't think Leo was violent but he was so angry.'

'That can't have been nice for you. Do you think whatever Rory said was to try and cause trouble between you and Leo?'

She shrugged. 'Yeah, probably. I've never seen Leo like that. It scared me.'

'But you've no idea *what* was said?'

'No, Leo wouldn't tell me, he said it was really vile – and just lies.'

I remembered Robert saying he'd heard from Marek that Leo was taking drugs; did Kai know? Were he and Rory accusing Leo of taking drugs? Would that cause him to react in such a way?

'Do you think Leo takes drugs?'

'What? Where did that come from, Mum?' She looked genuinely horrified, and it made me wonder if Robert had got it right. Had Marek?

'No way! He wouldn't even have some of Tom's weed the other night.'

'I hope you didn't either?'

She didn't respond, so I left it. I wasn't going to worry about that on prom night.

'Cheers, darling,' I said, clinking glasses.

'Cheers, I'm so glad you're my mum,' she said.

And that was the last proper conversation I had with my daughter. What happened later was so horrific, she stopped talking and hasn't spoken a word since.

I didn't tell Jill, because I knew she'd somehow use it against Olivia, say she saw something, or did something and her guilt was the reason she'd not spoken.

She'd use Olivia's extreme reaction to prove *she* was the one who murdered him.

What worried me most was that Jill could have been right, but while Olivia wasn't talking, we'd never know. But one thing I did know for sure was that Jill wasn't the only mother who lost her child that night.

NINETEEN

JILL

'What the actual fuck!' Wendy is shocked when I get back to the cottage. I must seem bedraggled and I'm still shivering. I'm not sure if it's cold or shock or fear – probably all three.

'I went out to look for you. I virtually combed the whole bloody area!' She hits her forehead with the heel of her hand. 'I'm such an idiot for not realising where you were. I should have realised you'd gone snooping round the Venableses'.'

'Sorry!'

'I was really worried. I even checked your room thinking you'd packed and gone.'

'I wouldn't have just left, this weekend's important to me,' I said truthfully. 'I texted you but there was no signal. I really thought I'd never see daylight again.' I grab a warm cardigan, wrapping it gratefully around me. 'I feel a bit shaken.'

'I bet you do. Come on, sit down,' she says more softly now. 'I couldn't get through to you either – no signal, this bloody place.'

She makes me a cup of tea while I tell her about the pictures on the wall and the weird behaviour. At every punchline, she's open-mouthed with shock and horror.

'Jesus, Jill, I can't take it all in. Seriously, what the *hell* is going on over there?' She's shaking her head slowly. 'A *bed*, what does he do on a *bed*?'

'And who *with*?' I murmur.

'The photo of Tim is a weird one though; are they somehow related?'

'I don't know, but Mrs V made it sound so random, that he collects "his little treasures". But what are the chances he finds a random photo somewhere that is the father of a schoolboy he met, and the husband of a woman in his cottage?'

'Can't you call Tim now and ask him?'

'No, I've no idea where he is. I don't want to be calling him at her house.'

'Oh, it's like that, is it?'

'Yeah.' Then I look at her. 'Are *you* still in touch with him?'

She flushes. '*Me?* No. Why would I be?'

'I don't know, just thought... you guys always got along.'

'No, I probably saw Tim over a year ago.'

I don't believe her.

She brings me my tea, and I take it gladly, seeking comfort. I'm cold, and not because it's winter; I'm cold *inside* after what I went through this morning. 'I wonder if something did happen when the kids were here – with Leo, I mean?'

'I don't know. He might be mentally ill; it could be dementia of some kind? Either way, I think you should call the police, Jill.' This is the woman who's criticised me for going to the police with my apparently 'crazy' theories about what happened with Leo.

'Not yet, not unless I can prove it has some relevance to what happened to Leo.'

'Mr V did say he'd been back to Worcester and seen him—'

'But Mrs Venables said he *didn't*, and if he *does* have dementia, then perhaps he just *thinks* he went back there?'

'Mmm. But from what you tell me, even if he *can't*

remember stuff, the police need to be aware of him. This is a dark sky area, lots of schools bring students here on trips; we can't leave it to chance. You should definitely call the police and tell them *everything*, Jill,' she repeats.

I'll do nothing of the sort. I don't want the police sniffing around. Especially this weekend. I find it interesting that she's now encouraging the idea of murder when someone other than her daughter might be in the frame.

'Do you think Mr Venables might have done something to Leo that night?' I ask. Having spoken with Mrs V and watched the way he interacts, I didn't get those vibes. I genuinely think he has dementia, but I'm intrigued at what Wendy will say here. Would she really throw a senile old man under the bus just to protect Olivia?

'He might have?' she offers.

It seems she *would*.

'But you've always said it was just an accident; are you finally coming around to my way of thinking?'

'I don't... er, it depends on who was there.'

'So you do think someone *did* something to Leo and it might be Venables?' I give it a moment, to watch the familiar flush rising from her neck right up to her jawline. A raggy redness an instant rash, the key to her soul.

She flushes when I mention my husband, *and* when I mention the murder of my son?

'It wasn't an accident, was it, Wendy?'

The flush is burning bright, and I must be a bitch because I'm enjoying her discomfort.

'You know what I think, but just because his death was an accident, doesn't mean Venables didn't harass him, or scare him in some way.'

'Can't see it myself.' I then look directly at her. 'Wendy, tell me again what happened that night, when Olivia called you?'

She sighs dramatically. 'Jill, I've told you and the police a million times. If they're happy why can't you be?'

'I know we've been over this, but indulge me,' I say, wide eyed. Surely Wendy can't deny a grieving mother.

'Don't you *believe* me?'

'I don't know *who* I believe any more, but please, just tell me again, I want to get it straight in my head,' I say, which I imagine is the last thing Wendy wants.

Another theatrical sigh, and she reluctantly begins her account, not without some hesitation so she can get her story right first.

'It was 10 p.m., and like you, I was expecting Tim to pick them up and bring them both home as arranged.' She looks at me, waiting for me to interject, say something negative about Tim's parenting. I'm tempted, but I let her speak. 'So, yeah... I was expecting that, but I get a call from Olivia to say Leo left. Tim hasn't turned up, so she's started walking home on her own. I immediately went to pick her up.'

'And when you got to her?'

I can see her mind still ticking away, and I wonder if her memory is good enough for the details involved.

'She told me where she was, and yes, she wasn't far from the river; she'd followed Leo there, as you know,' she added point-edly. 'I pulled up at the side of the road. She was upset, said Leo had stormed out of the prom.'

'And did she say why?'

'No, she said he was really upset and angry and she didn't know why.'

'But we only have her word for it. Leo can't tell us what happened from *his* point of view – can we assume she's telling the truth, Wendy?'

'Yes, we can! I believe her.'

'Do you really know your daughter?'

'I do. But do you really know your son? Because I think

there was a lot more going on that night, and it didn't involve Olivia.'

'No, she was front and centre in all this.'

'It's been well-documented by others at the prom that something happened that night to upset Leo; he was angry and confused.'

'And *your* daughter was with him all evening at the prom, so she *must* know!'

Wendy rolls her eyes. 'How many times do I have to tell you, she *doesn't know*!'

'She sent him a threatening text!'

'Yes, because he'd abandoned her, humiliated her.'

'I bet that made her angry?'

'No... it made her cry and phone her mum!'

We are both raising our voices now, two mothers fighting for their kids. I can feel the fury rising in my chest, because I *know* she's lying. I can see it in her eyes, and the rage of red, rising again up her throat and around her jawline.

'I don't want to get into this, because as you say, he isn't here to defend himself,' she starts. 'But Olivia told me he was moody, aggressive at times. And something she did say about the trip to Wales is that after the trip, he asked her if she'd keep it quiet about the two of them. He said if anyone asked, she was to say they were just friends. She was hurt; they'd been going out together for weeks, but he said he didn't want anyone to know.'

This shakes me slightly as I had no idea.

'So they'd been seeing each other since the previous Christmas?'

'Yes, around that time.'

'I was under the impression that the prom was their first night out together?'

'No, it wasn't, but Leo didn't want anyone to know. But by the time the prom came around he seemed cool with people knowing they were together; I guess he liked her enough to put up with any resistance,' she says pointedly.

'I wish I'd known. I just wanted him to concentrate on his schoolwork,' I say, knowing this sounds like an excuse.

'Like I always say, you can't force anyone to do as you say, even your own kid. And they were having a good time. They went to the cinema, the park, and often came back to ours after school, playing computer games, listening to music.'

'They weren't left alone; the rest of the family were there?' I ask, like it matters now.

'Sometimes, but they weren't monitored, if that's what you mean.'

'I know you don't care what your kids do, but I can't believe you were so disrespectful as to not even tell me. I should have had some say in what my own child was doing – he was fifteen, Wendy!'

'I didn't tell you, Jill, because your son asked me not to.'

This is like a physical blow. It's worse than Tim telling me he's in love with someone else. It's another betrayal, but so much worse. It's so humiliating: everyone hiding things from me including my own son. It hurts to know he had secrets. But then so did I.

'So what else did you hide from me?' I ask, trying not to sound tearful.

'Oh, Jill, don't be so dramatic. I didn't hide it. I told Leo he should talk to you, that you loved him, and if he explained that he was happy you'd have been fine. But you wouldn't, would you? Because it wasn't about him being happy, it was about keeping him to yourself – and away from Olivia. I know you didn't think my daughter was good enough for your son, but it wasn't about you – or me; it was about them.'

'About Leo and Olivia? The girl with tattoos and tight tops and public displays of affection in the close in broad daylight with Rory Thompson? Not on my watch, Wendy.'

'Wow! Okay.' She takes a breath, this time a real one, which indicates that what she's about to tell me now is possibly true, unlike the rest of her lies.

'I know you think Olivia's the bad seed, but your son wasn't perfect, Jill.' She raises her eyebrows in that know-all way she always does.

'Oh?'

'I heard Leo was in with a bad crowd?'

I shake my head doubtfully. 'I don't know where you heard that.'

'Robert, actually; he heard that Leo had been experimenting with drugs.'

I feel like I've been hit in the face, again. 'That simply isn't true. How could Robert *say* that?' I'm genuinely shocked and hurt.

'He wasn't the person *saying* that; someone else told him. Robert just repeated it to me,' she adds smugly, safe in her little world, the woman with three surviving kids.

'You see,' she's saying. 'While you were judging Olivia, your son was the *real* wild child. He may not have had a tattoo, but what he was into was far worse.'

'Leo wasn't interested in drugs, it wasn't something he'd do. I knew him; he told me everything.'

'He didn't tell you he was round at ours, in Olivia's bedroom,' she says, a smile playing on her lips.

I want to smack her hard across the face, I want to punch her and scream at her and tell her what I really think. But no, I have to stay calm, I need to keep her onside and unaware. She has no idea what's in store for her this weekend, poor, sweet, chaotic little Wendy with her bare summer feet and come-to-bed eyes.

TWENTY

WENDY

Sunday Evening

The weekend had turned into a nightmare. I was treading on eggshells with Jill, who went from fury to friendly in seconds and back again, and it was exhausting. And after the revelation about Olivia and Leo, though she was trying not to be angry, it was obvious that she was.

'Jill, I think I'm going to leave now instead of staying another night,' I said. 'This is so difficult, and for the sake of our friendship I think it's best I go and we just remember the good times.'

The old Jill would have said, 'Yes, get lost'; she'd have been too proud to ask me to stay, but she suddenly seemed to crumple before me, and became tearful and quite distressed, which was completely out of character.

'Please, please don't leave, Wendy. Everyone I've ever cared about has walked out on me or died, and I honestly don't know what I'll do if you go.'

She'd really changed; I'd never seen her like this before. She was a mess.

'After being in that freezing cold shed I've got a cold coming on, and if you go I'll just have to stay here on my own, with an unreliable phone signal.'

'Can't you leave too, go back to Lavender Close where there's a phone signal and neighbours to help?' I suggested. Despite her obvious distress, I didn't want to stay a minute longer.

She shook her head vehemently. 'I can't drive like this, I feel dreadful. I'm shivering and achy, and I don't want to be alone.'

How could I leave her like that? So I offered to make dinner, and set about cooking.

'Thanks, Wendy... for staying,' she said from the living room.

'It's fine, I just don't like confrontation and the situation is very – well, confronting. And I can't really leave you here alone with a cold after what you went through today.'

'God, don't remind me, I feel such a fool. I genuinely don't think he meant to lock me in, but I keep thinking, what if they'd gone away for a few days?'

'Yeah, or if old Ma Venables hadn't come back it would have been very different. He might have forgotten you were there, or worse,' I added, still campaigning to keep Mr V in the frame.

'He's harmless, he's just confused.'

'So how do you explain photos of a half-dressed teenage boy on his shed wall? God, and the weird little bed, not to mention the photo of your husband. What's *that* about? You don't think Tim is in on it do you?'

She seemed shaken by this, and I wished I hadn't said it, but I had to.

'Tim isn't, I mean he wouldn't... God, I don't know, I guess I'll never know.'

'You can ask him, Jill.'

'No, I told you we only speak through lawyers now. I can

hardly email his lawyer and ask if my husband was involved in my son's death.'

'Didn't Venables say he had relatives in the area we live? Is Tim a relative?'

'I don't recall Tim ever saying anything about a relative in Wales. Surely when he knew Leo was coming here on the stargazing trip he'd have said he has a relative here?' This hadn't occurred to her; she was clearly disturbed by the idea. So was I. This was so weird. She looked at me doubtfully over her cup of tea. 'None of it makes sense.'

'No... and if Venables is genuinely confused, and his wife doesn't know the answer, then the only person who could say why his teenage photo is on the wall of that shed is Tim.'

'You're probably right, but I'm not asking him. Such a shame that Mr Venables is so confused.'

'Or was that all an act – for you?'

'No, he's a confused old man who isn't even sure of his wife's name.'

'They might be in on it together. Both playing games covering for each other; is she Rose to his Fred West?'

'Hardly,' she murmured, but I knew I was scaring her.

'I think it would be a good idea to mention all this to the police.'

'I *told* you, I'm not telling the police anything until I have something concrete.'

'Okay, I understand.' I almost moved on, then remembered. 'I do wonder about Tim though; you told me just yesterday that he'd lied throughout your marriage. So what's to stop him lying about having a cousin or a weird friend here in Wales?'

'But why would he hide something like that from me?'

'Exactly, *why*? What is it about the relationship that he doesn't want people to know? You reckon he kept his affairs from you, so what *else* hasn't he told you about?'

I could see her mind whirring. This was making her uncomfortable, and she was beginning to question things. This was good; she might start opening her mind up to options other than my daughter, like Venables, or an accident. So, keen to build on this, I continued. 'I'm not saying for a minute that Tim had anything to do with Leo's *accident...*' I said, 'but he might be the link to Venables.'

For once she didn't push back on this idea, nor did she correct me when I said 'accident'. Perhaps she was finally beginning to accept or consider this option. God, I hoped so.

She didn't say anything for a while, but seemed pensive, like she was trying to work it all out. Then she picked up her phone from the nest of tables and stared at the screen. 'I don't know, I'm confused. I've googled Derek Venables' name with Tim's, but nothing.'

I shrugged. 'They might just be acquaintances? But *whatever* they are, it doesn't explain why Tim's photo is on his wall.'

She continued to scroll on her phone. I didn't think she was really listening. She never seemed to want to hear what I said regarding Leo, and this *was* about Leo. For Jill, *everything was about Leo,* that was the tragedy; with him gone, she had no one to love or nurture any more. Consequently she filled that gap with this obsession to track down the person who she believed was responsible for that loss.

'Yeah, the only stuff I can find on Derek is local newspaper headlines about his stargazing,' she was saying as if to herself. With her glasses on the end of her nose as she scrolled, and in the light, her face concentrating, her brow furrowed, I saw a little old lady hunched in an armchair. God, it was heartbreaking to see how much she'd aged; the grief was etched on her face and had crushed her once upright posture.

'He's written some articles for the local newspaper too. Apparently he's written a book, Mr Venables.'

'Really? What about?' I asked, pouring myself a second glass of wine.

'It's a book about stars he's seen in the area; seems he's discovered new ones.'

'Oh great, a book about everything he's spotted with his big old telescope through the bedroom window. That sounds like a bestseller right there.'

Jill chuckled at this, an echo of the old days when the kids were young and we'd both sneak a glass of wine and a giggle on our back steps once they were in bed. Our back doors faced each other; it was perfect really. Life was so much easier then. I wished we'd left things as they were.

But we were all humans, all flawed, and between us we managed to fuck it up.

I never meant to hurt her or make her feel inadequate, but when Leo was a baby, I made some mistakes. I could see she was struggling, and I wanted to help, but she made it very difficult. I guessed I felt guilty because I had two healthy boys at the time and wanted to just show her some love. But when she opened the door to me she didn't want to talk so I didn't stick around, just said I was there if she needed me.

I'd asked Robert what I should do, but he'd never had much time for Jill.

'Stop worrying about it, who cares? If she wants to struggle, let her.'

He was right, but I was concerned about my friend, and genuinely worried that she was fragile emotionally. So I did something I shouldn't have done and had a discreet word with Jill's midwife, who was a friend and colleague of mine. It wasn't something I'd ever done before, and I had to pretend to be sympathetic when Jill told me she'd been given an appointment for a psychological assessment.

'No way am I doing that,' she'd spat, ripping up the appointment letter.

I'd only popped in on my way to work, and I'd wished I hadn't been there when the letter arrived because I could feel my neck flushing. If ever I was embarrassed or put on the spot, my neck went red, which had always amused Jill, but I remembered her eyes wandering to my neck. 'Do you know anything about this?' she'd asked, furious.

'No, I'm not your midwife; it's nothing to do with me.'

'Christ, Wendy, I thought it was husbands who tried to gaslight their wives and get them locked up, not their friends.'

Regardless of whether or not she took the test, after my conversation with my fellow midwife, some safeguarding was put in place. A social worker was assigned to visit her, for both her and the child's sake, and despite her opposing it because she was worried they might take Leo from her, she had no choice.

Then one day I was having a coffee in Costa with Emily, her old midwife, and Jill walked into the coffee shop. It was awful. I remember Emily and I were giggling about something and I happened to look up from my coffee and she was there, standing at the counter. She looked over at us, and the look she gave me was pure hate, then she paid for her coffee and left. I'd implied to her that I didn't even know her midwife, and as she stood alone ordering her drink, we were sitting there giggling. Obviously we weren't giggling about her, but she must have felt so excluded, and probably did think we were laughing at her. She'd had so much pain in her life, losing her parents young, struggling to have a baby, miscarrying some of her children. Now she was worried that Leo was going to be taken from her, and though I'd meant well, she'd always suspected I'd told on her, and this meeting seemed to confirm it. For a long time after that she barely spoke to me, and apparently took to warning some of the other new mums to be careful how they behaved around their kids when I was there. 'She's a spy,' she told my other neighbour, Michelle. 'If she sees you doing anything she goes straight to social services to report you.'

I didn't think our friendship ever fully recovered after Leo was born. She'd changed, and I wasn't saying she'd become paranoid, but she certainly saw her friends through a different lens. This continued throughout Leo's childhood, and though there were still good times, there was always an undercurrent, like she didn't trust me around Leo. The more I thought about Jill's invite that weekend, the more uneasy I felt; what did she *really* want from me?

TWENTY-ONE

JILL

After my ordeal with the Venables, I was glad to get back to the cottage. Wendy and I then had a few words, and she threatened to leave. So I told her I didn't feel very well and pretended I'd caught a cold from standing in Mr Venables' shed. I really laid it on thick about people leaving me. I felt a bit guilty about that, but it was the only way I could get her to stay.

Anyway, we've both calmed down and she's not annoying me quite so much this evening. Perhaps it's because I know I won't have to see her after tomorrow, and after that it's goodbye, Wendy!

'Jill, I really think you should call the police; just tell them what happened yesterday. It gives me chills thinking that Venables could do that to someone else – some kid? And don't forget the Tim connection!'

You know a few seconds ago when I said she wasn't annoying me quite so much? Well, now she is, because she's trying to convince me that Tim knew something about Leo's murder. *The Tim connection* indeed! She must think I'm stupid; does she really think I have no mind of my own, that I'm so suggestible I'll just be convinced by everything she's saying?

She wants me to call the police and point the finger at Tim now, and given the circumstances, that's the *last* thing I'm going to do. Her influence might have worked twenty years ago when she told me to paint my walls blue, or pronounced that a kitchen island was the only way forward, but I've grown up and this is about more than domestic interiors.

Honestly, she's like a search light, constantly on the lookout for someone she can shine the light on so it will be taken off Olivia. It's always someone else – well, *anyone* else she can implicate. But my spotlight has never wavered, and regardless of what she says, or how weird the Venableses are, I will still be including Little Miss Perfect in my list of suspects.

'I'll admit it was a shock to see Tim's photo on the shed wall,' I concede. 'I think it's odd – but it isn't incriminating, and I'm sure there's a logical reason. Mrs Venables doesn't know, but I'll ask Mr Venables before I leave.'

'What... how was the relationship between Tim and Leo?' she suddenly asks.

I wonder what she's up to now. 'Fine,' I reply, irritated.

'It's just that I remember Tim saying Leo had become quite difficult and they argued?'

'I thought you didn't speak to Tim much?'

'It wasn't *Tim* who told me, Lena did. Marek said Tim told him that he and Leo weren't getting along.'

'Rubbish,' I say, 'they were fine.' I cast my mind back to those last few months of Leo's life; he'd changed towards both of us, and Tim had remarked on this several times after Leo's trip here.

'Everything I say is wrong. I can't seem to reach him any more,' he'd said. I felt exactly the same, but at the time, we'd both put it down to him being a stroppy teenager.

'Please don't take this the wrong way,' she starts, and I brace myself; I'm sure I'll take it the wrong way.

'Venables may be fine and Tim may not even know him. But

in that febrile environment after Leo's accident, everyone felt under suspicion, even when they weren't, because you accused a lot of innocent people.'

'Yes, because I was desperate to find who'd killed him, as any mother would be. You'd be the same, Wendy. I felt so alone, and God knows Tim was nowhere to be seen when I needed him. As always, it was left to me alone to fight for the truth about our son. The police were wandering around in a daze, like there was no urgency. They didn't seem bothered to check CCTV and DNA and... the police were a total waste of time.'

'They had it all under control and didn't need you to keep calling them with your suspicions. You did so much harm to our little community, Jill, and all everyone ever wanted to do was help and support you.'

'I didn't harm *anyone*.'

'You *did*. Olivia was devastated. She couldn't believe that "Auntie Jill" had told the police lies about her and tried to throw her under the bus.'

She's trying to sound calm, but the red rash is back, and it tells me all I need to know. She can't fool me; this is her rehearsed speech pleading for her daughter's life.

'All I want is to find out who killed my son and why. Is that so difficult for you to understand?'

She throws her arms up in the air, like she's given up trying to convince me. 'I'm going for a bath,' she says, grabbing her glass of wine and walking out.

She always has to be the one to storm out first; she has to have the upper hand. Over the years she's affected my confidence, made me feel like I'm not enough, like the poor relation. Wendy had everything, but still it wasn't enough; she wanted a slice of my pie too. It may have started with Tim, but it ended with Leo.

Neither she nor Tim ever admitted to anything, but I *knew*.

Only I could see what was going on; I was aware of the little whispers between them, which suddenly stopped the moment Robert or I appeared.

'Honestly, Jill, you're imagining it,' she said when I confronted them. 'We were talking about you. We're all really worried about you.'

She always liked to turn me into the victim so she could play the caring best friend, but Wendy never cared about me. She'd tried to get social services to take my child, she was trying to take my husband and before Leo died, she was using her daughter to reel my son in. I was shocked and hurt to discover yesterday that Leo had spent so much time at their house. I'd be waiting at home, thinking he was doing extra classes at school, when all the time he was messing about with her family next door. It was like all the times she'd invited Lena and Marek for dinner and asked them not to tell me because I 'wasn't much fun'. Fancy telling those two anything and expecting them not to blab.

And now she's trying to tell me I need to accept this, move on. She's expecting me to erase what I believe, and go with her story about an accident, or Mr Venables, or even Tim – anyone but Olivia. She won't even allow me to have my own opinions, my own theories; hell, I can't even have my grief, on *my* terms.

There was a police theory that Leo had killed himself, and his issues with both Olivia and his father were, for a while, seen as significant by the police. I worried about that too. I still do, because Tim and Leo had been at loggerheads after the stargazing trip. Leo was difficult and withdrawn with both of us at times, but where I skirted around things, Tim confronted him. He demanded to know what his problem was and gave Leo such a hard time. I can never forgive him for that. I can't tell Wendy any of this because it's none of her business, and she will see it as a golden opportunity to blame Tim for causing Leo

to throw himself in the river. And I don't believe he killed
himself, even if he did have issues with his dad – or Olivia, for
that matter. No, I will keep that family drama to myself and not
give Wendy an opportunity to call the police and set them on
Tim. It won't provide any answers, just more problems. My
husband was stupid to discuss his rocky relationship with Leo.
Marek and Lena are such gossips, and what was probably told
in the pub, in confidence while Leo was alive, took on much
darker implications after his death. And I'll always believe that
if Tim had turned up early that night of the prom, things would
have been very different, and my son would have survived.

Instead, he chose to prioritise his other woman over his
family, my husband's default position throughout our marriage.
Leo and I never came high on Tim's list of priorities. Even
before the stargazing trip, Leo had little respect for his dad
because of the way he treated me.

I think Leo picked up quite early on what his father was;
the place was a rumour mill and most of the information came
from Lena and Marek, and their son was Leo's friend. I
remember once Leo asking me, 'Does Dad have a girlfriend?'

We both knew that he had, but this was Leo's gentle way of
telling me, of letting me know.

'No, of course not, darling,' I said, wanting to kill Tim for
causing us both so much pain.

As Leo got older and more knowing, he was more honest,
and on one occasion, after Tim had left for the evening, my son
found me in tears. He hugged me and said; 'Mum, why do you
stay with him? He's a shit.'

Now I regret staying with him for as long as I did, but in
truth, I thought we could get through it. I'd taken my
marriage vows and they meant something to me, and though
he wasn't the best husband, I didn't want to be the one to
cause a messy break-up and ruin Leo's childhood. I also knew
the trysts were meaningless, and as long as people didn't

gossip, I could carry on being a good wife, a good mother and a good liar.

In the end, I wasn't surprised that Tim wanted to leave me. I was prepared for that. I think he would have gone years ago but it was a convenient little life, and I gave him no trouble; we rubbed along most of the time. But after Leo died, he had to escape from the baggage and the blame and the huge cloud of grief that still hung over our home. It follows me wherever I go, sneaks up on me when I'm alone at night in bed, wraps itself around me when I walk through Lavender Close. It even found me in the shower the other morning. It was a sudden tsunami of sobs and salty tears mingling with shower water, washing away the tiniest little dust particle of hope and bringing the cloud down around me.

Tim and I weren't the only casualties after Leo's death; Wendy's family disintegrated too. Wendy says it's all fine and she's coping, but she obviously can't bear to talk about what's happened with Robert. He left for Spain quite quickly and the house was soon sold, which makes me wonder what happened between them. I reckon she had an affair. She seemed to brush it away when I tried to get her to share how she felt.

Like Tim, Wendy was always on the lookout for someone else. She never had that fairy-tale love for Robert, but she *needed* him, wanted his adoration, his attention, his money. She was the princess, and he was always under her spell; what a fool he was to let her use him like that. Perhaps him going to Spain is an indication that he's finally come to his senses? But I was surprised to hear that Olivia had gone with him; that must have been a sucker punch for Wendy. She'd had to leave their beautiful house, to move into a flat, and apparently he has a villa somewhere near the coast.

I think we all reassess our lives when a young person dies. It makes us realise how cruel and short life can be, and how fragile. Wendy thought she was immune, that life couldn't touch her or her family, but look now how their actions are coming back to haunt them. I was devastated when the police dropped the case, but it doesn't mean I have to accept all her lies. If the police won't do it, I will. I invited Wendy Jones to join me this weekend for a reason, and however she tries to spin it, and however hard she fights it, I intend to see that through.

TWENTY-TWO

WENDY

Sunday Night Stargaze

'Are you going to have another?' Jill asked as I picked up the wine bottle.

'Yes,' I answered defiantly.

'Oh, I wasn't asking in a disapproving way.' She smiled. She was, of course.

'Good.' I smiled back as I began to pour myself a large one. Her mouth was tight and she almost winced as the wine landed in the glass with a splash.

'No, you carry on with your wine; you're obviously enjoying it,' she said through gritted teeth. 'It's just that I wanted to go out tonight to see the stars. I'd hoped to do it last night but— well, we had a little too much to drink, didn't we?' She giggled girlishly.

'Oh, why didn't you say earlier?' It was our last night at the cottage and I'd been looking forward to leaving the next day and planning an early night. Jill had said she was suffering from her cold and wasn't feeling well so we hadn't done anything in the day, just sat around while she'd interrogated me as usual.

I was irritated by her springing this stargazing on me; I knew it had been part of the plan, but I assumed with her cold that she'd changed her mind. But miraculously, her cold seemed to have gone now.

'I really don't fancy going out there now, Jill, it's freezing, and you're not very well.' I pushed it back onto her.

'Oh, I'm fine, just a sniffle.' She waved her hand dismissively while wiping her nose on a tissue with the other. 'Anyway, it's colder tonight because there's no cloud cover. It's the perfect night for stargazing.'

'Well, I'm sorry, mate, but you're on your own,' I said, pulling my cardigan around me and taking out my phone. 'Just the thought of it is making me feel chilly.'

When she didn't respond, I looked up to see her just sitting there, her face crumpled. I suddenly felt very guilty. This wasn't about going out into the freezing cold; it was about retracing the steps Leo took and finding his stars. I went back to my phone, reluctant to leave the warm cottage, but now feeling like a bad person, especially when she slowly stood up.

'You okay?' I asked, watching her stagger from the chair.

'Yeah, still just a bit stiff from being in that cold shed.' She rolled her eyes.

'A warm bath will help?'

'I had one earlier. I'll be fine once I start moving. I need to walk, so I'll head off.'

'What? You're going out on your own, now? It's after ten. I don't think you should just go wandering.'

'I'm not *just going wandering*,' she replied, holding on to the table as she made her way from the room. 'And the later the better for the stars.'

Martyrdom and emotional guilt were always top on Jill's playlist when she wanted something, like now when she wanted me to go with her on a freezing night to look up at the sky. I'd watched her use the same techniques on Leo, and to some extent Tim. Her husband just let her play it out and only responded if he felt like it, or it suited his agenda to do as she wished. But Leo had no choice; I would often remark to Robert how Leo was crippled with guilt. 'Why do you say that?' he'd reply, always reluctant to criticise others, even Jill.

I recalled the pleading eyes, the anxiety in Leo's voice, the awkwardness in his demeanour, all put there by his mother. 'He's always so secretive, doesn't want Mum to know when he comes here after school.'

'Does he come over a lot?' Robert had asked; as he worked away such a lot, he hadn't really been across everything that had happened.

'Most nights recently, he walks back with Olivia.'

'Why?'

'They're just friends,' I lied.

I planned to wait until Robert was home to tell him, but I was sure he'd be fine, despite hearing he'd got in with a crowd who took drugs. He'd known Leo since he was a baby, and he was a huge improvement on Rory.

I was delighted at their burgeoning relationship, and afterwards felt a wave of deep sadness just remembering the two of them huddled together on the sofa doing homework. Sometimes they'd watch films on Olivia's laptop and play videogames in her room; it was all very innocent. Over those few months, I watched, delighted as under Leo's influence my girl became softer, kinder, less rebellious. Another bonus was that she began to take more interest in school, becoming conscientious about revising for exams. It wasn't all one way either, because she gave Leo more confidence, and he didn't take everything so seriously.

Leo had always got along with our boys, and when he allowed himself to stay for dinner, he joined in on the banter and the jokey insults they threw at each other. He'd always felt like part of the family, but away from Jill, he was so much more confident, and relaxed.

I thought about this as I watched Jill put on her jacket. I missed the kids, and I couldn't begin to comprehend her loss.

She slowly put on her scarf, then her boots, one by one, and as she added each layer another layer of guilt was laid on me. How could I let her go out there alone in the dark at night? After all, the reason we were there was so we could see the stars, and Jill could feel close to Leo. She'd originally booked this weekend for her and Tim; they were going to sit on a rug and watch *Leo's* stars. And now she'd lost them both. How much loss can one person endure? Yes, she was bossy and judgemental and relentless, but she was my friend, and she'd been through so much. I admired her courage. Not only was she heading out into the pitch-black freezing-cold night, but also in doing this, she would be coming face to face with painful memories of her son. I couldn't let her do that alone.

'Will this help you feel closer to Leo? Do you think it will help you come to terms with... everything, Jill?' I asked as I reached for my thick quilt coat.

'I hope so,' she replied quietly, pushing her hand into a second thick glove, straightening her scarf. Even now she looked neat and tidy, short, straight hair under a woolly hat, scarf tied perfectly around her neck, a thick jacket zipped right up to the throat.

Meanwhile, I forced my coat hood over unruly blonde hair, threw a scarf around my neck and then we both looked down at my shoes. Bright-pink glitter, mud-splattered trainers that rubbed the back of my heels and were so old they may not last the night.

'I know, they aren't walking boots, Jill,' I chided before she could.

'You always preferred to be barefoot, didn't you, Wendy Jones?' she replied, smiling indulgently.

'What can I say? I hate wearing anything on my feet, so if I have to do it, only pink glitter will do.' She chuckled at this, and

I put my arm through hers as we walked out into blackness and the kind of cold that bites your face.

'Gosh, I can see why it's called a dark sky reserve; there's no light pollution at all,' I murmured, taking my phone from my pocket and turning on the torch.

'So you *provide* the light pollution,' she said, joking, but clearly irritated by this.

'Jill, we can't see a thing, I don't know where I'm going.'

'Okay, but when we get to the spot, you'll have to turn it off,' she said like a bloody school teacher. She was suddenly on edge again; her moods were so inconsistent.

'Fine,' I said, slipping easily into angry teen mode to her bossy mum.

We continued walking down the lane guided only by my phone torch splashing light ahead into the pitch black. I couldn't see behind me or to the side; it was unnerving. 'This is creeping me out,' I said. 'Anyone could leap out at us; I feel like there are eyes everywhere.'

'Don't be silly,' she snapped. She was obviously feeling on edge about this pilgrimage, and I had to be more sensitive, so I shut up for a while and concentrated on the walking. But all the time I felt exposed, vulnerable on that dark road, and all I could hear were our crisp foot falls on the ground. But on grass not even our footsteps could be heard; no sound, no light – and I remember thinking, is this what it's like to be dead?

'Come on, let's get a move on,' she commanded, striding on ahead, compelled to do this, to surrender herself to whatever was out there. We walked in silence, climbing up a hill and eventually arriving at her chosen spot. I kept my torch on until I'd checked it out. We were higher than I'd realised, and lowering the torchlight, I felt dizzy looking down. Below us were steep, craggy rocks. 'Be careful,' I warned, 'it's a sheer drop from here.'

'I told you about that torch,' she muttered, irritated.

'Sorry, but have you seen how steep it is? If I hadn't had my torch on, I might have taken a wrong step and ended up over the edge.' I moved away, turning it off, but it wasn't quite so dark up here, and when I looked up I could see why.

'Oh wow!' I said under my breath as I gazed at a sky I'd never seen before. It was crammed with so many stars it looked like the whole of the sky, both above and around, had been sprinkled with glitter dust. There must have been millions of tiny pin pricks of light creating a swirling, sparkling mass.

'I never imagined it would be this beautiful.'

'Leo told me, but I never thought it would be like this,' Jill said. 'I'm so glad you brought me here; thank you, darling.' I hadn't expected her to feel his presence; it took me by surprise, and touched me deeply, and for quite some time we both stared in silence, just taking it in.

'There it is,' she suddenly said, 'the Leo constellation.' She touched my shoulder and pointed upwards. 'Can you see the lion's head...? It's a crouching lion, see it?'

'Yeah, wow,' I replied, unable to see anything but sparkle dust, and she spoke again to Leo, thanking him, telling him how much she missed him.

'I know what I have to do, darling, and I won't let you down. You need to rest in peace,' she was saying to the sky.

I moved away to leave her alone with her thoughts and turned around and around, looking up at the sky. My mind returned to my own children, and to Olivia, in her beautiful prom dress, clinking glasses with Leo, both laughing, their lives before them. But then the sky seemed to darken, the stars dim, and my mind returned, as it always did, to later that night, frantically washing the blood from her prom dress.

TWENTY-THREE

JILL

I feel on edge. Am I doing the right thing? Is this what Leo would want me to do? Of course he would. We always had the same thoughts, my son and I; we were so alike, we finished off each other's sentences. I'd always been a loner until Leo was born, but that's when I understood what it felt like to be needed, to have a friend, someone who understood me, and I understood him.

'I'd never had a best friend until I met you.' I haven't admitted that to anyone before. Perhaps now is the time for truth?

'What about school? Didn't you have a best friend then?' She stops, stands still.

'Not really.' I shake my head and sit down on a rocky mound. I need to gather my courage before I do anything, and behaving normally, just talking to Wendy, will help me do that.

'Ahh, that's a shame.' She sighs.

But she doesn't understand, because she's always had friends and lovers and people who stay. There were other girls like me at school, ghosts in the classroom, invisible at playtime, our voices never heard, stories never shared.

'That's sad, I'm sorry,' she says, but her voice is absent, because at school, girls like Wendy never noticed, or cared. They were too busy dating boys and having fun with the other Wendys.

'I never went to a birthday party,' I heard myself confess.

'Shit... that's awful, Jill, why?'

'Mum didn't like me being away from home. I was never allowed to go to someone else's house.'

'That's rubbish.' She was still wandering around, gazing up at the sky; she looked like a teenager in love.

'It is rubbish,' I murmur, remembering the only time I was ever invited to a birthday party as a child. I sprinted home clutching the invitation, imagining my party dress, the candles on the cake, the games and the pretty little party bags. I'd only overheard whisperings of these things, and longed to experience them for myself. I threw open the door and dashed into the house calling for Mum, jumping up and down with excitement. But as she took the invitation from my hand, I saw her face and knew I wasn't going to the party.

'What about when you were a teenager? Did your mum let you go out with friends then?' Wendy asks.

'No, but she didn't *say* no. As a teenager I might push back, so she used emotional blackmail instead: "If you go out tonight I'll be all alone..." Stuff like that.'

She doesn't reply, but she moves closer, sitting down on a nearby rock. I can't see her face in the darkness, but I've already said too much.

'Your parents both died young, didn't they?'

'I was just nineteen when Mum died. I only took two days off college for the funeral.'

'That's crazy.'

'No, I was doing my exams. Mum wouldn't have wanted me to fail. She told me to go back to college. Dad died when I was six years old, so it had always been just Mum and me. We were close, and I wanted the same kind of closeness with Leo. Thing is, once he was born, I didn't need anyone else, and let's face it, as a husband Tim was a waste of space.'

'Yeah. You needed someone stronger, who loved you more.'

She's right; he just didn't love me enough. 'I felt like he was never really engaged with Leo and me; he didn't get involved in us as a family. I was always the one standing on the football pitch cheering Leo on. I was the one who picked him up and dropped him off. Tim didn't know his friends' names, or what subjects he'd chosen for A levels; he was like a lodger who just came and went from our lives. I'm glad he's gone!' I add bitterly.

Wendy knows what he was like, and she gets it, but I remind myself that I must be careful what I say to Wendy about Tim. I'm still not sure of their friendship and if she's telling the truth about not staying in touch with him after she moved away.

'I had a rubbish husband. I sometimes wonder if he'd been like that if my mum had been around.' I smile. 'She would have sorted him out for me.' I look at Wendy and we both giggle.

'She sounds quite formidable, your mum.'

'She was! I know she's with me now, here on this rock. She was waiting for Leo with her arms open when he left me. Mum always told me that she'd hear everything I say and see everything I do while she's up there waiting in heaven. I look up at the sky and swear I see the outline of her face. She's smiling; she's telling me I'm doing the right thing by my child, that she'd have done exactly the same for me.'

'So sad, your mum never saw you walk down the aisle,' Wendy suddenly says.

I drag my eyes away from the stars and my mother's face. 'Oh, she did.'

'Really?' Her voice is slightly incredulous. 'But wasn't she... dead?'

I smile to myself. 'Yeah, but Mum never left me, not really. She's with me now. And for my wedding she told me which dress to choose – as I stood alone in the changing room looking at myself in the mirror, I felt something touch my bare arms. I thought it was the veil, but it was just Mum telling me, "This is the dress."'

'Wow!' she exclaims, and I know she's thinking I'm mad talking to my deceased mother, but I don't care. It doesn't matter any more, because Wendy won't see me again.

'And is that the wedding dress *you'd* have chosen?' she asks.

'No. I hated it,' I reply. We both chuckle at this, and I wonder fleetingly if I should have been stronger with Mum after she'd died.

'I've seen the photos. Your dress was gorgeous,' she is obviously lying, it was hideous. 'Gosh, we were all just married when we met, weren't we? We were different people then. So much of life ahead, all white lace and promises as the song goes... And now we're splitting up and downsizing and worrying if our pensions will see us through to the end. It's so depressing. It all happened so quick. Who put it on fast-forward?' She groans at this.

'Yeah. Where did our lives go?'

Even in my well of sadness, I can supercharge it with extra sadness about Tim and our marriage. She's right; we had such hopes for the future, but it was just sand running through our fingers.

'Hard to imagine now, but I was so in love with Tim in the first years of our marriage; I was so insecure though. Everyone I'd ever loved had left me, and I just expected him to be next, and in the end he was. I know you all thought I was hysterical, accusing Tim of having affairs, watching him all the time. I thought I was going mad too. But all the years of humiliation, of him coming home smelling of someone else's perfume, drove me mad.

'Of course the aftermath of miscarriages and the process of IVF and all those extra hormones didn't help. The baby years turned me into an even more highly-strung wreck than I already was, but at thirty-two I finally had my baby, and I wanted nothing and no one else. I didn't want anyone else to come near him, to hold him or touch him.'

'I remember,' she murmurs. 'But you weren't well, Jill; it wasn't a healthy way to be.'

'That's what Tim said, he obviously got the idea from you,' I say accusingly, and before she can protest, I continue. Tonight is mine; the Wendy show is over. 'He said I created a bubble for Leo and me, and I never really let him in, but it wasn't helped by you contacting my midwife and social services, trying to get him taken off me.'

Silence.

'I know you wanted Leo yourself. You wanted him in your little family, didn't you?'

'No, you're wrong, Jill. I saw what was happening. I wanted to get you help. I wasn't trying to take him from you – I was trying to make you both safe.'

'You had everything, and still you wanted what I had. And hearing your boys next door swearing and shouting and fighting, I'm glad you didn't get your hands on him.'

'My boys are real, they live their lives, they aren't scared of upsetting their mother.'

'They are liars and cheats and they have no moral compass.'

'Rubbish!' she snaps in the darkness.

'I knew Leo was going over to your house in secret. I'd wondered where he was going. I'd been to the school once to pick him up and they said he'd left earlier. I got the same feeling as when I called Tim at work to be told by his colleague that he'd been off sick for two days. All the time I thought he was fighting fires, but he was *lighting* them.

'About a week before the prom, Leo called me to say he was at the library doing revision. So I went to the library, and when he wasn't there, I made a list of all the possible places. I imagined a drug den, a pub, a betting shop – but what I discovered was so much worse, when I knocked on your door under some pretext about a new fence.'

I can hear her breathing. She isn't responding, probably preparing her defence.

'You answered the door all tangled hair and tiny vest, barefoot as always and your usual frivolous but confident self. But unusually, you didn't throw open the door and expect me to follow you into the carnage that was your kitchen. You didn't perch on a stool in the middle of chaos and pour us both a wine or coffee depending on your mood. No, you stood warily in the doorway, smiling, while that red flush rose slowly to your face.

'I thought it was suspicious, but I silently chided myself. Tim had remarked on me becoming paranoid in recent months, or as he put it, "more paranoid than usual". But as I said goodbye and turned to leave the doorstep, I saw Leo's school bag in the hallway. It was hidden under all the other kids' bags, possibly deliberately, but I glimpsed it, and I knew it was his; I'd know it anywhere. I put his packed lunch inside it every morning; I knew every inch of that bag. What I didn't know was why my son wanted to be in your house instead of mine. I only discovered that when I was told who he was going to the prom with.

'I could forgive you for distracting my husband, but I will never forgive you for stealing my son from me before he died. Wendy I *know* you were involved in his death. I know you told the police you'd gone to pick up Olivia after she called you.'

'I did,' she says.

'You left the house at nine-thirty, so why was it almost midnight when you pulled into your drive? And why was Olivia sobbing, if she didn't know at that point that Leo was dead?'

TWENTY-FOUR

WENDY

It was absolutely freezing, and pitch black. The effort of walking uphill and the biting cold was making us both slightly breathless, and we carried on for a while in silence, Jill directing. When we came to slightly flatter terrain, I had more breath, so started talking. If nothing else I wanted to clear the air. We couldn't keep being angry with each other; it wasn't helping either of us.

'I'm sorry that you feel I stole your son,' I said.

She didn't respond, just kept walking.

'I know this hurt you, and looking back I should have sent Leo home, told him to ask his mum before he came to us. But he was Olivia's friend, our neighbour; we'd known him all his life. And I knew you would forbid it.'

'So instead you encouraged him not to come home.'

This wasn't true, but there was no point arguing with Jill. 'You'd always seemed fond of Olivia until you discovered she and Leo were dating, and suddenly she wasn't good enough for him.'

'If he hadn't gone to the prom with your daughter, he might still be alive.'

'I don't believe that.'

'I *know* it.'

'Look, they were happy, they were two young people going to the prom. If Leo was going to rush out early and fall in the river it had nothing to do with Olivia.'

'It had everything to do with her. You couldn't believe your luck when they started going out together. You were hoping to end your daughter's fascination for bad boys by foisting her on my son. You were hell-bent on them being together, and your daughter loved the novelty of going out with someone who didn't have a police record.'

'Is that why you wanted to split them up, because of her ex-boyfriend?'

'I had lots of reasons. That night I tried so hard to convince him not to go to the prom with her.'

'I know, I heard you. Even during the pre-drinks and photos at our house, you were taking him aside, whispering your poison about Olivia. Did you think we didn't know what you were doing? Have you any idea how that made Olivia feel? You behaved horribly, the kids were confused and I was surprised at how rude you were; you were so prickly and made everyone uncomfortable.

I'll never understand why you were *so* against my daughter?'

My words hung in the cold air; thick silence sat between us, the stars above.

'I just... didn't think she was right for him.'

'They were only going to the prom, they weren't getting married.'

'No, but it was *like* a wedding, you had the outfits... the drinks... the photographer!'

'It was supposed to be a special time in their lives, a memory to treasure for ever, a time to be celebrated, and I wanted to do that for them.'

'No, you didn't, you wanted to do it for yourself; it was all about you. With the new dress and the full make-up, you looked ridiculous by the way.'

'And you didn't in your JB Sports top and trainers? You looked like you were going for a run.

I don't get why you're still so irritated that I'd organised a professional photographer. I booked him to capture the moment, the kids in their finery, the garden blooming. I'd even hired a cleaner to clean the place. I'd spent a fortune in fresh flowers just for the photographs, and it was beautiful, Olivia in her prom dress, Leo looking smart in a suit. Yes, and I was in my new summer floaty, my hair done and make-up on. If that makes me an immoral, superficial person, then so be it.'

I hated that she had the cheek to look down on me like I was trailer trash for having a new dress, when she turned up looking like some weirdo in walking gear. It wasn't like it was even Sweaty Betty or Lululemon she was wearing; it was cheap viscose, stood out a mile. And her face was like thunder; she'd refused to even be in the photos until Leo coaxed her, and she never smiled.

As a mum of boys I knew it was hard to let them go, but she really was too possessive. And that night, I wondered if she might be losing it again, and I made a mental note to talk to Tim about her next time I saw him. Tim and I had always got along really well, despite Jill accusing us of having an affair on more than one occasion. There was no point in going over this with Jill now; it had hung over us for years.

'So, you never told me, what happened on prom night when you picked Olivia up?' she suddenly said. 'Why did it take you so long?'

I didn't answer; I didn't know what to say. There was the official story that we told the police, which was Leo left Olivia at the prom, and embarrassed at being dumped, she went outside alone, called me and I collected her.

And then there was the truth.

'All I can think is that, on the night, I must have dropped off in front of the TV, because my phone woke me up about 10 p.m.,' I started, unsure how I would address the two-hour interval unaccounted for in my police statement. 'I saw Olivia's name on the screen and picked up thinking she was just calling to say what a great night she was having. You can imagine how I felt to hear my daughter sobbing hysterically on the other end of the phone. "What is it, darling?" I was saying. "Calm down and just *tell* me." I was in bits, desperate to try and work out what the hell was going on. You know me, I can be calm in a crisis, but when it comes to Olivia I just go to pieces and now I'm pacing up and down the sitting room. "Calm down and tell me." I just kept repeating this like a mantra, walking round and round the room. You feel so helpless, don't you?'

She didn't respond.

'It took ages for Olivia to finally speak, and when she did it was through hiccoughing tears. "Mum, Leo's just gone, he's run away... I think he hates me. I don't know what I've done. He's gone and I can't find him."

'So I asked her where she was and I just jumped in the car and raced round to the school, but before I got there, I noticed something.'

'Oh...?' She was all eager, hoping I could give her a clue... Well, here was one.

'Yes, your car, hiding behind the trees. I saw you sitting in wait. Who were you waiting for, Jill?'

TWENTY-FIVE

JILL

I can't believe she saw me. I'd hidden the car so well; I knew I wouldn't turn up on any CCTV because there was nothing around, just trees.

'I never mentioned it before, because I didn't want you to know I was there.'

'Why were *you* there?' I ask.

'I was collecting Olivia, why were *you* there?'

I take a deep breath. I'm stalling for time, and I realise we're quite near a good area to stop – which will give me even more time to come up with something.

'Let's go over there, sit down, watch the stars for a bit, then go higher?'

'Higher? I'm no climber, Jill, as you know.'

'Don't worry, I know what I'm doing. Come on, park yourself here.' I pat the mound and she joins me.

'So go on...' she says.

'Well, I... I couldn't get hold of Tim. So I went out about nine to see if I could see him parked down near the woods around the school. I knew he was up to *something* that night, I just didn't know who with, but I thought it might be you. And when I saw you were all dressed up having drinks with the kids before the prom, I thought you might be dressed up for an assignation – with my husband.'

'*Assignation?*' She laughs. 'You are so 1950s, Jill.'

I don't respond, scared I might slip up.

'Still doesn't explain why you were sitting in your car behind some trees like a spy. You were very close to the woods. Are you sure you didn't see Leo?'

I am *so* anxious, I'm glad she can't see my face in the dark. I have to make sure I *sound* convincing. 'I parked down there because I was spying on Tim,' I lie. 'He was due to collect the kids at eleven and I just had this feeling that he might be meeting someone first.'

'Oh, Jill. You stalking your husband is no surprise, but – really? You've driven yourself mad for years – I'll say it again, I'm glad you two have finally split up, it's healthier, you can let it all go.'

'I'm sure you're right,' I concede. I think what I've told her is crazy enough for her to believe. The mix of disgust and pity in her voice is humiliating, but I can never tell anyone why I was there that night. I'll take it to the grave with me. I *have* to.

'So, I've confessed my stalking. Why were *you* so late getting back home that night?' I ask.

Now it's her turn to take a breath; I can almost hear her mind ticking over while she comes up with a reason; I'm just sorry I can't see her neck flushing one last time.

We're sitting on a hill in Wales, lying to each other about where we were on the night my son died; it would be funny if it wasn't so tragic.

'When I got to Olivia, she was in the woods. She was devastated because Leo had basically told her it was over. Apparently he'd received a text while they were dancing. He looked irritated, upset, and said to Olivia, "I just have to deal with this," and off he went. She said he was gone for more than half an hour, and when he came back he was visibly upset, but when she went to put her arm around him to comfort him, he shook her off. She had no idea why he did that.'

I know exactly why he did that. 'And she has no idea who sent the text or why he was so upset?' I ask, feigning surprise.

'No, she had no idea.'

'What about Rory Thompson? He might have sent Leo the text and then when Leo went outside to meet him, he threatened him or something?' I can't think he'd have been too chuffed to see Olivia at the prom with another boy.

'I don't know if he *met* anyone, or even went outside,' she says slowly, like something's dawning on her.

I hope I haven't slipped up.

The silence is thick between us, and I wonder if she's thinking about what I just said.

'Oh... sorry, I thought you said Leo went to see who'd texted him?'

'No. I didn't. Leo said, "I'll have to deal with this." Olivia had no idea what he did; I assumed he'd gone to text them back. Perhaps you know more than me?'

'No... I just misunderstood, that's all. So after he came back in, he... he just left?' I ask, moving on. 'And Olivia chased after him?'

'Not immediately. She was upset and ran to the toilets where her friends comforted her.'

It makes me sad to think no one comforted Leo. He just ran out into the night upset; his whole world had come crashing down. And it was my fault.

I think I hear something behind me, and turn around.

'Is someone there?' I say loudly.

Immediately, Wendy puts her torch on and starts throwing it around.

'Did you see anyone?' she asks, fear in her voice.

'No, I thought I heard someone, but I might have been mistaken.'

'I think we should go now, Jill,' she says, standing up.

'No, I'd like to stay a little longer.'

'I'm not being funny but you've seen the stars, we've talked about everything, let's just go back and get a glass of wine?'

'I knew you'd say that, which is why I brought this.' I take out my hip flask, filled with whisky.

'I figured you'd need a little top up. The wine should be wearing off about now,' I joke as she concentrates the light from her torch on the silver bottle.

'Cheeky.' She laughs, her spirits lifted slightly now she knows there's alcohol in her midst. I hand her the hip flask and she takes a long swig, throwing back her head. Then she takes another and moves away, twirling around, waving the torch, flashing it on my face. 'Hey, Jill,' she calls, 'we've got the stars, the drink and the dancing.' She starts to move, swaying her hips, waving her arms in the air like a stupid teenager. 'Wish we had the music!'

She's tipsy and silly and after more than twenty years of it, I've had enough. She's never going to admit that Olivia did anything, so there's no point in being here with her; she's wasting my time and hers.

'It's time,' I murmur under my breath, in case Leo's listening. This isn't spontaneous; I've wanted this for a long time. After I invited her for the weekend, I knew it would happen. I got to work with Google Earth and worked everything out, planned the route, this hilltop, not too high for her to climb but a beautiful sheer drop that no one could survive. My only concern was, would she drink enough to make it look like she fell? Silly me, I should have known Wendy wouldn't let me down there, and just in case, I pulled a slightly disapproving face each time she downed a glass before we left. Being Wendy, the rebellious child, my fake displeasure ensured she drank even more than usual. But I had to be careful she didn't overdo it, and as I know from experience, Wendy can be giggly one minute and in a drunken heap the next. She had to be able to walk here and get up this hill, which she has without too much complaining, and I'll take her by surprise. No one will ever suspect that timid old Jill has hurled her oldest friend off the top of a hill onto sharp, craggy rocks twenty feet below.

She's now dancing and throwing the torchlight around while singing 'Fly Me to the Moon'. Frank Sinatra must be spinning in his grave. Oh yes, it's definitely time. I stand up and she joins me, dancing, swaying, and being so stupid and annoying. This is going to be easy. I grab her by the shoulders, like we're dancing, and with one swift movement, I step forward and take her by surprise.

TWENTY-SIX

WENDY

I was in shock. I never expected that. One minute I was dancing on the top of a hill trying not to think dark thoughts and pretending I was at a pop festival, the next, Jill was trying to hug me. Then I started laughing, thinking she was messing about, but then she was dancing with me like a bloody ballroom dancer.

She was holding my arms and marching me towards the edge, but I couldn't see where the edge was, and I was feeling a bit tipsy and weak from the whisky.

'Jill, what the fuck?' I shouted as she seemed to be using all her wiry force to push me backwards into the darkness and down, and in that split second, I realised I'd spent far too long with my boys. Middle-aged women like Jill do *not* play-fight on rocky terrain in the dark, so what the hell was she doing?

'Jill!' I called, then, 'JILL!' but even as my foot slipped on the rock, I didn't believe she was trying to push me. I was so shocked, I couldn't get my breath. I was gasping and panting with fear as I lost my footing in those old trainers. I was falling. But despite my shock and confusion, some primal survival instinct kicked in and I grabbed at her. I felt wool in my hands –

her scarf. I'd grabbed her scarf. 'Jill, help me!' I was screaming as I began to slip down the side of the hill. But I still had hold of her scarf with both hands. She was being pulled down with me, and I couldn't let go. Even then I thought she might be trying to help me, until she started fighting me off, yelling, 'Let GO!'

We were now both on our backs sliding downwards in the mud and ice. Jill was above me and kicking me so hard in the head, I was stunned. Everything was blurred and started to move in slow motion.

In those last few minutes all I could think about were my children and how they'd cope without me. Olivia, my damaged daughter, sitting in the same chair, her face still and unmoving like a perfect doll.

'This is for Leo!' she was yelling. 'I know you covered everything up, and when you're gone I'll find Olivia and I'll get her to tell me the truth. You sent her to Spain so she was out of the country, away from the police, but she can't run for ever!'

This terrified me, the very thought of Jill getting to Olivia, accusing her, hurting her even more than she was already hurting seemed to give me the impetus I needed to fight.

We were both sliding down and I was still clutching her scarf. She was struggling, but had stopped shouting. I heard her gasping and wheezing as I held on tight to the scarf still tied round her neck. It was too dark and I was petrified. Then she kicked out at me again. I could feel her boot coming towards my head and letting go of the scarf, I moved quickly aside. I was crouched in the rocks waiting for the blow, but the force of her kick didn't land on my head; instead, it propelled her forward. I heard a muffled scream and felt her roll past me down the hill at some speed. Disturbed rocks and gravel rumbled after her, and I buried my face in my arms while holding on tight. Then suddenly a loud scream and a heavy thud from a long way down.

I stayed crouched in the rocks. Shock. Silence.

It had all happened so quickly, I had to wait a moment to gather myself together. Still clinging to the rocks, I somehow eventually managed to crawl slowly upwards. It was agony. My arms could barely hold on a second longer. As I gripped the rocks to heave myself up, my nails broke and bled, but I just kept going, my hands stinging from the cuts and freezing cold. Finally, I managed to pull myself back to the top and flat ground where I landed heavily, exhausted.

I hurt everywhere and couldn't move. I knew my phone was somewhere in the pocket of my quilted coat, but I couldn't yet stand up to try and find it. So I just lay flat on my back for a long, long time, gazing up at the stars, trying to work out what just happened and wondering if Jill was dead. And as I stared blankly, something emerged in the glittery sky. I couldn't make it out before, but there it was, as clear as anything: the crouching lion – Leo's constellation.

Eventually, I tried to sit up, locate my phone, but my back and arms hurt every time I tried to move, and I heard myself groaning in pain. My arms couldn't take the weight of my body as I leaned on them, and I kept slumping back onto the ground, exhausted and scared, looking up to the sky.

I called her name, but there was no response. I had no way of knowing how far she'd fallen. Was it a long way down?

I felt so vulnerable lying there. Had she landed and died, or was she just a few feet away, watching and waiting to come for me? Jill was a hiker; she was stronger and fitter than me – what if she was quietly climbing back up now? I glanced towards the edge, lit by starlight, imagining her hands suddenly coming into view. Fingers gripping the edge firmly, her strong arms easily lifting her slim body as she arose like a phoenix, stealthy returning for her prey. I wanted to look away, but couldn't; I had to be ready in case she was on her way back to finish me off.

I was terrified. I thought I knew Jill. She'd had her problems
in the past, behaved oddly at times, but I'd never in my darkest
fears imagined she was capable of killing someone. Leo's death
had affected her, but grief didn't turn people into monsters, did
it? She must always have had that capability, that detachment.
The killer lying dormant next door. I shuddered and made
another attempt to move. This time I rolled onto my stomach,
and finally, with some struggling, got to my knees. I started to
feel for my phone in the pocket of my coat. They were deep
pockets and the coat was thick. I pushed my throbbing hands
deep into the right pocket, carefully moving my fingers around
to feel for the phone, but nothing. Then I tried the left pocket,
which was less likely as I'm right-handed, but still in all the
madness God knows which pocket I'd pushed it in. I rummaged
around in the second pocket. It wasn't easy with the coat still on
me; it was long and I was kneeling on it. My big duvet coat and
slippery old trainers were a gift for anyone trying to murder me
up there that night. After more fumbling around, I gave up and,
groaning, I slumped back onto my stomach, but as I did, I heard
something. Someone was walking towards me. I looked up, but
could only see boots, couldn't lift my head high enough to see
who was stood above me holding my phone.

'Is this what you're looking for, Wendy?'

I knew the voice, and it filled me with dread.

'Mr Venables?' I heard myself murmur.

'Call me Derek.'

TWENTY-SEVEN

JILL

I've never felt so helpless, so out of control. I can't speak, can't move, can't communicate. I must be under sedation because I keep drifting off. It's either that or the head injury. I heard the doctor talking about it; apparently I fell from a great height. I don't remember much, but I do remember that Wendy was there.

God, I hate it in here. I feel like I'm strapped to this bed; there are tubes going into me and out of me. I can't see them, but occasionally I feel tugging, especially when the loud nurse with rough hands is here. She bathes me too. I hate it. The other one is gentler and quieter. I like her.

According to a conversation that's now taking place over my bed, I'm in trouble – medically speaking.

'She landed on her head,' a nurse is explaining to her colleague during what I presume is some sort of handover. 'As you know, an injury like this can cause the brain to swell after the event, and that's what's happening here.'

Silence.

'That's not good.'

'No, it's not looking good; she's on steroids and blood thinners but who knows? It's a tricky time for this one. Just hope she's still here on my next shift.'

Break it to me gently, why don't you?

She said it quietly, but my hearing is as good as ever, as well as my sense of smell and my sense of fear as I lie here, terrified, waiting for my brain to swell. I have so many questions, like will it ooze out of my skull? Will it hurt? Will I *know* if it swells, or will everything go black and that's me?

When will they know if I'm going to live or die? And if and when they do find out, will they bother to let *me* know? Probably not.

I know I'll be with Leo again. But I'm not quite ready yet. I'd like to clear my to do list before I go, which reminds me – what *did* happen to Wendy? Is she still alive, or did I succeed, and if she's dead – am I home and dry, or is there a police officer sitting on a plastic chair outside waiting for me to open my eyes so he can arrest me?

My eyes won't open. I can't speak, and I have so many questions I can't ask. It's beyond frustrating, makes me want to scream and cry and *move*. But I can't do any of that; I'm doing it on the inside though.

I wonder how long I've been here? It could be days or weeks, or even longer.

The last thing I remember was sitting in the dark on a hill with Wendy Jones. Then I fell – or did she push me?

I've also remembered *why* I was with her. I was going to kill her. I've wanted to kill Wendy for a long time, and that weekend away was all part of the plan.

If Wendy's dead, I wonder how Robert will feel?

Gentle nurse is cleaning my head wound. She talks to me sometimes, asks about my family.

You don't want to know.

Gentle nurse smells of peaches. My hearing and sense of smell have developed to compensate for me not being able to see. But I hear the nuance in voices, the significant pause in conversations. I'm blind, but I can see so much more, it's almost biblical.

Oh, the doctor's just arrived and from the sounds of breathing and shuffling, he's brought a team. It's hard to tell how many are now congregating around my bed looking at me, talking about me. It's not ideal for someone with anxiety issues; I feel very vulnerable and my paranoia is stratospheric. So along with the whooshing of my breathing tube and the beeping of a monitor, I can't think straight in the sudden cacophony of sounds and smells. Soft shoes on tiled flooring, sickly perfume, random throat clearing and the sugary chemical smell of fabric conditioner. The one with body odour is here again; ugh. The air is laced with sticky unpleasantness.

I'm trying to concentrate on what the doctor's saying. But as usual it's meaningless to a non-medical person – it's just about doses and milligrams and medication with long pharmaceutical names. He asks if there are any questions. Yes! I have one. *Am I going to die?*

As hard as I try to stay awake and make sense of what's going on, my body drifts off to sleep, which is frustrating but I can't help it...

I'm awake now, and it seems everyone's left. God knows how long I slept for; it could be minutes, hours, days even, but I'm suddenly lifted by the strong smell of disinfectant or something similar. As it fills my nostrils, I imagine I'm in a pine forest by a lake in Canada. Tim and I hiked there when we were younger, when everything was possible, before all the guilt and broken hearts came between us. It feels like another life now, the summer days of children laughing in the garden, the sweet smoke from a barbecue. The Christmases when both our families would come together on Christmas Eve, a huge, glittering tree and a houseful of excited children in pyjamas. I think now about how we'd leave the Joneses' late on Christmas Eve, me with arms full of gifts, Tim carrying Leo. One year I recall watching from the bedroom door as he gently took off Leo's Batman slippers, tucked him in and kissed him tenderly. He was as besotted with Leo as I was, but for me there was always the shadow of guilt, because I couldn't have another one, for Tim.

I might be crying. Is a tear trickling down my face? Would anyone even notice if there was? The machine forces air into my lungs. I smell the air that tingles with the scent of the forest and try not to think because it hurts too much.

Someone new just walked into my room... I can smell their perfume.

I know exactly who it is.

TWENTY-EIGHT

JILL

'Jill, it's me, Wendy.'

I obviously failed in my quest to kill her. I don't want her here. Do I have no say in who comes to stare at me? I really am in a bloody zoo!

'I thought you were dead,' she says. I feel her move slightly. The chair scrapes on the floor. Oh God, she's sitting down.

'Well, Jill, I don't know if you can hear me, or even understand me, but the nurse says it might help to hear a familiar voice.'

Trust me, it won't.

'It's been a difficult few weeks.'

You can say that again.

'I didn't mean for you to get hurt. I don't really know what happened, but because I grabbed your scarf it looks like I tried to strangle you.' She chuckles at this.

Oh no, she's crying now. I hear her rustling a tissue and giving her nose a blow. Nice.

'It was self-defence though, Jill. You were kicking me in the face. I can't get my head around what you were trying to do.' Then she lowers her voice. 'Jill, were you trying to kill me? It hurts me so much to think my friend only invited me away so she could end my life.' She's blubbing again.

Only Wendy could visit the dying and make it about her.

'Anyway, whatever you might have done to me, I called the police and the ambulance and they rescued you. They had to get an air ambulance.'

I'm furious. I've always wanted to ride in a helicopter, and the one time I do I'm out of it and miss the whole damned thing.

'You'll never guess who was there, who saw it all?'

Now I'm vaguely interested.

'Derek Venables.'

Oh?

'And it turns out he *does* have dementia. Well, it hasn't been diagnosed, but Margaret – that's Mrs Venables – told me all about it, and from what she said it sounds like he has some form of it.' She pauses. 'She doesn't want any outside agency involved though because she has her own way of caring for him.' She laughs a little.

Go on then, what?

'You know the shed? Of course you do, you spent several hours there.'

She stops talking; the chair leg drags across the floor. She's closer; I can feel her breath on my neck. She's talking quietly so no one will overhear.

'Poor old Derek's been suffering for some time, and as his sole carer, Margaret has had to find ways of coping with him.'

She puts her hand on my arm. I want to shake it off. It feels like such an invasion.

'Apparently, every night when they go to bed, she locks him in the bloody shed! Can you believe it? I mean, she makes sure he's safe and warm and has everything he needs, which explains the bed, and the books and papers you found. She says he pretty much sits up all night going through his notes on bloody stars.'

I'm intrigued, but what about the photographs? Did you ask about the photographs? Who is the half-naked boy? And why is my husband on his wall?

'She said that until she came up with the idea, she wasn't getting a wink's sleep; he doesn't really know the difference between night and day. He'd wander off in the middle of the night, and she'd have to go out looking for him. It wasn't safe for either of them, so she came up with the idea of the shed, so at night-time, or if she has to go out in the day, she just shuts him in.'

That does explain most of it, but still – what about the photographs?

'She asked me not to tell anyone about the shed. She doesn't want social services getting involved because she's worried they'll put him in a care home. She said life wouldn't be worth living if one was without the other. Sad, isn't it? Despite everything, they still love each other. I felt quite touched about that; a bit envious too, if I'm honest.'

It is sad. Looking at them, I thought they had nothing, but it seems they have everything.

'Weird, isn't it, how you can look at someone and you think you know exactly who they are, and they turn out to be completely different. They aren't trying to hurt anyone; they just want to keep living their little life in that strange old farmhouse with all that ancient furniture. Ugh, it gives me the creeps, but each to his own, I guess.'

Yes, and if they're happy, who cares how old their furniture is?

'Oh... there's another thing. The photograph of the half-naked teen you saw on the wall of the shed?'

Yes, yes go on?

'It's their son. He died. Apparently it was very sudden; he had a heart condition no one knew about. And the reason he has no top on is he was a keen boxer, only young, but apparently had great promise.'

That's tragic. I wish I'd taken the time to sit down with Mrs Venables; we would probably have been able to help each other. Only another mother who's been through it understands. So, what about the other photograph, Wendy? Don't bail on me now!

'Look, they aren't telling me anything because I'm not next of kin, it's still Tim, but all they are saying is that you're critical. You might not pull through, Jill.'

So tell me about Tim's photograph or I might never know!

'But it's made me realise that you and I have a short time left, and just in case there's a flicker of something left in your brain, I want to tell you...'

Yes?

'I know how it looks with Olivia, and I understand how you must feel.'

Oh, here we go, back to the same old song, 'my daughter is innocent'; I don't want to hear it.

'Thing is, I can't sit here and say hand on heart that Olivia didn't kill Leo...'

Ooh, is there a confession coming?

She's taking a breath, adjusting her chair again. I can feel her breath on my neck; it's revolting. 'Jill, I'm going to tell you something. I have wanted to tell you this so much, but I knew if I did, you'd go straight to the police, but I haven't told anyone.'

If I wasn't on a respirator, I'd hold my breath. As it is, I think my heart is pumping too fast.

'I've been lying about what happened the night Leo died.'

TWENTY-NINE

JILL

I'm not sure you can have bated breath when you're on a ventilator. But if you can, I have it, waiting for what Wendy is about to reveal.

'So when I got to the woods that night...'

And?

I wait for an eternity.

Is she still here?

She must have gone.

Oh, this is hell. There are lots of horrible things about being in my situation, only hearing half conversations between nurses and not knowing the person lying next to me. You see, there's another patient in the room; might be more than one? I don't know if they are male or female, dead or alive, but I can hear at least one other respirator, and the nice nurse sometimes talks to them. Or is she talking to herself?

Hang on, is that Wendy's voice I can hear in the corridor? She hasn't left yet! How long has she been hanging around? Or did I pass out and it's another day, another week? God, this permanent disorientation is tortuous.

Her voice is getting louder; she's coming nearer. I can feel my heart beating in my chest, hear the beeping of the monitor, the pumping of my lungs.

'So good to see you...' Is she talking to me? Her voice is blurry, but I can tell it's Wendy.

'I had to come, are you okay?'

Is that a man's voice?

'Yeah, I... I think so.'

He then says something in a consoling tone. I can't hear his voice as he's too far away.

'Oh God! It's so awful, so bloody awful!' This outburst from Wendy is loud enough for me to hear clearly. It's followed by what I think is sniffing. Is she crying? Either that or laughing; it would be just like her to have a good laugh at me.

They're talking very quietly. I can't make out their words, just a low hum. I lie here taking in the distillation of tears and mumbling, interjected by the deeper timbre of a man's voice. Who is he?

Sounds morph into other sounds; noise isn't making sense.

My heart rises as I hear the clatter of the plastic chair legs on the floor. She's moving closer to me. Can I feel her breath on my face? Is she *that* close? Is she going to confess?

'It's good to have you here,' she's saying, more clearly now. 'I didn't want to ask you to come. You have enough on your plate, but I'm glad you did.'

I can't hear his answer, just a low rumble. Definitely a man.

'Was the journey okay?'

He doesn't respond; perhaps he nods? I don't know.

'I can't take much more,' she's whining, 'I just want to be away from here.'

Tell me about it.

He says something like, 'You don't have to stay here.' I still can't hear him properly. He's talking much more quietly than she is, and it sounds like he's standing on the other side of the room. I still can't properly make out his voice or the words. *Who is it?*

'Do you need a break?' I think he asks. 'You've been here every day.' He's moving a little closer now. I can pick out words and fill in the gaps myself. I'm good at that now.

'Yeah, I could do with going back to the hotel...' She pauses, gives a mirthless chuckle. 'I say hotel, it's a room with a filthy shower.'

'That doesn't sound great, but not long now; we'll soon be heading back.'

'I can't leave her yet.'

'Why? She doesn't *need* anyone. Look at her, she's... there's nothing there. She's grey and cold, not a flicker of life; the machine's keeping her alive. I doubt she'll last the week.'

'Really?' There's a squeal of surprise in her voice; she seems genuinely upset. I'm almost touched.

'I think it would be a blessing; what does she have to live for now Leo's gone? He was her life.'

'But she can't die, what would happen to me?'

Oh... she wasn't upset. I needn't have almost felt touched.

'What do you mean?'

'What would it look like? I spoke to the police yesterday and they were really pushy, even asked about you.'

'Me? Oh... you didn't say.'

'It was late, you were travelling. That's the third time they've asked me to go in.'

'Did you have a solicitor with you?'

'No.'

'Shit, Wendy!' I think he sounds exasperated, but still his voice is murky. He's too far away for me to hear him; I'm just piecing together sounds.

'You *should* have had a solicitor with you.'

'But they weren't *arresting* me, and surely asking for a solicitor would have sounded like I'm guilty?'

He doesn't answer, which is frustrating because I want to hear him, work out who he is.

'Jill fell, I didn't push her,' she says. 'Don't look at me like that. I didn't.'

'I'm not saying you *did*, all I'm saying is you need legal advice; otherwise, you might say something you shouldn't.'

'I'm not stupid, I won't *say* anything.'

'You might just let something slip without meaning to.' He pauses. 'I think we should get away as soon as possible. Have the police said you can't leave the country?'

'No, but it would look odd if I jumped on a plane now, wouldn't it?'

'Wendy, it isn't about "looking odd", it's about getting the hell out of here. And if the police haven't actually told you *not* to leave the country, presumably you're free to go.'

What the hell?

'Look, I'm worried that if or when she dies, they might slap a murder charge on me – I'll look less guilty if I'm here, being sad.'

So that's why she's been hanging around my bed; it's all an act. It's always been an act, hasn't it, Wendy?

Silence, aching silence while my addled brain tries to process all this. Then Wendy suddenly speaks.

'Remember, they could re-open Leo's case any time, then where would we be?'

'Shh, don't *say* that in here,' he whispers.

'Don't worry there aren't any cameras. No-one can hear us.'

'You still have to *be careful!*'

'I know, but I don't think you realise how serious this is for me. Jill had ligatures around her neck; they were from her scarf but it looks like I strangled her. And Mr Venables keeps saying he *saw* me push her.'

'I agree, it doesn't look good, which is why I said it wasn't wise to hang around her bedside for weeks.'

Weeks? I thought it was days?

I hear muffled sobs, probably Wendy imagining the rest of her life in prison.

'Just stay calm. Everything's going to be fine, but you mustn't lose focus,' he urges, and even though his voice is muffled, I hear the edge of anger, fear even.

'Just looking at that monitor, you can see she's fading,' he continues. 'She won't be here this time next week... but neither will we. We'll be far away, on a beach drinking cold beers.'

In that moment, he's close enough for me to identify the voice. And it's only now that I realise who *he* is.

THIRTY

WENDY

I finally returned to the hospital a few days later. We stayed in the horrible hotel, but it wasn't as lonely now he'd flown back to the UK. We'd had dinners out, went for walks; it was romantic, and despite everything, I felt hopeful for the future – for our future.

I decided that I'd go back and see Jill alone, and this time I was determined to tell her. There wasn't much time; she was fading fast, and our flight was booked for the day after next.

'You okay, Jill?' I said gently, walking into the room.

Charmane, the ICU nurse, was checking her monitor.

'I just feel so helpless. I'm used to looking after people, but my speciality is bringing babies into the world,' I said.

'Mine seems to be helping them to leave the world,' she replied as we both gazed at Jill, as still as a statue.

'How is she?' I asked. 'I mean, nurse to nurse, the truth.'

She looked from me to Jill, then glanced around to check no one was within earshot. 'It's so hard to predict, but in Jill's case it's a severe traumatic brain injury, and if she survives there are likely to be long-term consequences.'

'Oh God, like what?'

'Anything from permanent brain damage, disability, even a shorter life expectancy.'

'Oh, it's not looking good,' I murmured. 'We go back a long way, me and Jill. I've known her more than twenty years.'

'Wow, that's tough.' She touched my shoulder. 'I think you might have to pray for a miracle.' She smiled sympathetically. 'I'll leave you girls to talk.' She left the room as I pulled my chair up close to Jill's bed. Looking into her sleeping face, I could see the faint lines and pores in her skin. The tiny scar on her cheek where she'd told me she'd fallen off her bike as a kid, a chicken pox mark, every flaw and freckle of a life lived, the scars we all carry, inside and out.

'Sorry I haven't had a chance to finish what I started telling you. I really wanted to, but with one thing and another...' I realised there was no point in telling her anything other than what I'd gone there to say. And as she slept, blissfully unaware of my presence, I was able to talk to her, tell her what happened.

'So, I pulled up where Olivia told me to, at the back of school, in a clearing that led to some woods and on to the river. I knew about this place because Josh had once been caught smoking there; apparently it was a blind spot for CCTV so the teachers couldn't see them.

'It was very dark there, and denser than I'd expected. I almost fell over the broken branches lying on the ground. I remembered someone saying there was a fungal disease in these woods, Ash dieback... All the branches were falling, the trees were dying.' I stopped for a moment. 'It's strange talking to you without you interrupting or contradicting,' I joked. 'Or judging, for that matter.' I touched her hand very lightly. It was cold, like alabaster. And so still, like she was already dead. 'I don't suppose you need to know this, but at the time it struck me how creepy it was to be in a dying wood in the dark, scrambling over dead branches searching for my child. I called her, but she didn't answer. Was I in the right place? She sounded so distressed on the phone, I'd dashed to get there and hardly asked any questions. I was so scared, had she been attacked? Apart from the distant thump of music coming from the school hall, it was deathly quiet.'

Jill's respirator was sucking and blowing constantly, and now and then the heart monitor showed a rise. It made me wonder if she would last the night, but then again, in her condition, an altered heart rhythm could mean anything, and nothing.

'I ran into the clearing, and the first thing I heard was Olivia crying, so I sprinted towards her. I couldn't really see her, but this weird, croaky uncertain voice spoke: "Mum? Is that *you*?"

'I reassured her it was, turned on my phone torch and manoeuvred it towards her and there she was, bent over something. I couldn't make it out, but I staggered towards her, cigarette ends and hash papers littered the ground, and I was in sandals, so the tree roots and broken branches cut my feet. But I felt nothing, I just waded towards her. She needed me!

'As I got closer with the torch, I could see she wasn't bending over *something*, it was *someone*. It was Leo. I got closer and focused the torch on his face, and what I saw will stay with me until the day I die. His eyes were wide open, his face covered in blood, and those eyes were staring into the light.'

I saw something flicker on the monitor and wondered if it was a reaction to what I was saying, but I knew it wasn't. Jill couldn't hear, or understand.

'I took one look and thought, *Overdose*. I was in a real panic, screaming in Olivia's face. "What's he taken?"

'"Nothing, Mum!" I can see her now, face wet with tears, her mouth open in horror as we both looked at each other.

'Olivia was distraught. She told me about him receiving the text and how when he came back, she said he looked at her "like she was the ugliest girl he'd ever seen". This broke my heart, and then he said he didn't want to go out with her any more and ran from the school. I told you the truth when I said I didn't know who the text was from and what it was that had upset him.

'I want you to know that I *did* try to revive him, Jill,' I said, suddenly realising how I needed to make this clear. If nothing else, it made me feel better to know I did all I could for him.

'I cleared the ground of bricks and branches and all the other detritus, slipped into nurse mode and checked him over. No pulse, body still warm, blood issuing from a deep wound in his head, which looked like it was coming from the sharp tree roots he'd landed on. But I didn't give up on him, love. I gave him mouth to mouth and cardiac massage and I worked on him for a long time. But he was gone. Trust me, if there'd been any flicker of life, I'd have brought him back.

'Through all this, Olivia just covered her face with her hands, whimpering. She was in pieces, just kept rocking back-wards and forwards.

'Now, I know what you're thinking, Jill, I thought the same – and I asked those questions. I asked if they'd fought? Did he slip and fall? Did she hit him? But she just kept saying no she didn't, that about twenty minutes after he left the prom, she went to find him. And she found him like that, on the floor, with blood pouring from his head.

'I know you probably will say that Olivia has a temper, she might have lost it and... Well, you know what I mean. She's quite a tantrum queen, always been the same since she was little. We used to laugh about it, didn't we?' I paused; it wasn't funny any more.

'I admit, Olivia *could* be lying to me, Jill, she could easily have followed Leo out there, furious, and they could have fought.'

I looked for a sign that she'd heard. But there was no glim-mer, no flickering of the eyelids, nothing.

'Jill?' I said, taking her hand. It was freezing; thick blue veins twisted along the surface under pale, thin skin, like the hand of a very, very old person. This wasn't Jill, my fit-as-a-fiddle neighbour who walked and hiked and talked and judged. 'Jill?' I said again. Not a flicker.

'Olivia's sometimes told untruths; she has "a good imagination", I think you once famously said? As offended as I was that you were calling my child a liar, I have to admit, even Robert called her Walter Mitty, but she only told white lies, and it was always to spare people's feelings. She isn't malicious, and the irony is, she doesn't even tell white lies any more -- what I'd give to hear her *say* anything.

'But that night, her voice was fine. She was desperately unhappy, but still our feisty, spirited girl. She'd been dumped, rejected, and – I know what you're thinking: she must have done something in anger? I've wrestled with this too – and in all honesty, Jill, I can't say, hand on heart, that she *didn't* hurt him that night.

'Mine and Robert's theory was that she might have *pushed* Leo, which *may* have caused him to fall and bang his head. The forensic people said the branch found near the scene was covered in Leo's blood and it was possible he'd fallen and injured his head on that branch,' I offered. 'This ties in with the theory of an accident. The head injury could have caused him to fall in the river the same way that too many drinks at the prom might have caused him to fall. *An accident,*' I stressed.

'Anyway,' I continued, aware the nurse could return any minute and time was limited, 'as you know, I'm good at being calm in stressful situations, like Olivia breaking her arm, and Leo falling from that tree when he was seven. I'm always the one who deals with things; Robert used to fall apart, get angry in a crisis, but I took it all on. I think that's why I'm so good at my job,' I added.

'So, I realised I had *two* choices: I could take Olivia to the police station, tell them what had happened, which could lead to her being charged with murder or manslaughter. Life. Ruined.

'Or I could remove the problem, never tell a living soul and make Olivia swear to do the same. I tried to stay calm and work out what to do. Would we get away with it? Was I missing something obvious?

'This wasn't an easy decision, Jill, and for a moment, I really considered calling the police. After all, Olivia would just tell the police what she'd told me, that she found him there.'

I knew Jill couldn't hear or comprehend what I was saying, but I didn't want to say any more. I didn't call the police because I suddenly heard her voice in the darkness. 'I hate him, I *hate* him,' she said in a low growl I didn't recognise as my daughter. It didn't even sound human. 'I'm glad he's dead.'

I shivered at the memory. She sounded like a wounded animal; it turned my blood to stone. She'd been so hurt. She loved Leo and he'd rejected her on what was supposed to be the most magical night of her life so far. As her mother, I understood, but the police wouldn't.

In this retelling, I was back there. In the torch spotlight I could see her face, damp with tears, mascara around her eyes, lipstick smeared. She looked like a monster, the damning bloodstains stamped on pale-blue chiffon. All I saw in the torchlight was fury, pure, raging fury. It was only then that I realised my beautiful sixteen-year-old daughter could, in that state, be capable of anything. Even murder.

THIRTY-ONE

JILL

Wendy said she had to pop out; she'd had a text apparently.

'I feel much better for telling you all this, Jill,' she whispered before she left. She seems to love offloading on me, using my catatonic body like a sponge to soak away her guilt. I wish I felt better, but hearing that nurse tell Wendy how she had to pray for a miracle made me wonder if they should just pull the plug now. But not until I hear the rest of what Wendy has to tell me.

She must come back; she can't leave me in limbo like this, just as she was about to finally tell me the truth. I long to know what happened, but at the same time I'm scared to hear it. But I can't choose not to hear it. I'll *have* to listen.

Having now heard some of the truth of what happened that night, it's unearthed all kinds of thoughts. And with all this time on my hands to do nothing, and all the silence and space, I'm playing around with different scenarios like a detective. If Olivia told her mother the truth that she just found Leo there, and we take that as read, then that means someone else hurt him, or hit him over the head before she got there. So taking this idea to its logical conclusion, someone else was hanging around that night waiting for Leo. If so, who? And why?

Once the kids had left for the prom that night, I went home and paced the floor, constantly going to the window to check the road outside to see if Leo was walking up the drive, having come back early. And while I was doing that, I remember looking through the window and seeing Josh, the Joneses' eldest ambling out of the house with Robert. When I'd been at the house earlier, Wendy had said Robert was due back, but his flight had been delayed and she was so disappointed as he'd miss the kids all dressed up. But as I stood there being jostled by Wendy and her photographer, having Prosecco thrust in my face, I wondered if Robert was deliberately late.

I was thinking this as I watched them climb in the car. Robert was driving, and he seemed to be muttering to Josh, neither of them smiling. I wonder if that's significant? Where were they going? I make mental notes in my head, storing things in document files in my brain.

And what about Tim? I know he wouldn't harm a hair on Leo's head, but he said he was at work, and when I phoned to remind him to pick them up from the prom, he didn't answer. So I called the landline, and his colleague said he'd already left work; it was only 7 p.m. I guess I'll never know exactly where Tim was that night – but I know he was with a woman; my only query would be which one?

I have so many questions, and it's agony not being able to ask. I miss such a lot lying here, but what I miss most is a pen and paper to write down those questions, and the ones arising from Wendy's account of that night too.

It would seem that the medical staff are writing me off. I've heard so many conversations where they say I may not make the next twenty-four hours. But they don't know me; I don't give up easily. Hopefully I'll be able to open my eyes soon. I may not be able to talk, but at least I could communicate by blinking.

I used to think I need more time, and now I have all the time in the world, and I can't do a single thing. I'm exhausted. Just trying to stay conscious to hear Wendy's recounting of that night has wrecked me. I took in every word, each one a precious diamond I wanted to hold, analysing the facets and watching them catch the light. I'm trying to keep everything in my head for when I'm better. I just hope my memory doesn't let me down.

'You know something, Jill.' That's Wendy's voice; she's back. I must have fallen asleep.

'You look like a stone saint lying there,' she's saying brightly, like it's a joke that I'm in a coma.

'Me garbling my confession over your wasting flesh reminds me of my last moments with my mother,' she says.

'I told you about my mother, didn't I? She was a staunch Catholic who regularly confessed to her priest. She wanted to be forgiven, saved, just like I do now, but if I'm honest – and that's what confession is all about' – she stops a moment, presumably to process this – 'I'm not religious, so it doesn't matter – but I don't think me or my daughter will go to heaven.'

No, Wendy, I think that train has gone, and you're both heading on one going in the opposite direction!

'So, where was I?' She took a tortuous few moments to recall, during which time I couldn't give her so much as a hint. 'Oh yes... so I didn't call the police. Olivia was so distressed I couldn't let her anywhere *near* them; there was every chance she'd incriminate herself whether she was guilty or not. My instinct was to get her home, remove the damning stains from the dress, make her have a shower and wash everything away.'

I feel sick, but it must be psychological; I don't think I'm biologically capable of feeling anything.

'So I told Olivia to take off her shoes,' Wendy continues. 'She was still kneeling by Leo's body, and looked up at me like I was mad. At first she refused to take them off, but I just told her to do as I say. I remember my hands shaking as I bent down to untie Leo's shoelaces. Fortunately, he was still pliable, no sign of rigor mortis yet, so it was easy to pull the shoes off. I handed them to Olivia and told her to put them on.'

What the hell?

'She knew not to argue and reluctantly pushed her feet into Leo's shiny new shoes; she was whimpering. It was just horrible.'

This breaks my heart all over again. I took him into town to buy those shoes. They were a little tight, but he wanted them so much he didn't care. How precious those nothings are now, like dandelion clocks. I reach for them, trying to hold on to the nothings that become everything.

But Wendy's voice machetes through my head, taking me back to the horror, my son's body on the ground, my neighbour, her daughter. The dandelion clock has disappeared.

'We were both crying, and I longed to hug her, but there was no time. The prom finished at eleven and some party-goers were bound to walk back home that way as it was a short-cut. So I began lifting his shoulders.

'"Are we taking him to the river?" Her voice was small, scared, as she picked up his legs and I told her not to drop them. If his feet had dragged that would be curtains, evidence that someone had moved him. That's why I swapped their shoes because I needed to take Olivia's footprints *out* of the frame, and at the same time make it *look* like Leo had *walked* to the river.'

It was something I'd seen on a detective programme, but what I hadn't realised in the drama was that my footprints might be there too. I was in soft ballet pumps, they hardly made a mark, but I took extra precautions and used a leafy branch to sweep the ground *I'd* walked on.'

She adds this with some pride. Well done, you fooled the police and saved your murderous daughter. Go Wendy!

'But she was all over the place, and crying again now, so I had to give her a good talking to. You know how she is, Jill: ever since she turned thirteen she's argued with me about every-thing. You used to say I was too soft, and you were probably right. I was too soft with her, wasn't I? But she was my girl, you know.'

Oh yes, I know. And he was my son!

'Weird, but I was waiting for you to say something then,' she said. 'One of your rants about how all children need *bound-aries*? You had a point. Perhaps I should have set more bound-aries: Josh might be less egotistical and kinder; Freddie might not demand money all the time and be hateful when we say no. And Olivia... Oh, where do I begin with our only girl? She hasn't turned out quite the way we'd hoped. You were right, I spoiled her.'

You spoiled them all, and consequently, they're all bad kids.

'We did our best, you and me, but I don't think either of us got parenting quite right, did we?'

I wish I could say I disagree, but it's true. We both tried, and both failed, in very different ways.

'I don't know how we did it *physically*,' she continues. 'There are anecdotes about how the maternal instinct is so strong, a woman is capable of lifting a heavy truck off her child. Is that true? Who knows, but it's medically proven that under extreme stress, humans are capable of performing feats of strength they couldn't ordinarily achieve. And that night, I did just that.

'While Olivia struggled with his legs, I took his upper torso under the arms and between us with great effort, we lifted him. It was awful. Once or twice she nearly dropped his legs, which made me yelp. I didn't want any drag marks along the ground. We needed the police and forensic team to think he'd either slipped or taken his own life, that no one else had been there.'

You were my friend. How could you? I may look like a statue, but inside I'm alive with disgust and hate and an overwhelming grief that wracks me with sobs that no one can hear. My feelings are so visceral and raw, I'm amazed she can't see the tsunami of hurt and rage bubbling just beneath the surface.

'God, I can still feel the heft of his young dead body as we heaved and pushed to get him to the river, and once we were there... It makes me shudder.'

And it makes me howl inwardly. Silently.

'I didn't want to do it, and Olivia certainly didn't. "Let's just call the police and tell them the truth," she said, but as I pointed out, it wasn't about the *truth*; it was how this *looked*!'

She stops talking. It's a relief; my injured brain is overwhelmed with information and the implications of what she just told me.

'I cried, Jill, we *both* did,' she continues, still star of her own show. 'I couldn't believe that just a few hours before, you and I were waving them off in a limousine.' She pauses, presumably to take that in.

I can't allow myself such indulgence. I want only revenge.

'We couldn't actually see him in the dark, but as we dropped him in, we'd heard the splash, so we knew he was in the water.

Your daughter killed my son, and you covered it up?

'I was horrified, but I just kept telling myself it was the *right* thing to do. Even if Olivia *had* pushed him, it was an accident, therefore it wouldn't be fair for her life to be ruined over an *accident*, would it?'

No, of course not. We can't have Olivia's life ruined for murdering someone.

'There's a chance that Leo had tripped and fallen before Olivia got there, and now she was in the wrong place at the wrong time. She couldn't take the rap for that,' she added. 'I know you've always seen my moral compass as being slightly off-key, Jill, but I know what's right and wrong. It's just a matter of perspective, and...' She paused. 'God, I thought I saw your eyelids trembling. Jill? Jill?' She pauses again.

I feel movement next to me; I think she might be pouring herself some water.

'This probably sounds so brutal to you, but what you have to understand before you judge me – and I know you would if you were here – it wouldn't just be Olivia's life ruined if we'd left the body there and called the police; our whole family would be decimated if she'd been convicted of murder,' she continued, like this justified what she'd done.

Her moral compass isn't off-key any more; it's non-existent. She's a psychopath!

'Robert couldn't continue his work if Olivia had gone to prison, and the boys... What would happen to them? Both her brothers are hoping to go to university next year. They're finally getting their lives on track and this would be like throwing a bomb into everything. God, it doesn't bear thinking about. What could happen to *them* with a convicted murderer for a sister? So you understand, don't you? I had to think of everyone.'

No. You had to think of the Joneses. No one else mattered; they never have.

'I know you can't hear me or understand, but I have to explain all this, what my thought process was. And by the time I arrived, it was too late for Leo, and I had to save Olivia. You'd have done the same, Jill. I know you would.'

I hear her chair scrape along the floor. She's going now, but before she leaves, I feel her lean over me. My heart soars. I haven't felt this intensity before; and yes, I really feel her breath on my cheek as she leans in and whispers.

'You don't have long, Jill. I'm glad I told you everything, even if you can't hear me. I know you resent me because your child died and mine survived, but you're not the only one who's suffering. Since that night, I've lost my daughter too.'

THIRTY-TWO

WENDY

When I left the hospital that day I was in bits. Reliving that night was so hard, not just because of Leo's death, but because of what I asked of Olivia.

My daughter was devastated, but in that moment in those dark woods, I felt it was the safest, best option to move the body, get rid of the evidence. Leo was already dead; it was too late to save him, but Olivia was alive, and as her mother, I had to save her.

I would probably never know if he was already dead when she got to the woods, but for what it was worth, I believed Olivia when she said she didn't do it. I just had no evidence to prove that. Either way, I shouldn't have forced her to move Leo's body and I should have called the police.

I held on to that guilt for a long time, and felt so much better after explaining it all to Jill. I felt like a weight had been lifted; that now I'd told her, I could move on with my life without being saddled with that awful secret. It was over, for me at least, and it would soon be over for Jill too.

Robert and I were going to a new life; we'd planned it all

and I couldn't wait to start the next chapter. Our flights were booked and we were leaving the day after next.

* * *

The following morning, I woke feeling happier than I had in a long time. I hadn't realised until now, but the secret I'd been keeping had weighed heavily on me, and finally I could see the light at the end of the tunnel. There was something comforting about walking through those big double doors, breathing in the bitter smell of antiseptic laced with fake pine. It was a smell so familiar to me, and as a nurse, it felt like home wandering down endless corridors to ICU for the last time. Today was the last day I'd visit Jill; I wanted to see her just one more time to say goodbye.

Charmane had just finished giving her a sponge bath and was chatting away to her when I walked into the unit with a string of pink balloons bought from the hospital shop. Flowers weren't allowed in the Intensive Care Unit, and despite Jill being unaware, I wanted to mark the last time I saw her. My friend was dying, and I was leaving the country.

'Oh, how beautiful!' the nurse said admiringly. 'Let me help you.' She took them from me and tied them to the bottom of Jill's bed.

I looked at Jill, her monitor beeping, her face ashen; I'd seen dead bodies, watched people die in front of me, and in my opinion, she was close to death. I'd known for some time that these were her final days, but this wasn't a patient, it was my *friend* I was grieving for. My eyes sprang sudden, unexpected tears.

'You feeling okay, Mrs Jones?' Charmane asked from behind the pink balloons, which looked slightly ludicrous and too celebratory on Jill's death bed. Less a kind gesture, more a cruel prank.

'I just hate to see her like this,' I said, which was true, but deep down I was also grateful that this was coming to an end.

'You're a kind friend,' she murmured in her lilting Jamaican voice. 'I'm sure she's loving these balloons.'

I sighed. 'What a shame she'll never see them.'

'Oh, you never know, she might.'

'I'd like to think so too.' I nodded, going along with her fake optimism. We all did it, us nurses; it was important to give friends and relatives hope while managing their expectations.

'Last night I swear I saw a faint smile on her lips.' Her kind brown eyes were a mixture of sadness and hope. 'I called the consultant, and he came to see her, checked her vital signs.' She came closer. 'I don't want to build up your hopes, but he thinks she might be rallying,' she said excitedly.

My heart clanged, and my finger ends tingled. *What?*

'Oh? I... I assumed that was impossible,' I said, my mouth going dry. 'I talked to one of the nurses the other day and she implied that Jill would *never* wake up.'

She shrugged. 'Well, it's hard to say. Never say never. We might *think* the patient is unaware, but you can never be *absolutely* sure... Some patients just come through, despite all the odds.'

'Oh... really?' I asked, trying to give what I hope looked like a smile, but was probably more of a grimace.

'Yeah, yeah, you'd be amazed. I'm medically trained, not supposed to believe in miracles – but I've seen them in here.'

'Yes, I see miracles in midwifery too,' I replied. 'But Jill's been in this state for weeks now, surely even if she woke up... her brain...?'

'The human brain is amazing, so complex.' She leaned against the foot of the bed, the balloons wafting around her as she delivered the killer blow. 'Patients like Jill often present as being unaware, beyond reach, and even though she looks like she isn't with us, she might hear and be aware of everything, but just can't communicate yet.'

Fuck!

'So there's a chance she might wake up?' I asked, unable to look at her, worried she might see the terror in my eyes.

She looked at me, concern on her face as she stroked my arm. 'I don't want to get your hopes up, but my colleague said she blinked yesterday, which could be a sign that she's starting to emerge.' She was smiling, her hand still on my arm, her face too close to mine. 'The consultant is very positive. He's scheduled her for a brain scan later.'

Before I could say anything to show my delight at this potential 'miracle', she turned away.

'Oh look, another visitor. Hi there.'

'How is she, Charmane?' He looked into the nurse's face with apparently genuine concern. I was amazed. I never realised he was such a good actor, and the nurse was clearly taken by his charm, fake or not.

'She's stable,' she said. 'We mustn't give up hope. I was just saying, there are signs she may yet pull through.'

'Yes, Charmane's just explaining that one of the nurses saw Jill blink yesterday, and she's going for a brain scan later,' I said, glimpsing panic in his eyes that matched mine. I couldn't understand why; after all, he had nothing to panic about, unless he'd guessed that I'd told Jill everything. I felt so foolish.

'Well, that's something isn't it?' He looked away from Charmane and gazed at Jill, while I tried to compose myself. I could feel Charmane's eyes on me; was she watching, or was my guilt causing me to *think* she was?

As soon as she'd gone, I beckoned him to move away from Jill's bed; I wasn't risking her hearing another word.

'I'm worried. If she wakes, she'll say I tried to kill her, I know she will,' I whispered, which quite honestly was the least of my problems. 'I think we should go now!'

'She can say what she likes, but it's your word against hers. It wouldn't stand up in court.'

I felt such an idiot for talking to her. What was I thinking? I had to tell him; he had to be prepared.

'Look, I told her some stuff,' I hissed quietly in his ear.

He looked at me with a confused expression. 'What are you talking about?'

'That Olivia might have pushed Leo... That I put his body in the water.'

'What the hell?'

'I just wanted to get it off my chest. I hoped that—'

'You told her Olivia found him? About you putting him in the river?' he whispered through gritted teeth.

'You guys okay in here?' Charmane popped her head round the doorway.

We both nodded while offering subdued smiles.

'It's a lovely day, very sunny and warm for March,' she said, wandering in, checking Jill's notes, looking at her watch. She wasn't going anywhere, just shooting the breeze with us and chatting away about how she couldn't wait for the summer.

Panic rose in my chest. I wanted to scream.

'I think I'll head off,' I said, hoping he'd take my cue.

'Oh... okay, I'll come with you then,' he replied.

After saying goodbye to Charmane, I didn't kiss Jill on the cheek as I had been, for fear of waking her. My heart felt heavy as I left that small, white antiseptic box, and once out of there we almost ran through the hospital corridors. When we got outside, I let the sun shine on my face in an attempt to soothe myself. It didn't work; my heart was banging in my chest. I took huge, deep breaths of cold air to try and calm down, while he stood close, agitated.

'What the hell made you think it was okay to tell her?' It was clear he was trying not to sound angry, but his words stung.

'I'm sorry,' I said. 'I feel *such* a fool.'

'Let's not talk about it now. Take your car back to the hotel. I'll follow on in the hire car.' He looked at his watch. 'I think I left my wallet in the room,' he said, checking his pockets, those little veins standing out in his head when he was stressed.

'Do you want me to come with you?' I offered.

'No... no, you can't ever go back in there again, if she lives or dies. You need to stay under the radar now. I'll see you back at the hotel.'

'Okay.' I felt like a child who'd been told off by their dad for doing something stupid. I had; I'd done the most stupid thing I'd ever done in my life. And there was a chance both me and my daughter would have to pay for it.

THIRTY-THREE

JILL

The gentle nurse is called Charmane. I heard one of the other nurses call her by that name yesterday. I'm definitely hearing things better and I feel less blurry and confused, and I don't know if I dreamt it, but I think Charmane told Wendy that I was rallying. What a beautiful word that is. It's music to my ears. And I might be mistaken, but I swear I felt my finger twitch. I was hoping my visitors might notice it and alert the nurse, but they obviously didn't see it – or perhaps it didn't happen after all. But still I feel exhilarated at this spark of possibility, that there might finally be a hint of colour in what I imagine is a very white room.

Charmane always takes her time, talks to me, even asks me questions; with her, I exist. Wendy talks *at* me; she doesn't really care what I think or how I feel about what she's saying. I'm just an empty bowl for her to pour her guilt into.

She might think she's unloaded that guilt, but she's still carting it around with her. She'll take it to her grave, but if I have my way, she'll spend some time in prison before then. I have to survive; I have to drag myself out from this quicksand.

Apart from Wendy and Olivia, only I know what happened that night, and only I can make sure justice is done.

'Hello, Jill.'

It's him.

My stomach flips. I haven't had such a visceral reaction to anything since I came in here. Is he alone? Or is Wendy with him?

'I had to come back. I just wanted to see you.'

I don't understand. Why now after all this time?

I hear the familiar scraping of the chair as he drags it towards the bed.

'I feel bad about everything. I can't begin to tell you how what happened affected me. I've lived with this, as of course you have, but just holding on to it was... *is* exhausting. I felt so guilty, and it weighs so heavily, I sometimes wish we'd just told them, got it out in the open and dealt with it. Who knows? By now it might all be healed.'

I don't want to hear this. Not now. It can never be healed; we opened up that wound and it can never be closed.

He takes a breath. 'I remember you and Wendy having the babies within weeks of each other; we knew they'd all be great friends. It was bittersweet watching the kids playing together, the boys too, Josh helping Leo with maths homework or Freddie showing him how to bowl at cricket. I'd see them with you and Wendy, our two happy families and think: *If only they knew.* There were times when I'd sit at those big family Sunday lunches and have intrusive thoughts; just one sentence could blow everything up.'

I can't bear this. There's no point. It's all too painful. I don't want to hear it. I want to run. God, how I wish I could run out of here and away from him.

'But at the end of the day we were *two* families. I loved Wendy and you loved Tim, and despite caring for you, it would never have worked, Jill.'

This terrible secret that pulls us together also tears us apart. Like Wendy's pink balloons mocking me at the end of the bed, both scared to untie them, always watching in case it floats away and the secret's out.

'Secrets are so destructive, aren't they? I held on to that secret for so long I felt like it was burning a hole in me. I could barely look at Wendy and the boys, found it hard to relax in my own home. That's why when Leo was born, I chose to work away. I thought after a while it would get easier, but one year slipped into another and I'd missed so much, my children growing up, our lives together...'

That day, when we met, you walked to the back of the van, opened the doors and within seconds you were moving my furniture. I was sad that Tim had let me down – again, and I fell in love with you, that first day. And over the years, that love grew, but it didn't make me happy; it made me jealous and miserable and uptight. Was it the same for you?

'Thing is, Jill, what happened between you and me was about two people caught up in a grown-up world we wanted to escape from. You felt let down by Tim, and I was so crazy about Wendy, and so insecure, I lost my way thinking I couldn't give her what she wanted. Then you came along. We hit it off, laughed a lot, and I felt I could tell you anything. Being with you felt right. It was easy; I didn't have to try.'

I never told you how I felt about you because we were both married, but if I could speak, I'd tell you now. It wouldn't be too late; we're not married to other people any more and I think I'm getting better. Perhaps this is our time, Robert? You and me together at last; it's all I've ever wanted.

'I don't know if Wendy told you, but our marriage was rocky for a little while. I think Leo's death affected everyone remotely involved; it was such a terrible, terrible thing.' He sniffs; I think he's upset. 'But... you know, we've got back together for the kids, for Olivia really. She's struggled – you know? Well, we all have; poor Wendy is a mess.'

Is she really? Poor Wendy.

'I don't know why I'm telling you this. I was angry with Wendy for blabbing, but you know what she's like. It's her beautiful chaos, her vivaciousness, her chatty, optimism that draws me to her.'

Oh...

'I know she tried to change me; she still does. You accepted me for who I was, and our friendship meant the world to me, but after that night, and the pregnancy, I lost you as a friend.'

A friend?

'I remember you once saying how alike we were, you and me, complete opposites to Tim and Wendy the "party people". But as our marriage has grown, I've come to realise that *party people* need wallflowers to calm and organise them, keep them safe, and the wallflowers need the fizz and of those party people. Truth is, Jill, Wendy is the love of my life, and I've spent the last seventeen years torturing myself for one night when I betrayed her with you. It's one of my biggest regrets.'

I didn't think I could hurt any more. I'd cry – if I could.

THIRTY-FOUR

JILL

I was his biggest mistake, an inconvenient extra in the movie of his marriage to Wendy.

I was the child who lost her parents, the girlfriend who got dumped, the wife who was cheated on, the mother who miscarried. All my life I've been the woman nobody wanted or wanted to *be*. Even my so-called friends only hung around me because I made them feel better about themselves, their marriages, and their own lives.

But earlier, when Robert came to see me, I really believed he would be the one who turned it all around – that he'd come to save me.

I'm not a passionate woman given to obsession and jealousy; I love quietly, secretly. My feelings for Robert burned deeply, consistently, calmly, never wavering through the long years.

Having Robert in my life got me through the envy of pregnancy, the agony of babies, and christenings, and first days at nursery before I had Leo. During the seven long years of trying for a baby, everyone else's life continued, and the children's watersheds and celebrations were painful, but as long as he was there, I could cope. He was so different from Tim, and I felt like he was the first man who loved me. Except it turns out, he didn't.

I suppose it wasn't fair, but having Robert around, I constantly compared the two men, and Tim never came out well. They were chalk and cheese. Robert was intelligent, well-read, reliable, and drank only good wine, and never too much. My husband, meanwhile, was insensitive, loud, had never read a book in his life, and after flirting with every woman at every social event we ever attended, he'd drink so much beer, I'd have to help him home.

It sounds rather immature to be besotted by someone who was happily married, who saw me as a friend, who I could never have. But loving Robert from afar was enough for me. I could turn away from my husband in bed at night and imagine it was Robert lying next to me. I could live the scenarios in my head about us having a secret affair, leaving our partners, going to live in a cottage by the sea. It was all so long ago and far away, but until today, I'd continued to live with a little secret hope.

On those nights I felt wretched. It wasn't just the longing for Robert; my longing for a child had become entangled in all my feelings. Tim refused to have fertility treatment; he didn't want a child like I did. 'Why are you always looking at other people's lives and wishing yours was the same?' I couldn't tell him it was because I was with the wrong partner. Before I was pregnant with Leo, I'd sit alone in the garden on summer evenings, listening to them next door. Their garden was always sunnier than ours, which seemed darker, more closed in. I imagined ours to be colder than theirs. Wendy would be calling from the kitchen, their double doors wide open, letting in the sunshine, their laughter and conversation tumbling out onto the garden. Her boys were tiny, but very lively; they'd be playing football or diving in and out of a little paddling pool. The dog would be barking.

'Christ! I can't hear myself think!' she'd yell from the

kitchen, and I'd envy that so much, because I *could* hear myself think, and it went round and round and round my head.

If Robert was home, I'd hear his gravelly voice, which had this quiet authority that made me swoon. He'd be telling the boys to calm down and asking Wendy where the olive oil was and I'd smell the barbecue, my heart soaring just knowing he was there. So near and yet so far. Their lives were busy and Wendy dashed from childminders to work, to nursery and back again. Often her mother would appear like Mary Poppins and turn everything into Disneyland for adults and the kids.

I wanted everything Wendy had, everything she was; even the madness of two kids and a job and a husband away seemed like bliss. Meanwhile, I might meet a friend or stay for drinks after work. I even joined a book club at the local library but I was the youngest there, by about a hundred years. Tim was either at work, or at the pub, and sometimes when I was home in the evenings and the laughter was too much next door, I'd go in and close the door. I'd sit inside watching *Coronation Street*, wishing I had the kids and the dog and the leaky paddling pool and the reliable husband. I thought having a baby might transform Tim into a family man and we could have some paler, quieter version of the Joneses' life. But as I soon discovered, having a baby doesn't make someone a daddy. And by the time Leo arrived, I had to face up to the fact that I'd ended up with the wrong man, in the wrong life.

It never occurred to me that Robert would ever look at me; with a wife like Wendy, why would he? But then, one evening, we were over at the Joneses', just the four of us, having a few drinks and nibbles in the garden. Tim and Wendy had been giggling all night, and Robert and I had been talking about politics and he'd been telling me about his medical work with Médecins Sans Frontières. Earlier I'd half-jokingly accused Tim and Wendy of having an affair and she was clearly angry about this. 'How could you even think that?' she said in her drunken haze. She could barely stand up as she swayed and yelled at me, 'I flirt. I flirt with everyone. You don't even flirt with your own husband, that's why he does it with everyone else – perhaps you should try it sometime, Jill!'

She staggered off to bed soon after, while Tim fell asleep on a deckchair, both so pissed they'd forget everything the following day.

Robert apologised for Wendy's behaviour, but I didn't care; I wished Tim and Wendy would get together. That would leave the way clear for Robert and me. He was kind, intelligent, and reliable – everything Tim wasn't. I thought he'd felt that same invisible spark. That evening we talked for a long time about our lives, his hopes for their two boys, my dream of being a mother. It was that late-night, slightly tipsy kind of conversation when you say things that you probably shouldn't.

'I sometimes think you and I married the wrong people,' I heard myself say into the fairy-lit silence.

He turned to me, smiled. 'You might be right.'

That's all he said, but that gave me some encouragement, and I flirted, told him he was handsome and that I admired him, which he seemed to enjoy. And later, he offered to walk me home, leaving Tim still out of it on the deckchair in their garden. We staggered down their drive and stepped over the flower beds to our house, where we had a clumsy drunken kiss on the doorstep. Despite my inebriated state, I was euphoric, and I invited him in. Nine months later, Leo was born.

Finding out I was pregnant was wonderful, traumatic, and devastating. I was so mixed up, torn apart by guilt, jealousy, shame and sheer, unbelievable joy. It was the kind of joy that catches at the back of your throat whenever the source of that joy comes into your head.

This joy was obviously tempered and dampened by the guilt, and I felt this sense of injustice – why couldn't I just be with the man I loved and have the baby I'd longed for? At the same time, I couldn't look at Wendy without loathing myself. When Leo was born, I told Tim I didn't want any visitors because I was feeling so low. So she sent me a beautiful basket of fruit to the hospital that sat on my bedside table on the ward, like a fat reminder of what a bad person I was. And when I returned home with Leo, she left flowers on my doorstep, sent texts, tried to call, but my shame and jealousy had boiled up into a dark rage against myself, and I couldn't face anyone. Especially Wendy.

Like everyone else, Tim thought I had post-natal depression, and was actually quite concerned, but I imagine his concern was based on wondering who was going to look after the baby if I was poorly. He took time off work to look after Leo and me, and for a few weeks he even stopped going to the pub every evening. I found out later that he'd told Marek the reason he stayed home with me was because he worried I might harm myself or the baby. How funny; I was more likely to harm *Tim*!

I'll never forget the first time Robert saw his son. Wendy had thrown me a big surprise party in their garden for my birthday. I was thirty-two and suffering from post-natal depression, but Wendy wanted a party. I happened to have a birthday, and she was determined to have some fun. But it was the last thing I wanted to do; I was distraught.

She had said 'no kids' and given Tim phone numbers for people who'd look after my two-month-old baby.

'Sorry, if she wants me there; she can have Leo too,' I'd said when Tim objected to me taking him to what I thought was just a dinner party with the four of us. I would never leave my son with a sitter, and definitely not at two months old. I didn't even want to go next door; the only reason I'd agreed was so Robert could meet his son.

Wendy's face was a picture when she saw Leo at her fancy party, clearly furious that I'd disobeyed her party rules, but desperate to seem reasonable in front of all her friends. They were all shouting 'Surprise!', and I felt attacked.

I plonked myself on some outdoor furniture and spread my baby kit on the table. She didn't want to photograph my breast pump or nappies; Wendy only ever did pretty.

So I waited at the table alone, nibbling at photogenic canapes while waiting for the father of my baby to turn up. Eventually he appeared and I called him over to meet his new son.

THIRTY-FIVE

JILL

He's still here, and I can't help but wonder what he's thinking.

'Thing is, Wendy feels we should go back to Spain now, thinks we're risking everything hanging around here. She's worried that she's told you too much and you'll wake up. But you won't.'

I will. I will wake up, and when I do I'll tell the police what she told me, and I'll tell everyone who Leo's father is. I've had enough of holding on to other people's secrets; they eat you up inside.

'Oh, Jill, I wish things had been different.'

He takes a long breath. I can see him in my mind's eye, running his fingers through his beautiful hair. He's almost fifty, but still has thick, curly hair and boyish good looks, from what I remember.

'I deeply regret what happened.'

Oh...

'I was horrified when you told me that night at the party. I'm ashamed of my reaction; I rejected you and the baby. But you have to understand, I couldn't risk hurting Wendy and the children.'

He sounds just like Wendy, protecting his own at the cost of others. They don't care what the consequences are, as long as they are all safe. It seems to me that feelings and fates of the Jones family always come first when it comes to other people's lives... and deaths.

'You and me were a drunken mistake that should never have happened, but I want you to know, I'll never regret Leo.'

My eyes are burning. It's a weird sensation, like when Charmane puts the drops in to stop them drying.

'When you told us he wanted to be a doctor, I almost blurted, "Just like his dad". And when he did so well in his exams or won a medal at sports' day, I knew, usually through Wendy, and I gave a silent cheer. She was so fond of Leo, always said he was like part of our family. I suppose he was.'

I think this gets to him. He's quiet for quite a while. I wonder if he's crying. Does he feel the loss of our child as much as me? When I wake up I'll ask him.

'I don't know why I'm telling you this now, I haven't told a soul, but my secret's safe with you. God, I still go cold remembering the night you told me I was Leo's father at the party. Wendy had gone to so much trouble; she'd created this beautiful space with these beautiful people, and suddenly, I saw you.'

I remember that so well. Our eyes met through the crowd of dancers and you were drawn to me, finding me there alone with your child. I thought you knew Leo was yours, that some primal instinct had told you this was your baby.

'It was weird; you looked so out of place, this frail little woman in dark clothes holding her baby, while everyone else danced around you, like you weren't there. I remember walking towards you and thinking you looked like a ghost, and I wanted to check you were okay. I bent down to ask you if you'd like a drink and you whispered something in my ear. I remember asking you to repeat it because I'd obviously misheard.'

He stops a moment and I wait for him to carry on, and I hear the tears in his voice when he speaks again.

'"This is Leo," you said. "He's your son."'

How could I have got it all so wrong? What meant everything to me had meant nothing to him.

'I knew you'd had problems getting pregnant, but it had never occurred to me that the child could possibly be mine. I'd naturally assumed it was Tim's; then I thought you'd used me to get pregnant; that's why I was so... hostile.'

You assumed the fertility problems were mine, and that I'd slept with you just to have a baby?

'I was so relieved when you agreed we'd never tell anyone. It had to be our secret.'

I treasured 'our secret'. It was the only thing we had exclusively, just the two of us – this big secret that bonded us forever.

'Here's the thing,' Robert's saying. *I always like the way he uses that phrase, often before a joke or something light-hearted, or profound. I've always waited eagerly for whatever he says after this opening phrase, and today is no different. Except I know this isn't going to be light-hearted, and it certainly isn't going to be a joke.*

'That night at the party when you told me Leo was mine, I was devastated. I felt so bad I drank far too much, and confided in Marek. I remember waking up the next day feeling sick, not just about the fact I'd made the next-door neighbour pregnant, but that I'd *told* Marek!'

The next-door neighbour. That's all I ever was.

'I know, I *know* he's the *last* person I should have confided in, because he and Lena are like a damned podcast.'

And all the time I thought it was our secret, but you told the last person you should ever share a secret with. Nice work. And I thought it was Tim who was the idiot.

'So the next morning, I told Wendy I was going for a run and popped over to Marek's. I took him aside and told him to

forget what I'd said and never repeat it to a soul, even Lena.
And I really believed he'd done that.'

Why do I feel a 'but' coming?

'But then Olivia came home from that stargazing holiday in
Wales and mentioned some trouble between Leo and Rory
Thompson.' He pauses. 'You might remember him, not exactly
a parent's dream for their daughter. Here's the thing: Rory was
making fun of Leo, and Olivia was confused by this, but Rory
kept saying Leo's father was the next-door neighbour. Olivia
said, "I know it's just Rory being vile, bullying Leo because he's
mean."

I agreed, said it was absolute rubbish, and also slander, and
I'd have words with Rory. She said she thought he might be
jealous because of the rumour she was going out with Leo.'

I can feel my heart pumping faster now.

'I tried to hide my horror and asked her if it was true. She
denied it and said she and Leo were just friends. "He's like my
brother, Dad," she said, which triggered me but placated me, for
obvious reasons. I then got in touch with Rory and arranged to
meet him, and he told me about some odd things that had
happened on the school trip.

'We met in a coffee bar and I said if I ever heard that he'd
been saying anything like that again, I would take him to court,
and with his record he'd end up in prison for the rest of his life.
Yes, I exaggerated, but he's so stupid he believed me. I asked
him where he'd heard this "lie", and he said Marek's son Kai
told him on the school trip and he thought it was only right to
let Leo know what Kai was saying about him. I doubted very
much that Rory was so compassionate, and was actually
taunting Leo.

'Rory's a bully; he said Leo was a mummy's boy and never
had any friends because his mother never allowed him out after
dark, stuff like that. Then he told me that when they were on
the school trip, Leo hung around with some old guy in his

bedroom. At first I was shocked, but apparently this guy lived near the campsite. He was a stargazer who had a telescope in his bedroom.'

Mr Venables.

'Apparently Leo told this guy what Rory had said about his dad, and the old fella threatened to kill Rory. I'd like to shake that man by the hand.' He chuckles. 'According to Rory, the old bloke was a bit loopy, and while they were all there hanging out at this farmhouse, he asked Leo if he could see a photo of his dad. Leo showed him a picture of Tim when he was about his age. He had it on his phone and the old guy got him to send the picture over to him. This bloke then printed it out on A4 and put it next to Leo's face. He was obviously being kind, trying to reassure Leo and told Rory to stop telling lies, because Leo and his dad were the image of each other.'

It's starting to make a weird kind of sense. It's two years since the trip, and in that time the old man's deteriorated, but kept this random photo because he thought it must be someone he knew.

'I thought the problem was over; I'd stopped Rory bullying Leo, and also kept the secret safe. But when you texted me the day before the prom to tell me that Leo and Olivia weren't just friends, I panicked and came home early to see for myself and to try to work out how to deal with this without anyone finding out the truth.

'I got home after the kids had gone and told Wendy I wasn't happy about the relationship. I had to continue a lie I'd started after the stargazing trip when I thought there was a chance they might get close. I told Wendy that Leo was into drugs; I hoped it would scare Wendy and stop her from pushing them together.

'But by the time I got home, things had obviously developed. I was angry and she was accusing me of being "just like Jill", not wanting our kids to be together.'

Robert's phone rings, and he answers. 'Yes, I found my

wallet. I won't be long. Look, I'm dealing with it!' he adds, clearly irritated. 'I'll sort it. I promise, look – just trust me, okay?' He ends the call. 'That was Wendy,' he murmurs. 'I should have told her years ago – *we* should have. And on the night of the prom, I was planning to tell Wendy everything, but Josh was there and he wanted a lift, so I begrudgingly drove him to the pub.'

Around the time I saw Robert leave with Josh, Tim called to say he couldn't pick them up because of a fire in Malvern. I knew he was lying, but I set off to the school hall. It was then I made the biggest mistake of my life, and texted Leo. I told him to meet me outside the school hall because I had something to tell him. I thought I was doing the right thing, that to keep it a secret any longer was immoral now he was older. But what I didn't realise then was that this would set off a chain of events that would ultimately lead to my son's death. But when did my son die, and who was the killer?

THIRTY-SIX

JILL

'I was sitting in my car outside the pub when you called to tell me that you'd texted Leo,' Robert says. 'He'd come out of the prom to see you, and you'd told him. Just like that you'd told him Tim wasn't his dad, that it was Uncle Robert.'

I had to, I was worried the two of them would fall in love and take things too far, and if it hadn't already, it might happen that night. After I told him, he cried, then he yelled at me, said some terrible things, and throwing open the car door, he just ran back to the school hall.

'After you called me, I was concerned about Leo. I knew he would be devastated, so I set out to find him. I'd hoped it would never have to come to this, but then we never expected them to fall in love, did we? At the time, I was angry with you, but I understand why you told him. You had more courage than I did, Jill.'

I wish we'd talked. I wish we'd shared this problem. If we had, Leo might still be with us.

'I was worried Olivia would tell Wendy and the boys, so I decided to find Leo myself and try to talk to him. I drove near the school and saw him running down the back road towards the woods.'

I never knew Robert was there that night. Oh God, this is all beginning to fall into place...

'I expected him to be upset, but when I walked towards him and tried to put my arms around him, he shook me off with such force I almost fell. "Fuck off!" he spat, and then he was scrabbling around the ground and picked up a big tree branch.'

My poor child. I can never forgive myself for telling him; if I hadn't he would probably be alive.

'I just wanted to calm him down, tell him I loved him, and all the things I should have told him before. I wanted him to know I was proud, and when the dust had settled, that he and I could be father and son. He had a ready-made family; he was a Jones too.'

He already had a family!

'But he was so mortified and upset about his relationship with Olivia; he said we'd humiliated him, that he felt like our dirty little secret. He assumed you and I had been having an affair and we'd betrayed Tim, who he said was his only dad. "You'll *never* be my dad," he said, and it hurt so much, Jill; his voice was filled with such hate and disgust.'

My body is tingling with grief. I feel like I'm reliving that night. Around the time he was in the woods with Robert, I kept calling Leo, but there was no answer, so I waited at the school, assuming he was still inside.

'Leo was just standing there, ranting at me, filling the air with a torrent of rage and hurt, and shame. Quite rightly this was all aimed at me. And as he lashed out, I stood and took it. I wanted him to punish me – I deserved it.'

He's crying now. I don't know if I want to hear what happened; at the same time, I am desperate to know.

'I didn't mean for it to happen, Jill. God knows I loved him like my other kids; I wouldn't harm a hair on any of their heads. But while he's yelling at me, he's still holding this huge tree branch and I suddenly see it coming towards my head. My instinct took over and I simply swerved to avoid it, but he was lunging at me, and when I moved, it caused him to lose his balance. He landed so heavily, Jill. I can still hear that horrible sound, the crack of his head on a tree stump. But before I could go to him, I saw Olivia emerging through the trees. I couldn't bear to see her. I couldn't explain; I wasn't thinking straight, so I did what I always do: I avoided the problem and escaped.'

Like you did when I told you Leo was your baby: you went halfway across the world to work – because you're a coward.

And that night in the woods, knowing your son was injured, possibly dead, you abandoned him. And ran away.

'I imagine Wendy told you the rest, but of course Wendy and Olivia have no idea what had happened, or that I was involved. Olivia was telling the truth when she said she just found Leo there, and it's my dearest wish to clear any doubts and tell the truth. But if I told the truth I would break everyone's hearts – Olivia would be devastated like Leo, the boys would never speak to me again and Wendy would definitely leave me. We'd all be so broken. But as it is, we are patching ourselves together, and they have no idea of what really happened, or of my relationship with Leo.'

He's quiet for a while. I think he's sobbing into his hands. I'm sobbing too, silently.

This man, the man I thought I loved, was made of straw, like beautiful barefoot Wendy and their three perfect kids in that gorgeous house – it was all a lie.

'So, Jill, I apologise if by any chance you *can* hear me. Wendy's panicking that you might wake up and talk to the police. But I know you won't.'

I want to kill him.

'Wendy and I are flying back to Spain tonight; we've bought a place out in the hills. We got a good price for our house on the close, I imagine Wendy told you – we were able to buy a really lovely villa with its own pool.'

I'm thrilled for them; they'll just jump on a plane, fly themselves out of trouble. I can't let him leave, they mustn't get away with this, but I'm feeling so weak, like I did when I first came here.

'We're so happy there: beautiful weather; lovely fresh vegetables and fruits. We all live a healthier life there. Wish we'd done it years ago.'

So do I.

You and Wendy killed Leo between you, and in doing that, you've ruined Olivia's life too. I'm not guilt-free but I know what's right and wrong, and I have to wake up, I have to.

'Here's the thing, Jill, I think there's a chance you might just wake up. I checked all your vital signs, I've studied that monitor, but what really worried me was your twitching finger yesterday. I couldn't let the nurse see it; she'd have brought in the doctors and they'd be filled with false hope – I say false, because you are never going to walk out of this hospital. I've decided you aren't going to wake up. I can't let you ruin our lives. We're finally free and happy, living in the sunshine; you wouldn't deny us that, would you? So I'm going to put a little something in your IV bag just to help you sleep. It's a slow-acting opioid, not easily detectable, and given the unpredictability of brain injuries like yours, I don't think anyone will be surprised when you slip away.'

I'm trying to open my eyes; inside, I'm screaming.

'Charmane's gone for the day, and the other nurses don't seem to have the same concern for you. They're all enjoying the gift basket of chocolate I brought in earlier for looking after my old friend and neighbour. There are no cameras in ICU as one has to consider the patients' privacy, so no one will ever know. See, I've thought of everything. I'm going to get off now. It won't take long and I don't want to be here when the alarm on your monitor bleeps. Night, night, Jill.'

NO! Please, no!

A YEAR LATER

THIRTY-SEVEN

WENDY

Our white stone villa in the Spanish hills is truly paradise. We wake each morning to sunshine and a spectacular view over ancient olive groves and lavender-dusted hillsides. Surrounded by mountains and rolling countryside on one side, and the glittering Mediterranean on the other, I feel like I've finally found what I've been looking for. It's like another world.

Despite it being late January, the weather is so mild here; we eat breakfast together every morning under a canopy of lemon trees. In the evenings we eat alfresco on our decked patio, and occasionally I take leisurely evening strolls downhill to the vibrant little village for drinks and tapas with new friends.

Josh has now joined us here in Spain, after a few issues with a dubious crowd at medical school who apparently enjoyed the drugs more than the lectures. Despite being innocent of any drug involvement, Josh was asked to leave the university and threatened with legal action if he didn't. He had absolutely nothing to do with the ketamine haul found hidden in his halls of residence; as he said, it was obvious he was framed.

So I took the next plane out to the UK, moved him and his stuff out of there, and he's now living in Spain with us, along with Freddie, our middle child, who moved to Spain with me after his exams. Now the whole family are back together and living in Spain. Apart from Robert, of course. I don't like to talk about it. I wasn't going to tell my friends here in Spain either until the biggest Spanish news site published this – available internationally, and in English too. Unfortunately, they had it covered:

EL PAIS

A local doctor was today convicted of 'spiking' an IV bag, almost leading to the death of a patient not in his care. Dr Robert Jones, from Worcester in the UK, was visiting a former neighbour and old friend, Jill Wilson, in the ICU department at Cardiff Hospital when he committed the crime.

Dr Jones, 52, and his wife Wendy Jones, 49, moved to Spain two years ago to start a new life with their three children. In January last year, Wendy Jones returned to the UK to spend a weekend in Wales with her former neighbour Jill Wilson, 50, who suffered a brain injury while hiking during their trip. This led to Mrs Wilson being airlifted to the hospital where she'd been in a coma for almost three months before Jones attempted to administer what could have been a lethal dose of opioids into the IV bag.

But Senior ICU Nurse Charmane Oke, 54, who happened to be in the hospital to meet a friend on her day off, checked on Mrs Wilson while she was there. During her visit, she was concerned to see Doctor Jones leaving the clinical supplies room with a carrier bag and immediately alerted her manager, who contacted the police.

'He was behaving suspiciously, and something told me he was up to no good,' said Charmane, who's worked at the hospital for twenty-two years.

'I kept an eye on the visit and heard Dr Jones tell Mrs

Wilson that she wasn't going to wake up because he'd put opioids in her IV bag and he was about to attach it.'

That's when the quick-thinking medic immediately ran for help.

'I removed the bag just in time while my colleagues held Robert Jones down until the police arrived,' she said.

Nurse Oke raised her concerns earlier when she'd over-heard conversations Dr Jones and his wife had with the victim.

'They had been neighbours, but there had obviously been issues over the years,' said Charmane, who's still in touch with Mrs Wilson, now safe and well back in the UK.

Det Insp John Jenkins, who led the investigation, said: 'The terror that Jones inflicted on this vulnerable woman reveals a deeply disturbing and calculated nature. This is a particularly shocking crime due to the fact this man was a medical doctor.'

Robert Jones's career in medicine spanned twenty-five years working across the world for Médecins Sans Frontières in countries of war and conflict.

He has been jailed for life with a recommendation of a minimum of twenty years.

Whoever would have believed that my husband, the doctor, would now be in prison for attempted murder? I refused to believe he'd even contemplate something like this, but there were witnesses. And finding out that Leo was his... that Robert and Jill had... well, it destroyed me for a while. I will never, ever forgive him.

Fortunately, my new friends here have supported me, and without them I'm not sure I'd still be here. And there are my new fans... Of course, I'm teasing, but my inbox is full after appearing on *My Husband, The Killer,* a true crime TV show out here. I've become quite the celebrity and male admirers are always slipping into my DMs.

Living here is about healing as a family, and I honestly feel happier and more fulfilled than I have in a long time. The children are here with me in Spain, the boys are taking a couple of years off work and study to travel, but first they want to start a band and bum around Spain for a while. My boys need some time and space to chill and kick back; they're creative souls who've had their issues but hopefully will come through the storm. We've all had a lot of stuff to deal with, and a year on, I'm still recovering from that terrible weekend with Jill. Yes, she tried to kill me, but she was confused; grief had addled her mind.

Poor Jill had little to live for after Leo died and Tim left. That long weekend in Wales had been bittersweet, and not the nostalgic girls' trip I'd envisaged, reliving the past and talking about old times over a few drinks. Jill had changed; she was even more uptight and on edge than ever that weekend. Now I know the reason for her anxiety. My old friend and neighbour was planning to kill me on the Sunday evening under the stars. That was the whole point of the girls' weekend!

Of course the biggest shock was finding out about Leo's paternity. I was devastated, as were the kids, and I couldn't bring myself to speak to Robert or Jill for a long time. But Robert begged to see me, and I finally agreed to talk to him in a supervised prison visit, when he described what he did as an act of kindness. 'Jill was desperate for a baby; she'd had lots of treatment, but had no luck. She begged me to give her a baby. I wanted to see her happy, to give her the greatest gift a man can give a woman.'

I wanted to vomit; what a pompous self-important liar my husband is. And how could he leave his biological son bleeding on the ground and run away – add coward to that list of traits. So the next day I wrote a long, forgiving letter to Jill.

Jill wrote back to me saying it was a one-night stand they both regretted, and no, she didn't ask him to impregnate her. 'I was as surprised as anyone to discover I was pregnant,' she wrote, 'and though I wish it had never happened – I'm glad it did, because I had Leo, and he made me a mum.'

I cried when she said that. I reckon Jill might have had a little crush on Robert. But it wasn't reciprocated; she'd misinterpreted my soon-to-be ex-husband's charm for something more meaningful. 'I see the way Jill looks at you,' I used to tease him. 'She's definitely got a soft spot for Doctor Robert.'

The irony was, all the time she was accusing Tim and me of having a secret affair, she was lusting after my husband, then carrying his baby! She was barking up the wrong tree there: I wasn't interested in her husband, Tim was never my type. He was a beer-drinking, skirt-chasing man-child who couldn't look after his own wife, let alone anyone else's. No, I only had eyes for Marek, tall and dark and handsome; he looked after me in the bedroom all those years when my husband was away.

Talking of Tim, I had a call a little while ago from someone trying to locate him; apparently his new partner reported him missing. I couldn't help it, I laughed out loud. 'I'm not at all surprised about that,' I said. 'He hasn't gone *missing*; he's gone to live in Australia with another woman. I spoke to his ex-wife Jill only last week. Apparently he's on the Gold Coast. He soon moves on; you should do the same and not waste your time on him.'

I don't know how or why Jill put up with him for so long; he made a fool of her, but she was so besotted with Leo (and probably Robert), he got away with it. He only had to drop Leo off at school and he'd leave the playground with another mother's phone number. And in between his affairs, he was sleeping with Marek's wife Lena on and off throughout their marriage. Marek didn't mind; it gave us more time together. I often wonder if I married the wrong person, lived the wrong life. Perhaps we all did? I miss Marek, but after Leo's death we all retreated back into our bunkers; life as we knew it ended that night.

Sometimes, when the memories overwhelm me, I lie on the floor in my beautiful white villa, the cold marble under my back as I wind through the film of years; newly married, new homes, new husbands and wives, new horizons, young sapling trees swaying in the garden. The friendships formed sitting on doorsteps, talking over fences, drinks on the patio, then the babies, sleepless nights, and cosy dinners. But I always come back to Leo or Olivia and the darkness descends, because in the end it all came down to those two babies lying on a rug in the garden. So I try not to go there, and turn my mind to the endless summers at the park, on the beach, by the river. *The river they dragged to find his body.* And I'm walking through the dark, and through to the clearing where I can hear her screams, and there she is, Olivia standing in a wood of dying trees clutching Leo's body, her powder-blue prom dress stained with his blood.

THIRTY-EIGHT
WENDY

My attempt to 'save' my daughter from being accused of murder has been catastrophic. More than two years later, she still hasn't recovered from that night, when we moved Leo's body. She is with us all in Spain physically, but not in spirit.

Olivia didn't come to Spain for fun, or travel, as I told Jill. She was taken out by Robert, while I stayed behind to work through my notice, and Freddie's final college exams. We simply had to get her away from Lavender Close and the UK. When Robert returned, during Jill's time in hospital, he left her here with Josh, who had to lock her in her room most nights to stop her running away.

We made the decision to bring her here after she threatened to go to the police and tell them we'd thrown the body in the river. This would have been damaging and pointless; the case was virtually closed and everyone had gone back to living their lives. To go to the police would have been at best disruptive, and at worst would result in a potential prison sentence for both Olivia and me.

Jill changed all that, of course, along with Nurse Oke, who seemed to spend more time listening in to Robert's and my conversations with Jill than doing any nursing. She's now being hailed as a hero because she told the police everything she'd overheard. Robert was arrested immediately, and Olivia and I hauled in for questioning soon after.

Just after Robert's court date, Olivia and I had one of our own.

I'm just grateful that the courts were more lenient with Olivia and me, but as we didn't actually kill Leo, I suppose it's quite right that we should only receive suspended sentences. Again, the Spanish news website *El Pais* were kind enough to report on bloody everything, so my new friends could enjoy the facts, and I had no place to hide.

MOTHER AND DAUGHTER WHO THREW BOY'S BODY INTO RIVER GET SUSPENDED SENTENCES

Today former midwife Wendy Jones, 50, and her daughter Olivia Jones, 18, were given suspended jail sentences for perverting the course of justice by concealing the death and disposing of the body of Leo Wilson, 16.

The mother and daughter threw the young man's body in the river in an attempt to conceal their potential involvement in his death during a prom night attended by both teenagers.

The police were alerted when Senior ICU Nurse Charmane Oke was concerned the death was suspicious having overheard conversations the mother of three and her husband Dr Robert Jones had with the patient, Jill Wilson.

Speaking after sentencing, Det Insp Emma Hoxton said the pair's decision to not seek medical attention and move the body was a 'cruel and heartless act'.

Jones was given a four-year suspended sentence, while her daughter Olivia Jones's sentencing has been delayed by a month for psychiatric reports.

I hadn't been honest with Jill; it was easier to say Robert had left me and we were having a separation than the truth. I didn't want her to know that we were whisking Olivia out of the country because that would be a red flag to her, nor did I want her to know what had happened to Olivia after that night. I had to keep her off the scent, and as she seemed to take pleasure in the idea of my marriage failing and Robert abandoning me, I let that one play out.

We assumed that after a few months of therapy and time with her father, Olivia would come to her senses and agree not to contact the police or tell anyone about moving the body. Except she didn't come to her senses. She stopped speaking and eating and... it breaks my heart to see what she's become.

Jill used to judge Olivia for her loudness, her heart tattoos, short skirts and bad choices. I worried about those things too, but now I'd give *anything* to have that loud, messy, feisty girl back again, because that's who she *was*.

But Olivia isn't who she used to be. My daughter has been changed by everything that happened. It's like her mind went dark, she slipped under, and now we can't reach her. We live in a beautiful villa on the edge of a mountain; the views are breathtaking, the walks are gorgeous, life is good, but my daughter spends her days staring into space.

I've taken her to doctors, psychiatrists, psychologists, and acupuncturists; you name it, we've tried it. And the general consensus seems to be that she's suffering from acute stress reaction. This is a psychological response to a traumatic event, and it's as if a key was turned that night, and she became locked in to her mind and body, and both mentally and physically she is unreachable.

I've acknowledged to the health professionals how much of an impact Leo's death had on Olivia, but can't bring myself to talk about the removal of the body, the splash as it landed in the water, the horrible aftermath of holding on to this horrific secret. I have nightmares, and I'm triggered by everyday sights and sounds; like yesterday, when I saw a teenage boy in a café and immediately thought of Leo. I sat drinking my coffee and feeling the weight of his body in my arms, and the sounds of my daughter's whimpering. Her face in the light of the torch, the bloodstains on her dress, and the fear in her eyes that reflected my own.

I try to reassure Olivia, but it's hard because when I try to tell her she's a good person and good people make mistakes, she doesn't respond. I wonder if that night I should have let her do what she wanted to do: call the police and take her chances. I've always said children should be free to follow their instincts. But that night my maternal instinct kicked in and I just had to take over, make everything better. So I *made* her move the body and keep the secret. But in removing one problem, I created another, and this new problem is far worse.

The advice is to keep her safe, structure her day, and hopefully she will come through, and with the help of my sons, that's what we're doing. Josh plays hoops with her on the patio, and Freddie goes for long walks with her. He says the silence is hard, but he just keeps talking to her, hoping it stimulates a smile, or a word – ironically, it worked for Jill.

There are good days and bad, and we hope for recovery but nothing is promised; we take joy in the rare moments she makes eye contact, or takes a can of Coke from the fridge. But the other night I woke with a start, aware of a presence in the bedroom. It wasn't until my eyes got used to the dark I saw someone move in the corner of the room, and suddenly I realised it was Olivia, standing very still, silently watching me from the shadows.

I shivered, because that person living alongside us, that spectator, watching and waiting, isn't my daughter. She's a stranger existing in the shadows of our lives. I feel like the last time I truly *saw* my daughter was on a July evening almost two years ago; she was waving from the limousine on her way to the prom. I haven't seen that girl since then, and I miss her and want her home, but today, I'm in the garden planting bulbs in time for spring, and as I look up, I see her standing by the window. Our eyes meet, and to my utter joy, she smiles in recognition, for the first time since that dreadful night. My heart is overwhelmed with happiness and I finally dare to hope. It's such a small thing, and yet for me it's huge; I'll never take her smile for granted again.

My child did nothing wrong, but the adults let her down. Her father left Leo to die, and then her mother forced her to move his body. In trying to save her, I lost her. And as she lifts her hand to wave, I wave back, tears running down my face. I think today my daughter has finally come home from the prom.

EPILOGUE

JILL

It was late summer 2005 when my third pregnancy ended in miscarriage. I was devastated. I wanted a baby more than anything in the world, but having gone through extensive tests, the consultant couldn't find anything wrong with me.

'I think in order to deal with this issue, we now need to test your husband,' she'd said. 'Miscarriage and failing to conceive can be caused by damaged DNA in sperm or a chromosome condition. It could even be a lifestyle choice: drinking, smoking. But we can work with it, and it can be treated,' she'd added. 'A minor op, some tests, no alcohol, no smoking...'

I was elated. Along with Tim, I'd blamed *my* body for not carrying the children we'd conceived, but the idea it might not be me who was faulty had given me hope. I drove home that day feeling like another door had opened, and we might after all be like other people and have children.

But my optimism and happiness were soon shattered when Tim refused outright; he wouldn't even agree to go for initial tests. 'I am not infertile, I'm not giving up beer, and I'm not prepared to go through operations and invasive medical tests to be told I'm fine.'

I should have known he was the kind of man who saw infertility as a reflection of his manhood. And all the pleading and crying in the world made no difference; he immediately shut the conversation down.

Then, a few months later I missed my period, so I took a test and it was positive. I was scared and thrilled at the same time. What if I lost this one, but what if I *didn't*?

I finally had a little chink of light in the darkness. To grow the tiniest seed of hope I now held, I planted a tiny apple tree. My maternal hormones were surging and needing to nurture. I told myself, if this didn't work, at least I'd have apples next summer.

The sapling apple tree reminded me of a little deer with spindly legs. It looked so vulnerable, I worried that when the wind blew it might break, so I taped it up with supports, and checked it every day.

And when the blood came, I went out into the garden and sat by my baby apple tree.

This happened again and again, and each time I channelled my grief into learning how to grow the tree, how to mulch the roots and feed the tree regularly, checking the soil to make sure the conditions were perfect. I nurtured that tree like I would the child I yearned for. It helped to fill the emptiness of my longing.

Years later, holding my new baby son in my arms, I would sit with him under that apple tree, rocking him, telling him how precious he was. My happiness was complete. I was just grateful that Tim never did the maths, because I knew Leo wasn't his.

That apple tree has been in my life now for almost 20 years. It's survived my only child, and will probably survive me. I'm grateful for its beauty in the spring, shade in the summer, russet cornflake leaves in autumn, and frosted winter branches.

Tim wanted to cut the tree down to build a small home

gym. 'But it's Leo's tree,' I'd said, horrified that he hadn't remembered, but did he even know? Had he ever heard me? Did he even care?

After several arguments, I suggested he build his gym *next* to the tree instead and eventually he agreed. Somewhat belligerently, he started digging up the garden to put in foundations for his gym. That was early autumn, and by the following January, as often happened with Tim, he'd abandoned the idea, and we had a huge hole in the garden, about three feet deep.

At first I nagged and complained and asked him to either finish it or fill it in. But eventually I gave up, just glad I'd saved the tree, because in its own way this tree has been a friend to me, always there, reliable and sturdy, unlike my husband.

Then one day, I decided to fill up the gaping cavern myself, and set about it with my spade, but while I was doing this, I had a thought. Just a few days before, I'd heard from Lena that there was a rumour Tim was planning to leave me, and this got me thinking.

You might remember, when he told me he was going to be with Angela, I suggested he stay one more night?

'Look, I tell you what, why don't you stay for tonight?' I'd said. 'I'll cook us a nice dinner, we'll drink our favourite wine. One more night together, and then we say goodbye?'

Of course he agreed; why wouldn't he?

'That sounds perfect,' he'd said, dumping his new girlfriend, who was waiting patiently for him to dump his old wife.

So that night I cooked a meal to remember: two delicious homemade chicken pies, one laced with oregano, the other with a lot of my prescription sleeping pills crushed in the pestle and mortar along with some garlic and salt. 'You hate oregano so I haven't put any in yours,' I told him. 'I've made a little pastry flower on mine so we can tell the difference. We don't want you being poisoned with oregano,' I joked, rolling my eyes. He disliked oregano so much he'd make a fuss if it was ever in his food. Little did he know he was eating far worse than an aromatic herb in his dinner that evening. As he enjoyed my shortcrust pastry and delicious gravy, he complimented me on the food, which was unusual. Then again, he thought he only had to be nice to me for one more night, so the criticism was kept to a minimum.

Straight after we'd finished, I checked my watch for timing, and when he started to turn pale and sweat a little, I said; 'Can you just do one last thing for me before you leave?

Could you just move the planks of wood you've piled up in the garage, the ones you were going to build the gym with?'

He looked a little sheepish. 'Yeah, I might take them at some point; Angela works out. We thought we might build the gym in *her* garden.'

'Great,' I said, 'but if you could just move them to the side, because I can't get in the garage, and I can't lift them.' Of course I could lift them; I'd been doing weights in the gym for years. I could probably lift heavier than him, but he'd never noticed.

He was obviously not feeling great, but I insisted, 'I need you to move them tonight. You'll forget tomorrow and just go. I want to put my car in the garage. Without you here it might get stolen,' I said, as if his masculine presence was so big, it deterred car thieves.

His ego fed, he reluctantly agreed, and we both went out into the cold dark night. Before going to the garage, I wandered over to the cavernous hole in the middle of the lawn and flashed my torch. 'What the hell is that?' I gasped, and immediately he marched over, his chest out, my knight in shining armour.

Not likely.

'What? I can't see anything.' He sounded anxious, confused, and as he grabbed my phone to use the torch, I noticed his hands were trembling. *Good.*

'You okay, Tim?' I asked, taking my phone back as he stood there in a daze.

'Yeah... don't feel great,' he said as he staggered around the hole by my apple tree. 'Be careful,' I said, pretending I was going to reach for him, but then I moved quietly behind him and picked up the heavy garden spade. He was now very usefully teetering on the edge of the hole, and I clutched the spade, bracing myself. I took a breath and went to lift the spade, then I lost my nerve and brought it crashing down. I couldn't do it, so turned away from him, and began walking slowly back to the house.

'Jill!' he called. 'Where the fuck are you going? I'm not doing this on my own.' His voice was slurry. 'Lazy cow,' he muttered. And that was it. I decided in that moment, he was never going to speak to me or anyone else like that again, and I turned around, and picked up the spade. Walking towards him in the dark, I remembered all the times he hadn't come home, wedding anniversaries spent alone, the smell of other women's perfume, all the nights he'd chosen someone else instead of me. And being so much stronger than he'd ever imagined I was, I lifted that spade high in the air, and, just as he saw me, I brought it down on his head. That's all it took for him to fall groaning into the grave he'd dug for himself without realising.

After that, I got to work and, with the same spade, I threw all the soil back into the hole and on top of him. It was dark, the garden is very private and back then, before my accident, I was very fit, and *very* handy with a spade.

A week later, when I knew he wasn't going to emerge from the soil, and I was safe, I left for Wales. Encouraged by my success in the garden with Tim, I'd arranged our girls' weekend, where I'd hoped to avenge my son's death further by pushing tipsy Wendy off a hill. But I think that first time with Tim was beginner's luck, and it didn't work a second time with Wendy. Fortunately, no-one suspected that I'd tried to kill Wendy, except of course, Wendy. But she had enough to deal with when Nurse Oke told the world what she and Olivia, and Robert had done, so she hasn't come after me.

I'd gone to Wales in January, planning to be away for a weekend, but returned home in March having spent almost three months in hospital. To say I was relieved to see the garden just as I'd left it, is an understatement. The soil has settled nicely, there's even a bit of grass growing on it now, and when Lena asked me why I'd filled in that great big hole, I explained that I planned to build a vegetable garden. 'I thought Tim wanted to build a gym?' she asked.

'Yes, but he's not coming back, so the house is mine, and it's *my* decision about what happens now,' I said. Then I made up some story about his new life on the Gold Coast with another new woman. No one's going to be looking for Tim any time soon.

It's over two years since I lost Leo, but I feel close to him here, and in the morning I often bring my cup of tea out into the garden and sit by the tree talking to him.

This morning it's crisp but sunny, and I run my fingers along the bark, admiring the little pale-pink clusters of sweet-smelling blossom scattered on the branches and the ground like confetti. Later the warmth of summer will bring me apples for crumbles and jams, and my tree will teem with hope and fruit and life, because I planted that seed, with all my love.

I lost my father when I was six years old, and it was the most painful loss I've ever suffered until I lost Mum, then my babies, then Leo. Each loss chipped away at me, at who I was and who I am, and now I'm someone quite different; I'm shaped by loss. But here in the garden, I can talk to Mum and Dad, my babies and Leo – even Tim, who tried to leave me, but I couldn't let him go. So he stayed here, and after twenty-five years, I'm finally secure in my marriage. I know exactly where he is every night, he's now the faithful husband I always wanted.

Tonight, I'll stand by the apple tree, look up into the sky, and see a scattering of stars glittering in the night sky. It's Leo's constellation. And when the wind rustles its leaves and branches, I hear his voice, and when the sun pokes through, I see his smile, and I smile too, knowing that, for sixteen years, I was the luckiest mum in the world.

A LETTER FROM SUE

Thank you so much for choosing to read *Wife, Mother, Liar*. If you enjoyed this book and want to keep up to date with all my latest releases, just sign up at the following link. Your email address will never be shared and you can unsubscribe at any time.

www.bookouture.com/sue-watson

I've always wanted to go stargazing, and recently I had the opportunity to stand on top of a hill, at night in a Dark Sky Reserve where the lack of light pollution turns the sky into bonfire night. There were more stars than sky, scattering, twinkling, shooting and it was so unreal. We were alone in an isolated landscape that was so dark, with no one around for miles. This was a special sky, and just breathtaking, but being a thriller writer, I also saw potential. It was the kind of sky that is begging to be the backdrop for a murder, and as I looked at those stars, the story began in my head.

After a long chat with my editor, I was soon bringing two good friends to spend a long weekend under that murderous sky, and even I wasn't sure who was going to live to tell the tale. This is a story about the good the bad and the ugliness of friendship, how, like a love affair, it can be a long honeymoon, but it can also turn sour. And when that friendship has already turned, a long weekend can seem like a lifetime.

I hope you enjoyed reading *Wife, Mother, Liar* as much as I enjoyed writing it, and if you did, I would be so grateful if you could write a review. It doesn't even have to be as long as a sentence – every word counts and is very much appreciated. I love to hear what you think, and it makes such a difference helping new readers to discover one of my books for the first time.

I love hearing from my readers – so please get in touch. You can find me on social media.

Thanks so much for reading,

Sue

 facebook.com/suewatsonbooks
x.com/suewatsonwriter

ACKNOWLEDGEMENTS

As always, my huge thanks to the wonderful team at Bookouture, who are amazing, supportive and expertly transform my ideas into ebooks, paperbacks and audiobooks.

Thanks to my fantastic editor and friend Helen Jenner, who lets me talk for ages about anything and everything during our brainstorms, with 'virtual coffee'. But thanks to her, we always end those conversations with a fully formed idea for the next book!

Huge thanks to lovely beta reader Harolyn Grant, who always reads my work with such a detailed eye, sees so much that I miss, and always makes me laugh with her hilarious notes. And Harolyn, please continue to be what you call, 'picky,' it's your super power!

Huge thanks to Su Biela, who spends an envious amount of time on lovely holidays, but is kind enough to squeeze in a beta read between her sunshine breaks; she also has a forensic eye and picks up on so much! And a special thank you to Anna Wallace, who did a brilliant final read through with her particularly fine toothcomb!

Thanks as always to my wonderful family and friends who are so kind and supportive and listen to me going on about how many words I have still to write, when they all know if I did less talking and more writing, I would get my books written far sooner!

PUBLISHING TEAM

Turning a manuscript into a book requires the efforts of many people. The publishing team at Bookouture would like to acknowledge everyone who contributed to this publication.

Audio
Alba Proko
Sinead O'Connor
Melissa Tran

Commercial
Lauren Morrissette
Hannah Richmond
Imogen Allport

Cover design
Lisa Horton

Data and analysis
Mark Alder
Mohamed Bussuri

Editorial
Helen Jenner
Ria Clare

Made in the USA
Coppell, TX
22 January 2025

44792317R00152